Novak Raven

(Harper's Mountains, Book 4)

T. S. JOYCE

Novak Raven

ISBN-13: 978-1535104265
ISBN-10: 1535104260
Copyright © 2016, T. S. Joyce
First electronic publication: July 2016

T. S. Joyce
www. tsjoyce.com

All Rights Are Reserved. No part of this book may be used or reproduced in any manner whatsoever without written permission, except in the case of brief quotations embodied in critical articles and reviews. The unauthorized reproduction or distribution of this copyrighted work is illegal. No part of this book may be scanned, uploaded or distributed via the Internet or any other means, electronic or print, without the author's permission.

NOTE FROM THE AUTHOR:

This book is a work of fiction. The names, characters, places, and incidents are products of the writer's imagination or have been used fictitiously and are not to be construed as real. Any resemblance to persons, living or dead, actual events, locale or organizations is entirely coincidental. The author does not have any control over and does not assume any responsibility for third-party websites or their content.

Published in the United States of America

First digital publication: July 2016
First print publication: July 2016

Editing: Corinne DeMaagd
Cover Photography: Kruse Images & Photography: Models & Boudoir
Cover Model: Matthew Hosea

DEDICATION

For you.

If you are reading this, you have let the Bloodrunner Crew into your imagination, and that means the world to me.

The raven is yours.

ACKNOWLEDGMENTS

I want to give a huge thanks to Corinne DeMaagd, for helping me to polish my books, and for being an amazing and supportive friend. I don't know what I would do without her. And to my man who does so much behind the scenes so that I can chase this dream, and who never wants credit for it. He's a secret badass, and I am a forever fan of his.

And last but never least, thank you. You have done more for me and my stories than I can even explain. Every share, review, recommendation, sweet message…I read them all, and you keep me going. Like 1010, you have my heart.

ONE

Twenty-six dollars.

Twenty. Six.

It might sound better if Avery Foley imagined her dwindled life savings in pennies instead of dollars. Twenty-six hundred pennies.

She frowned as she shoved the dollar bills and change into her wallet and relaxed back into the booth of Alana's Coffee & Sweets. Since it was the only place open this early, the newspapers were delivered to this shop first. She knew because she had woken up early every Sunday for the past five weeks and watched the delivery van make the rounds on sleepy Main Street. The weekly newspaper meant new job listings. It meant maybe she could keep her freedom for a little while longer because Bryson City was her haven.

The Bloodrunner Crew kept her safe, and they didn't even know she existed.

Avery perked up at the white delivery van headed this way. In the back of it, there was a stack of newspapers with hope written between the lines of the classified section. A buck fifty for the newspaper just to see the job listings, and there was her breakfast money right there. But if she could find a job, all her troubles would be over. Well, until the council found out what she'd done.

When the stink of fur and dominance hit her nose, Avery gasped and slammed herself against the booth wall. *Don't look it in the eyes.* She clenched her shaking hands under the table and averted her gaze when the curvy woman with the soft brown eyes and the scar on her lip poured a cup of coffee in front of Avery.

"I-I don't want any," she stammered. "Anything. Don't want it. I'm fine."

"Now, miss, I've seen you come in here every Sunday for three weeks, and I've never pushed you to buy anything. I'm not starting now." The woman pitched her voice low. "I saw you counting your money. Breakfast is on me."

Avery's words were clogged in her throat as she panted and pressed her cheek against the cold glass. "You're one of those...those..."

"Shifters?" There was a deep frown in the woman's tone. "My name is Alana. I won't hurt you."

Liar. Liar. She is a liar. She was too dominant to be a lesser shifter like Avery. Alana was a big cat, at least. "W-what animal?"

"It's not polite to ask that," Alana said softly.

Avery's breath came too shallow, too fast. She would pass out if the monster didn't leave soon. How had she not smelled her before? True, Alana had always stayed behind the counter when she'd come in, and it was across the shop. And true, Raven senses weren't as heightened as other shifters. And true, the scent of vanilla overpowered everything in here, but Avery had made a grave mistake in letting her guard down.

Avery dared a glance at the woman. She was pretty with skin the color of smooth, rich chocolate, and petal-pink lipstick painted her full lips. Her hair was in curls, and the front waves that framed her face were highlighted the color of honey. Too bad this was just a pretty shell that hid a terrifying beast. "Are you a Bloodrunner?"

"Yes." The woman's dark, delicate eyebrows were furrowed, as though she couldn't figure Avery out. And she wouldn't either. That was one advantage to being a flight shifter. Feathers didn't carry a smell like fur did.

A freaking Bloodrunner! It was one thing to use their presence as safety. It was another to cross paths with them. They would kill her if they knew what she was. That's what predator shifters did. They were violent and unreasonable and snuffed out anything less dominant than them. It was their way.

The porcelain of the plate Alana pushed toward her made a grating sound against the bright green table. On it sat a bear-shaped pastry. She should've known. A freaking grizzly bear. Avery closed her eyes so she could pretend she wasn't under the stare of one of the most terrifying of the shifters right now.

"If you need anything else, you just ask, okay, sugar?" Alana asked.

Avery whimpered and nodded once, hard. Alana's dominance pressed heavily on her shoulders as the woman stood there staring a few moments more, probably deciding whether to eat her or not.

But then she left. Just like that. Alana was polite as she poured coffee for the seven seniors across the café, and she was double polite to the newspaper delivery guy, whose nametag read Trevor. And she had given Avery free coffee and a pastry. And said pastry did smell mouth-wateringly delicious.

Perhaps it was poisoned. Predator shifters were very good hunters.

Avery poked it. Still warm, and the frosting coated her finger. Carefully, Avery lifted the pastry to her nose and sniffed it, but it didn't smell of anything other than dough and cherry filling—her favorite. When she nibbled a crumb off the corner, it was like heaven in her mouth.

Eyes on the delivery man filling the newspaper dispenser, Avery bit into the breakfast carefully. It tasted as good as it smelled. She hadn't eaten a thing since the dollar quesadillas at five o'clock yesterday at Drat's Boozehouse.

"Keep one out for me?" Alana asked Trevor.

"Sure thing," he said with an easy smile.

Everyone seemed so nice here. Nicer than the

community Avery had come from, but that was because she was a low ranking member. Low ranking members were scorned, punished, and pushed to marry up to lift their family's station. She wasn't angry about it. That was just how raven shifters worked.

Which was why she was here, avoiding the hell out of Benjamin and pretending to be something she was not.

Her phone vibrated against the table, the device clattering toward the ledge. Avery picked it up and answered right away. "Hi, Mom."

"Hey sweetie," Mom whispered, which meant Dad was still in the house. Why wasn't she calling when he was out?

"Are you okay?" Avery asked, lowering her voice to match her mother's. The last thing she needed was the Bloodrunner overhearing anything personal about her.

"Yes, yes, I'm fine," Mom murmured. "I need to tell you something, though. The council..."

Dread blasted through her chest. "Yeah?"

"They are talking about paying you a visit to make sure your courtship is going ahead according to plan."

According to plan? "No, no, no. Mom!" Avery glanced over at Alana, who was walking back into the kitchen. She cupped her hand over the speaker and whispered, "He wouldn't know me anymore, and he wouldn't understand. He was raised with predator shifters. He's the son of Beaston! I don't actually plan on meeting the Novak Raven."

"You mean your fiancé?" Mom whisper screamed.

"What else was I supposed to tell the council? They weren't going to let me go, Mom. And Benjamin is…" Terrifying. "I can't make a nest with him, can't build a life. I won't survive it."

Mom's deep sigh tapered into a helpless noise that said she was crying again. "I know. I just wanted to warn you. Get your story straight, honey. They're coming sooner rather than later, and your father will back them up." Because Benjamin's name would raise their station, and that was the most important thing to Dad.

A good daughter would've done her duty. A good daughter would've dug her family out of their hole. A good daughter would've married up the second she came of breeding age, but what had Avery done? Lied about a courtship with a raven shifter she'd only met once, years ago.

"Should I just come home, Mom?"

"No. Benjamin *will* have you if you come back."

"But the backlash will fall on you and Dad."

"Then convince the council you are really in a relationship with the Novak Raven. They're scared of his family. Scared of his crew. Scared of his father. As long as he doesn't marry another and register her to his crew, the council won't dig too deeply."

"And what do I say when they get here and the Novak Raven isn't with me?"

"Tell them he is out of town, or busy with work, or anything. Baby, it would be different if it was anyone other than Benjamin who asked to court you, but I've heard things. Awful things, and he was so mean to you when you were kids. I want you safe."

"But our rank—"

"Fuck our family rank if it means you get hurt."

Avery drew up like she'd been slapped. Wow. She'd never heard Mom say "fuck" before. She was timid like all female raven shifters, but there had been a shift lately. Mom had become stronger-willed, more outspoken, and that change had come about the day Benjamin had come into their home uninvited and demanded Avery's hand. Dad had been all for it. Mom had sat there quietly with this horrified look on her face as Dad promised him Avery would give her newly betrothed as many children as he wanted and Avery would be a good, submissive, and doting mate to a man with empty eyes.

Bile crept up the back of Avery's throat at the thought of how happy Dad had been to give her away to a brute.

"I'll figure it out, Mom, don't worry," Avery promised.

"Hannah!" Dad yelled in the background.

"I love you, honey. I have to go," Mom rushed out in a whisper. And then the line went dead.

Avery sighed miserably as she watched the glow of her phone fade to black.

Alana slapped a newspaper onto the edge of her table so hard Avery startled and dropped the phone onto the seat beside her.

"I've circled the jobs that haven't been filled, and here is a list of a few more that my friends in town have said will go in next week's newspaper." She jammed a red-painted claw at the purple sticky note stuck on the classifieds section. "Maybe you can get lucky and sneak in there before the jobs are posted."

For some reason Avery couldn't explain, her response to Alana's abrupt arrival had caused her to grab her own boobs in fear. Fantastic. Cheeks on fire and heart hammering against her sternum, she released the fondle-hold on herself and rasped out, "Th-thank you."

Alana nodded and strode off.

"Why are you being so nice to me?" Avery asked in a rush.

Alana turned at the counter and gave her a crooked smile, the deep scar on her lip stretching with it. "Because it sucks being the new girl in town. Maybe this can make it easier."

Stunned, Avery dragged her gaze away from the bear shifter and studied the jobs she had circled. Slowly, she plucked the sticky note off the newspaper.

Alana's Coffee & Sweets (barista, part-time)
Sugar's Ice Cream Parlor (cashier, part-time)
Dante's Traditional Pizza Pies (dishwasher, part-

time)

Big Flight ATV Tours (scheduling manager, full-time)

Chills blasted across Avery's forearms when she read the last one. She was a firm believer in signs, and every instinct in her body said this was a big one. Big Flight? How fitting for a raven shifter to work at a place with such a name. Working in a tourist town for an ATV tour company sounded fun, and it was the only full-time position, which she desperately needed if she was going to secure a rental cabin around here.

This could work. She could stay out of the Bloodrunners' path of destruction while maintaining her independence and securing a job, a house, all of it. She could have the life she'd always wanted.

All she had to do was convince the council she was off the table for a match and make sure the Novak Raven never found out about her.

Big Flight ATV Tours was her ticket to freedom.

TWO

"Excuse me," Weston Novak said to the woman in front of him. He handed her the purse she'd let slip from her shoulder and onto the ground. "You dropped this."

The woman in front of Weston turned and seemed to look right through him. It was her eyes that made him stop walking. They were hollow and so sad, so hopeless, that a heaviness settled over him. She began walking again without taking the purse he offered. City lights illuminated the night on the other side of the bridge they were walking on, and the recent rain made the asphalt under his feet shiny and reflective. No cars were driving on the bridge, and up ahead, the woman's long, floral sundress whipped around her ankles. Why wasn't she wearing shoes?

Weston's fingers moved on their own, rifling through her purse. *Stop!* He pulled out a wallet and opened the button, flipped through a plastic sleeve of pictures. There was one of a smiling man with a beard and thinning hair, and one of a little blond boy. There was another picture of all three of them, and the woman's beaming smile was genuine. She was happy. So what had changed? Why did her eyes harbor a thousand ghosts now?

The next plastic sleeve held a folded newspaper article. Weston pulled it out. Why couldn't he stop himself?

Slowly, he unfolded it and read the headline and first few sentences. It was an obituary.

No. Weston looked up at the woman. Her shoulders were shaking, and she was wiping her cheeks on the thin sleeve of her dress as she walked away. She'd lost her little boy.

"Ma'am," Weston warned as she climbed onto the railing. Shit. "Ma'am!" He bolted for her. She was sobbing uncontrollably now, chanting the little boy's name, chanting how sorry she was.

This couldn't be happening! He reached her in

time and grabbed her hand, but his fingertips went right through hers as though he was an apparition. No, no, no.

"Look at me!" he yelled. "It's going to be okay. I'll make sure it's okay. Just come down. Let me take you home!"

Balanced with her back to the churning water far below, she was looking at something right over his head. She couldn't see him at all.

"Jean!" he yelled, reciting the name from the obituary. She'd survived her child. No parent should go through this. Weston scrabbled at her legs, her arms, anywhere, desperate to be solid. To pull her back down and hold her and tell her everything would be okay eventually, even if it was a lie. Even if he knew she would never get over this, she had to live. "Jean, please look at me!"

Jean's face fell, and tears streamed down her cheeks like rivers, and then she did. She lowered her gaze and looked right at Weston, right into his soul. "Thanks for being here," she whispered. "I didn't want to do it alone."

And then she launched herself off the bridge.

"Noooo!" Weston screamed, bolting upright in bed.

His skin was cold and clammy, and his legs were all tangled up in the sheets. Desperately, he kicked out of them and rolled over, buried his face against the pillow, and yelled as loud and as long as he could. His voice grew hoarse, but it didn't help release the vision of Jean from his mind. She was a stranger, and he hadn't been able to help her. She was probably alive still, but he'd done this over and over, tried to fix the future, and every time, he somehow made it worse. If he tried to save Jean, she would still take her own life, and it would be even more gruesome. His visions were non-negotiable. They existed for no fucking reason other than to torture him with fates he couldn't change. With people he couldn't help. He punched the mattress over and over as hard as he could. Then stood and ripped the lamp cord out of the wall and chucked the lamp at the doorframe. It shattered, but still didn't erase the prophesy.

He needed to Change. He needed to Change and fly, drink himself to oblivion, or do something that could remove the image of her streaming tears, of the hopelessness in her hollow eyes from of his mind.

He fucking hated the sight. Hated it. His father had had it, and his grandmother, too. He'd thought it had skipped him, but six months ago he saw his alpha in a dream, telling him to come home. Since Weston had come to Harper's Mountains, the floodgates had been opened.

He wasn't okay.

His phone vibrated on the nightstand, and for a moment, he considered throwing that, too, just to hear the satisfying sound of it shattering against the wall. But there was already a massive mess of glass shards to clean up, and his cell phone was ringing again. Maybe whoever it was could be his savior.

"Hello," he answered in a scratchy voice.

"H-hello? Did I wake you?"

Weston glared at the glowing green time on the alarm clock. *6:15*. The answer should've been 'yes,' but Jean had woken him first. "No. Who is this? No, wait. Don't tell me." Talking to a stranger would be better.

"Okay." There was a long pause before she murmured, "Are you okay?"

No. "Yeah, I'm fine, just…" He sank down on the bed and ran his hand over his face. "Do you ever have bad dreams?"

"Uuuh." Static sounded on the phone. "Sometimes. I used to have them more when I was a kid."

"I never had them until I grew up."

"Did you have one tonight?" she asked. Her voice was pretty. Soft and hesitant, but with a clear tone. She probably sang well.

He should stop talking. He didn't know her, didn't recognize her number, and she could be anyone. Hell, she could be one of the vamps or wolves for all he knew. But her question came across the line so easy, as if she did care, and damn, he wanted to believe that someone, some perfect stranger, could ease the tightness in his chest. God knew, he couldn't talk to his crew about this or how bad it was getting.

Harper was going to have to put him down someday.

That thought drew him up short. It felt so true, so final. Someday, he would be driven mad by the sight, and there wasn't a damn thing he could do about it.

"What were your dreams like?" he asked, because he sure as shit didn't want to detail the one he'd just had to the nice-sounding woman on the other end of the line. Her voice was frail, and she was likely submissive. She wouldn't be able to shoulder a vision. Pity because, right now, he really wanted to unload on her.

"I used to have dreams about animals chasing me through the woods. You know the ones where you're running and running, and you never get tired, but neither does the thing that's chasing you? And then, right when the animal was on me, right when it was about to bite, I would wake up."

"What kind of animals?" he asked.

"Bears. Always bears."

Weston frowned at the wall. Yeah, she definitely wouldn't be able to handle his dream. Bears weren't even a blip on his radar of scary animals. There were three bear shifters in his crew, and his dad was a bear shifter. Hell, most of the crew he'd grown up with had massive bruins inside of them.

Silence stretched on as he laid back on his bed and rubbed his eyes. At least talking to this woman had settled his heartrate some.

"So," she drawled hesitantly. "I called for a reason."

He stared up at the exposed beams in his cabin ceiling and sighed. Right, she hadn't just dialed a wrong number to talk to a stranger at the ass-crack of dawn. "Okay."

"I heard you have an opening for a scheduling manager for your ATV business. I was wondering if I could fill out an application for it."

"Scheduling manager for... Where did you hear that? I haven't posted for the job."

"A Bloodrunner told me. Uuum, Alana." Her voice went all weak and shaky on her answer. Strike one against her. A scheduling manager not only had to be good with people on the phone, but also face-to-face. Plus, she was going to have to deal with his partner, Ryder, and he was a relentless pervy joker whose brain stem was connected directly to his dick. He would have her crying in no time. Add to that Weston just had a somewhat personal conversation with her, and he in no way wanted to meet her in person. Ever.

"Sorry, but I'm not hiring at this time." The line went so quiet, he thought she hung up. He checked the screen of his phone, but the call hadn't disconnected. "You still there?"

"Yeah, it's just, I really need this job." At least she

had a little steel in her voice now, so maybe she wasn't a complete pushover. "I've been looking and looking, but it's tourist season, and all the jobs get filled right before I apply. All I'm asking for is a chance. Just...let me come in for an interview, and if you feel like I'm not the right fit for your company, I won't beg or make it weird. I'm good at interviews. I just can't get in for one. I *know* I can do this job." She swallowed audibly over the line and whispered, "Please."

Weston let off an irritated sigh. He'd really imagined a roughneck man to be handling scheduling, so he could help keep the ATVs running and assist with building and clearing trails, too. This woman sounded like a splinter would end her life. She was begging, though, and he didn't want to feel like a total dick. "Fine. Can you come in tomorrow?"

"I can come in today and start immediately," she said in a rush.

Weston wasn't really in the mood to conduct an interview today. More like he wanted to drink a fifth of whiskey and work on his property alone, but fuck it. He had to hire someone soon, and getting the first interview done and out of the way might distract him from the stupid visions.

"I'll text you the address. Be there at noon."

"Oh, thank you! Oh my gosh, thank you so much. You don't know how much this means to me. Everything has been so shitty lately. Oh, no. I said shitty. I mean...I'm really grateful for the opportunity. I'm going to go. My mouth won't shut up. See you at noon. Okay, bye. Don't forget to text me the address. Sorry. You know what you're doing. Okay then. Toodles. Toodaloo. I mean bye."

More static blasted across the line, and then her muffled voice came across. "Oh, yeah! Oh, yeah! Eeeee!"

Weston winced away from the celebratory squeal.

"Fuck you, *Benjamin*! Take that, and that!"

Weston could just imagine her flipping the bird to an imaginary Benjamin.

"Oh, no." More static, and then in a much clearer voice, she said, "I thought I hung up. Please tell me you aren't still there."

Weston snorted. "I'm still here."

The woman cleared her throat delicately and murmured, "Good day to you, sir." And then she hung up.

Baffled, Weston canted his head and stared at the phone as a smile stretched his lips. Huh. He texted her the address and dropped his phone to the bed. Crossing his arms over his chest, he chuckled up at the ceiling.

What an odd bird.

At least her interview would be amusing, and even more importantly to Weston, distracting.

THREE

Avery's beat-up old Civic wheezed and coughed around the final mud pit before the clearing. The hand-carved sign above the dirt road read *Big Flight ATV Tours, Welcome.*

Thank God, because her GPS had basically laughed at her a few miles back and then refused to guide Avery an inch farther. No surprise since the building looked just barely finished. A man balanced on his knee on a half-built porch where he was sawing off the end of a board.

She'd expected an older gentleman from how gruff the voice was on the phone, but this guy looked like he was around her age. Maybe he was the owner's son. He wore sunglasses, and a good thing too because sawdust was spraying everywhere. Safety first, she always said. A camouflage baseball cap covered his head and, holy macaroni, he wasn't wearing a shirt. His powerful legs were hugged by jeans that were riddled with strategically placed holes. Tattoos covered his arms and part of his chest, and if she wasn't severely mistaken, Mr. Sexyman had his nipples pierced. Real piercings! She'd never seen a man like him, all tanned, gleaming with sweat, and tatted up. Raven culture didn't condone body modification, but suddenly she was thinking her community was a gaggle of morons because this fine specimen of a human was sexy as hell. His sweat probably smelled like evergreens and tasted like sugarplums.

When he looked up suddenly, she remembered herself and squeaked, slamming on the brakes a few feet away from the porch.

Great first impression, Avery. You almost destroyed the building.

"Were you planning on stopping, or no?" he asked rudely as she got out of her car.

"You aren't wearing a shirt," she said dumbly, like that was a valid excuse. "Uh, is your dad around?"

The man set the saw on the porch and stared at her with his mouth hanging open. "No. Why?"

"Because I have an interview today."

The man shoved his work glove down and checked his watch. "We agreed on noon."

Shoot, *he* was interviewing her? She hunched under his angry glare. At least she thought he was angry, because his sunglasses hid his eyes. "I wanted to be punctual," she admitted in a voice an octave too high.

"You're an entire hour early."

The tattoo on his chest said something too small to read from here, and a single drop of sweat slowly trickled down between his defined pecs. Down, down to his perfect little belly button between his perfectly flexed abdominals.

"Lady!" He covered his dick with his gloved hands and cocked his head.

"I wasn't looking at that." *Just your belly button like a normal person.* Avery turned her back. In a murmur, she pleaded, "Can you put on a shirt? It's r-really unprofessional to conduct an interview like this."

"Again, you're an hour early."

"Right. Sorry." She turned and looked at him over her shoulder as he was pulling a white T-shirt over his head, and this time she could see a faint trail of dark hair leading down into his jeans. Holy hell, she wanted to ride it down like a Slip 'N Slide. Forcefully, she turned back around. "Should I go and come back in an hour?"

"No. You almost drove through my porch once. You're good."

Geez, he sounded testy.

His work boots echoed hollowly on the porch, so she peeked around again. He picked up a half empty beer bottle from a table between two rocking chairs. Whoo, his man-butt looked good in those jeans, too. She opened her mouth to begin listing her good qualities as a future employee, but he entered the building and let the swinging door slam behind him.

Okay. Carefully, she padded up the stairs and around the power tools, lifted her knuckles to knock, decided against it, and stepped inside. "Hello?"

"Back here," the man said in an irritated tone. Her heart sank to the floorboards under her feet. She was definitely not getting this job.

Buck up, Avery. You need this. Win him over!

Most of the building was a single, large room with a counter along the back wall and a souvenir shop at the front. It looked like there was a gear room through the side door, and on the opposite wall was a room with a sign that read *Office* in hand-painted yellow letters above the door. That was the one Mr. Bitable Nipple Bars had disappeared into.

Avery scampered in behind him, determined to have a good interview from here on, but he'd taken off his glasses and hat and, holy shit, it was him. Weston Novak, the Novak Raven himself.

Avery slammed back against the wall beside the door.

"What's wrong with you now?" he asked, looking completely baffled.

His face was the same, just older. It was his body that had thrown her off and made him impossible to recognize on first glance. His bright green eyes were still the same, the color of his father's, but she knew from experience they turned black as night when his inner raven was worked up. He had a dimple on one cheek when he smiled big enough, and he was naturally quiet. He was a dominant brawler, which was at complete odds with his raven nature.

Weston's eyes narrowed to slits. "Do I know you?"

"No," Avery blurted out.

"What's your name?"

"Beth. Bethany. Bessie." She was panicking!

"Well, which one is it?" he asked, hands on his hips as if he wasn't buying anything she was selling.

"Hey, boss," a redheaded man said from the open doorway.

He'd appeared out of nowhere, and Avery startled hard. Oh, she knew him, too. He was none other than *the* Air Ryder. He had a huge online following, had spent half his dang life in the news conducting interviews, and was one of the rarest shifters on the planet, a snowy owl. He and the Novak Raven were the two most famous, most battle-proven, and most volatile flight shifters in the entire world, and here she was, caught right between them. Fuck, oh fuck, oh fuck.

"What do you want?" Weston gritted out.

"Barbecue and dick kisses," Ryder said without missing a beat.

"I don't mean what do you want out of life, Ryder," Weston said in a pissed-off tone. "I mean, what are you doing here?"

"Oh, right." The redheaded muscle-bound behemoth held up a stack of paperwork. "We've got trouble."

"What kind of trouble?"

Ryder cast Avery a calculating look, then twitched his head to Weston, gesturing for him to follow, and disappeared out into the main room.

"I'll be right back," Weston muttered as he passed. Great googly moogly, that man was tall. And his shoulders were almost the width of the dang door. He could squish her head like a blueberry if he wanted to. The Novak Raven? Hell. No. "Take your time." *While I climb out the window.*

But when Avery tried the only escape, it was jammed.

She grunted and pushed and grunted some more. Holy hell, this thing wasn't moving.

"You know you have to unlock it, right?" Weston said from behind her.

Avery froze, and as seconds ticked on, she couldn't muster the courage to turn and face him.

"I can still see you."

Heart banging against her chest, Avery rolled

sideways until her back pressed against the log wall. "Hi."

Weston's dark eyebrows arched up, and he gave her tight smile. "Hi." Gesturing to a chair in front of the desk, he said, "Have a seat so we can get this weird-ass interview over with."

Quiet as a mouse, Avery forced her feet one in front of the other until she reached the chair, bumped it back a couple feet with the backs of her knees, and sat gingerly on the edge, ready to bolt. Why? Because the Novak Raven was the son of Beaston, raised in the most violent crew of shifters that existed, the Gray Backs. And she'd heard whispers of the battles he'd seen. The battles he'd been in. Just recently, he'd been a part of evicting an entire coven of vampires from Asheville, and the Valdoro Pack of psychotic werewolves, too, but from here, she saw zero scars, which meant he was scarier than the other monsters. It meant he was better at war.

The council was wary of him for good reason.

The man took a long swig of his beer, condensation dripping from the bottle and onto the desk. While he chugged it, he watched her over the curve of the bottle, and when he'd finished every last drop, he hissed like his beer had hit the spot. Gross. Beer tasted like piss. "I'm Weston Novak, and that was my partner, Ryder Croy."

"Air Ryder," she blurted unhelpfully. "And you're the Novak Raven."

"Yes, okay. So you know of us. Great. Anyway, we're starting up this business and already booking clients. We're hiring a scheduling manager because we will be out a lot on tours." He gestured to a phone on the edge of the desk. "Job responsibilities will include answering the phone, keeping track of tours and deposits, running the shop when we're out, making sales, helping to fit clients with gear, making sure the vending machines are stocked, running the cash register for the souvenir area, and sometimes closing up shop."

Avery couldn't meet his eyes anymore. The Novak Raven was terrifying, and his voice was steely, but that wasn't the current problem. The issue was he was very attractive and making her forget how dangerous he was by talking like a normal man and not a War Bird in disguise. She had to force her next question past her tightening vocal chords. "Will I ever do an ATV Tour?"

Weston snorted. "Have you ever been on an ATV?"

He was laughing at her, making fun of her, and she didn't like that. She wasn't in the raven community anymore where she had to absorb rudeness. "No, but I would like to. I'm a quick learner."

When she cast her glance at him, she got trapped there. His head was cocked, his eyes gone dark and tight in the corners. His lips were set in a grim line, and he was leaning on the desk, his hands clasped in front of him. "What's your name? Your real name?"

A whimper wrenched up her throat. This was it. She couldn't lie with him so tuned to her. He would hear it. But her name was unique, and he would definitely recognize her as his pen pal. They'd written back and forth for years. She was so busted.

"Avery," she admitted in a murmur.

Something flashed through his eyes so quickly she couldn't decipher his reaction. It was there and gone in an instant, and his following words were so cool, so steady, her heart sank even further.

"Are you scared of me, Avery?"

He didn't recognize her. Not at all. Not her face,

not her name. Perhaps she hadn't really been pen pals with him. Perhaps it had been some sick joke, and she'd written to someone pretending to be him. That would explain why he'd been so cold the one time they had met in Saratoga.

Her eyes prickled with tears, which was stupid. Weston didn't know it, but he'd ruined her life. He'd made her want too much, made her reach too far for things she could never have. He'd made her feel too much. She was a female raven who had grown a bond with a man who didn't exist. A one-sided bond that had made her avoid boyfriends and courtships until Benjamin and the council had drawn up a marriage contract. Until Benjamin got tired of her brushing him off.

With every childhood letter from the Novak Raven, she'd grown further away from her own people and what was expected of her.

His fault, and now he didn't even recognize her.

"Are you crying?" he asked through a deep and disapproving frown.

Avery dashed her knuckles under her eyes and gave her gaze to the wall. Her stomach growled loudly. She would've been embarrassed, but she felt too numb to be. It was her body reminding her why she was here and why she was desperate for this job, no matter who owned the company. There was little risk in taking a position here because it was clear as day there would never be anything between her and this man. No spark of familiarity, no reminiscing on letters from their youth. She had needs—food and shelter—and a job here could give her those. And she was so damn tired of living in complete uncertainty. She needed stability so her animal would feel more settled. So she could stop wondering if she was really strong enough to leave Raven's Hollow. Maybe the Novak Raven didn't need her for this job…but she was at the end of her resources, the end of her savings. Avery really needed this to work. "How much is the hourly pay?"

"Ten an hour to start out, and paychecks come out every two weeks. Why do you want to work a job like this?"

Defeated, she inhaled deeply and explained in a soft murmur, "My whole life I was supposed to stand still, be quiet, and look pretty. Only I was born plain, and I got tired of standing still and being quiet. I have nothing, Mr. Novak. I will put everything I am into getting your business off the ground. Give me a chance, and I'll be here early every day and leave late if you need me to. I want independence, and I can't have that without a steady job. I'll be a good employee because I'm ready. Ready for this, ready for the responsibility, ready to be a part of something bigger than myself, ready to see Big Flight ATV Tours thrive." She'd meant every word, but she felt nauseous when she'd said them. Admitting she had nothing to a man who had shunned her friendship all those years ago was hard.

But what did she have to lose now? She was sleeping in her car, and soon she wouldn't have money for food or gas, and her only option then would be to go back to Raven's Hollow and marry Benjamin. She would be a broodmare for a man with cold eyes and no affectionate feelings for her. She would be broken slowly there if she couldn't build a life here. Because ravens—female ravens—didn't just escape Raven's Hollow or the reach of the council. The last time that had happened was over twenty-five years ago when Aviana King had chased down Beaston Novak, claimed him as her mate, and cut ties with her people.

This was Avery's stand—however pathetic it might be.

"Honestly, Avery, I don't think you're right for this job—"

"Wes! I need you, man," Ryder called from outside.

Weston's nostrils flared in irritation before he yelled, "What do you need?"

"You! I already said that!"

"Mother fucker," Weston murmured as he stood. "Look, I need a strong back who will be able to juggle and manage a lot here—"

"Wes!" Ryder yelled again.

Weston growled a terrifying sound and strode toward the door. "I'll be right back," he muttered over his shoulder.

But what difference did it make if he came back or not? Weston was denying her the job. She'd laid it all out there for him, and now her ticket to freedom was fading to nothing.

FOUR

When Weston strode out onto the porch and into the sunlight, the tension in his chest finally eased.

Avery. Goddammit, he knew he'd recognized her! She had the same shade of deep brunette hair with sun-washed highlights that said she liked to be outside. She'd piled it on top of her head in a tight, painful looking bun. She wasn't much taller than he remembered and still frail looking with hunched shoulders, as if she was trying to make herself even smaller. She'd grown curves in the years since he'd seen her, but did a damn fine job of hiding them under that baggy sweater she was wearing. A sweater! It was eighty-five degrees outside, and she was covered up completely. Her dull clothes couldn't hide that striking face of hers, though. Plain? Ha. She was clearly fishing for compliments he wouldn't give. Her eyes were a vibrant aquamarine blue, made even brighter by her thick, dark lashes, and she'd obviously forsaken the make-up today because her stark freckles stood out on her cheeks and nose. Her nose was just as tiny and pert as he remembered from the pictures she'd sent. She'd slathered her lips in some cherry-scented gloss that made him even angrier. Tempting little temptress, but he saw right through that shit.

The memory of the day they'd finally met made him want to rip a fucking tree out of the ground.

The girl who had ruined everything was here, begging a job from him? Fuck! He couldn't breathe. Weston pulled at the collar of his T-shirt and jogged down the stairs. He needed to get her out of here as fast as possible. Out of Nantahala, out of Bryson City, out of his life.

Today had sucked. First the dream, and now Avery freaking Foley was back to demolish him the rest of the way. He wanted to Change. No…he *needed* to Change. Desperately, he pulled off his shirt, tossed it to the ground, and bolted for the woods.

"Where are you going?" Ryder asked, appearing from nowhere and hooking his immovable hand onto Weston's bicep. He had his phone up to his ear. "It's ringing."

"What?" Weston asked, confused.

Inside the building, the landline trilled a long ring. Ryder waggled his eyebrows and mouthed, *I'm testing her.*

"Um, Mr. Novak?" Avery called timidly from inside. "The phone is ringing!"

Weston shot Ryder a dirty look and moved to go tell her she needed to leave. Ryder stilled him and put it on speaker, then pressed his finger to his lips.

On the third ring, Avery answered. "Big Flight ATV Tours, this is Avery, how can I help you?"

Weston drew up straight. Huh. She sounded a lot less shaky on the phone than he'd expected.

"I was wantin' to know about booking a tour for my family," Ryder drawled in a deep-south accent. Weston tried not to smile but failed on account of Ryder's accent being so thick and unbelievable. "I have eight kids, ages six to nineteen, and a wife who likes to get mud in her crack. Do you have anything that can accommodate me, ma'am?"

Avery let off a surprised-sounding giggle. "That's a great question. Let me see here." The sound of shuffling papers blasted across the phone, and after a few moments, she recited a sentence of wording off the stack of pamphlets Weston had left on the desk. "Ages fifteen and up only for safety reasons. I'm sorry sir, but we'll only be able to book a tour for you, your wife, and the kids over the minimum age requirement of fifteen."

"Oh, well that's a mighty disappointment."

"We do have tour packages in different lengths of time, though, so if you can find someone to watch your younger children for an hour, that is our shortest tour. And they are welcome to hang out around here. We have a hiking trail and a set of horseshoes out back. Picnic tables, too, if you want to bring a lunch for them."

"But you don't have one of them playgrounds or nothin' for my little angels?"

"No need for that in the Smoky Mountains, sir. The woods are the playground here."

Ryder nodded his head like he was impressed, and honestly, Weston was, too. All of her terrified demeanor had disappeared on the phone.

"Hired. You're hired," Ryder said into the phone. "Wait. What?"

No! Weston mouthed, shaking his head. Ryder didn't understand. She wasn't what he thought. She wasn't just some human looking for a job. She was a fucking raven shifter probably sent from the council to keep tabs on him.

Ryder rested his hand on his hip and wore a big dumb grin on his face. "When can you start? Wait, we're coming in." Ryder jogged across the clearing and inside the building, leaving Weston to trail after him.

"We need to talk about this first," Weston said, but there was Avery, standing in the open office doorway with a hopeful smile on her lips. And holy fuck, her smile stopped him in his tracks. She'd worn braces the first time he'd met her, but now her teeth were perfect. Her lips curved up so pretty, and her eyes were that bright teal that made his dick swell. Oooh, Avery was dangerous. The council knew exactly what they were doing.

"I can start right now!" she exclaimed excitedly. "Today!"

"Perfect," Ryder said. "We can give you the tour

right now."

"No. No. No, we can't," Weston said, yanking Ryder to a stop. "My vote is still no on this. She isn't right for our business."

Avery's face fell. "Why not?"

Because she was a fucking traitor! "You're just not."

Ryder's ruddy brows lowered over his narrowed blue eyes. "What's your problem, man? She's good on the phone. She's hot."

"You can't say that about employees."

"Why not? It's how I talk, and she'll have to sink or swim." Ryder rounded on Avery. "Do you mind me calling you hot?"

Her cheeks blushed bright red. "Well, no. No one has ever called me that."

Ryder pointed to her and called, "Bullshit. Plus, a hot girl in the store will sell more. It's scientifically proven."

"By who?" Weston yelled too loud.

"By scientists!" Ryder turned to Avery again. "I'm sorry for his behavior. He's never had a girlfriend before and doesn't know how to talk to women."

"Ryder, shut the fuck up," Weston gritted out. His

love life definitely didn't need to be discussed by the raven council.

"So, what should I wear to work?" Avery asked, her attention directly on Ryder, the weak link.

"Spaghetti-strap tank tops and push-up bras would work. Do you have cut-off short shorts? I can make them for you if not. My mate has lots of scandalous clothes. I could dress you like a saloon girl if you want. Wait, maybe I should order tank tops with our logo on it. Why are you wearing a fucking sweater in the summer? Your skin is as pale as a vampire. What colors do you look good in?"

Avery was nodding her head like a bobble-head doll, and her eyes were round like tiny moons in her face. "Uuuh, blue or green. Black? I should tell you I've never worn cut-off shorts."

"Why the hell not?" Ryder asked, looking appalled. "Everyone should wear them from time to time. I do."

Avery giggled a pretty tinkling sound and tugged at the hem of her green-brown burlap sack of a sweater. "Immodest clothing isn't allowed where I come from." She cast a quick glance at Weston's bare torso. "Or tattoos or piercings either."

Yeah, well, Raven's Hollow was a cult.

Avery's cheeks were now roughly the shade of ripe cherries.

"Ryder," Weston drawled, "this isn't an appropriate discussion, and you are getting way ahead of yourself. I want to conduct more interviews."

"Fuck you, man. I pick Avery. Vote on it. Who wants Avery to work here?"

Ryder held up his hand, and in a rush, so did Avery. Her sweater inched up and exposed a strip of her bare, creamy stomach. Fuck, she looked soft under all that fabric, and now Weston's traitor dick was knocking on the seam of his pants. Temptress.

Ryder cocked his head and looked victorious. "Sorry Wessy, two against one. We win."

Damn it all, Weston wanted to peck down a tree with his bare beak just to work off the frustration. Unable to win, he yelled and turned, and stomped out of the building.

Freaking Avery was going to demolish him, and now Weston's best friend, his blood brother, was going to help it happen?

Weston gave the raven his body, embracing the

blast of pain that ripped through him. Beating his wings against the air currents, he left his pants behind and aimed for the sky to escape the woman who had betrayed him. Who had *used* him.

There was a reason he was twenty-five and had never had a serious girlfriend.

And that reason was Avery Foley.

FIVE

Weston Novak hated her.

Avery tapped her pen in quick succession on the counter as she watched him out the big front window. One week of working for Big Flight, and he'd said maybe three full sentences to her. Ryder had taken over her training completely because Weston could barely stand to look at her.

What an utterly confounding man.

A pathetic part of her wanted to believe he was just an angry person and hated everyone, but he and Ryder joked around constantly, and now watching him converse with their first clients hurt her even deeper. He was perfectly polite and charming with the two couples and a family he and Ryder were about to take out on a two-hour ATV trek through the wilderness.

This morning had been busy, and she and the guys had been running around like chickens with their heads cut off to prepare for the first tour. The phone had been ringing off the hook for new tours since Air Ryder had announced the new business on his social media accounts. These mountains would be a feeding frenzy of hungry women in a matter of days, and something about that really bothered Avery. Ryder was happily taken, paired up with a human he called Sexy Lexi, claimed and everything, which left Weston as the only single between the two.

She would have to watch him flirt with clients and eventually settle down. Just the thought of that made her stomach hurt. She wasn't supposed to like the Novak Raven, but over the past few days, she'd seen him smile, joke, and work on this place relentlessly. He seemed to know what needed to be done and did it. When plumbing needed fixing, the electric needed work, or an ATV gave them trouble, he just solved the problem. He didn't look to others for help or stand around looking confused. He got the right tools and worked until it was done.

She'd never met a more capable man, and there was something eternally sexy about that.

In Raven's Hollow, everyone depended on everyone else. That was the culture—one of complete dependence. Their society didn't work if any of them grew too independent.

But though Weston was a raven through and through, he had been raised in a community where independence was cultured and encouraged. And that used to scare her—the idea of a society where everyone did what they wanted, but now she thought maybe the Gray Backs had the right of it.

Weston was out here on his own, fixing any and everything. He didn't need anyone to do anything for him, while she barely had any life skills at all.

The more she observed him, the less he scared her and the more she admired him. That didn't change the fact that he obviously hated her, though. She was stupid to care for a man who had hurt her so deeply all those years ago, but her heart apparently didn't give two smelly shits about learning lessons.

Outside the window, Weston clapped an older gentleman on the shoulder and jogged toward the shop. Avery jolted upright and tugged at her shorts, checked to make sure her boobs were still covered by the low scoop of her teal tank top. She still had no idea how Ryder got them printed so fast. The logo across her boobs had an owl and a raven flying on either side of the company name. Ryder probably hadn't meant to, but the birds were each positioned right over her nipples.

The second Weston walked through the door and saw her waiting, the smile dipped from his face. Something about that change in his expression broke her heart.

His bright green eyes dipped down her neck to her chest and back up. He looked startled for a second, before a frown marred his face once again. "Can you hand me a couple of waters?" he asked gruffly.

Avery ducked her gaze so she wouldn't see the hate in his. "Sure." She turned, pulled two bottled waters from the glass refrigerator, and handed them to Weston.

He took them, careful not to touch her hand in the exchange. It was too much.

"Why do you hate me?" she blurted out.

Wes froze, his back to her.

"I mean, I'm trying really hard, and I've learned everything I'm supposed to. I know you didn't want to hire me, but Ryder says I'm doing well, and I've booked three new tours in the last hour alone. I just don't understand. You're so nice to everyone else."

"I don't hate you," he said in a careful tone, giving her the profile of his face. "I just don't trust you."

She huffed a hurt laugh. That was rich. He didn't trust her?

"You find that funny?" he asked, narrowing his eyes at her over his shoulder.

"Yeah." Feeling ill, she leaned back on the counter and crossed her arms over her chest like a shield. "Hilarious. You hurt me deeply—"

"Bullshit. Don't you play the victim, Avery."

The venom in his voice stung like a slap, and she grimaced, diverting her eyes to the floor.

"I never hurt you," he gritted out. "I don't even know you."

"I'm proud of you," she rushed out on a breath.

"What?" He rounded on her.

Ashamed, she pitched her voice low. "Even though you hate me, I don't hate you. I'm proud of what you've become." She dared a look up at him.

"Congratulations on your first tour, Weston."

He licked his lips and looked like he wanted to say something, but he didn't. Instead, his eyes turned darker and darker until they were black, sparking with intensity. He lifted the water bottles in a strangle-hold and muttered, "Thanks for these."

"Sure thing," she said as he left.

When the door banged closed behind him, she jumped at the sound. She hated that everything frightened her. It had only gotten worse as she tried to make her way in the world outside of Raven's Hollow. Determined, Avery made her way outside and smiled politely at the clients, who were sitting on their rumbling ATVs, chattering happily in a line, the lesson on riding over. Weston stood on his quad, his powerful legs locked as he bent over the handlebars and eased his thumb onto the throttle. He wore a gray T-shirt with the company logo and sunglasses to hide his raven eyes. His camouflage baseball cap was on backwards, and he hadn't shaved in a couple of days. His tattoos were stark against his flexed arms as he made a wide circle and led the group past the porch. His attention stayed locked on her as he drove by, and she could see herself in the reflection of his sunglasses, one hand resting on her collar bone, one up in a tentative wave. And just before he turned away, he jerked his chin once in a silent farewell. Avery gasped. Progress. Perhaps he wouldn't be cold to her forever if she just kept trying with him. Perhaps they could find some common ground, and he could eventually treat her like he did other people.

Perhaps someday, he would smile and she would be the cause.

The tour rolled by, engines rumbling in the little parade, and as Ryder pulled up the rear, he was frowning at her. He slowed, then stopped in front of her. "You like him."

Heat blazed up her neck and landed in her cheeks and ears. "I do not."

Ryder canted his head and squinted his eyes at her. "Lie."

A shrill whistle sounded from up ahead.

In a hurry, Ryder told her, "It's his birthday tomorrow. I'm taking him to Drat's Boozehouse tonight to celebrate. You should show up around eleven." Without waiting for her to answer, Ryder gunned it and disappeared into the woods after the others, trailing dust behind him.

Oh, she'd known it was Weston's birthday tomorrow, but she'd assumed he hated celebrating it like he had as a kid. He'd never liked extra attention, but she was a fool for thinking Weston was the same little boy she'd known. They weren't comparable.

Whatever life the Novak Raven had led from then until now had changed him from the bones out.

I don't even know you.

His words rang so true, and she understood. He didn't remember her, didn't recognize her.

She was beginning to think she didn't recognize Weston either.

SIX

Weston would fire her in a New York minute if he knew she was using the showers at Big Flight for personal use. She was fine sleeping in her car, but personal hygiene was a must for her. She needed to be clean, or her raven would revolt. Already, she'd been Changing more than normal because she felt so unsettled. Her inner animal didn't do well with chaos. She liked routine. She liked having a steady nesting place, a steady resting place.

After gas and the minimal amount of food she could get away with, and after a really silly last-minute birthday purchase for Weston, she was down to $7.62. Things were getting desperate. She didn't know how she would make it another week until payday, but tonight, she had big plans to forget all her problems for a little while.

Besides, there were bright sides to her life now. The hopelessness was gone. She was earning money every day, and all she needed to do was get to that first paycheck, and everything would be fine. She'd even started looking at rental properties in the newspaper and had a couple of options. Sure, she would have to wait a few paychecks to be able to afford the deposit, but in a month, she would look back on this time in her life and be proud of herself for what she'd been through. There was light at the end of the tunnel. She could see it. She just had to be strong enough to reach it now.

Tonight, though…tonight she was going to be brave and open her mind to the possibility that not all predator shifters were bad or naturally violent people as she'd been trained to believe. The world was much bigger than Raven's Hollow, and not everyone was the same. Not everyone was terrifying like the raven shifters thought. Alana had proved that with her kindness in her coffee shop, and Ryder…well, when his eyes glowed gold, he was terrifying, but he had also been hilarious and really patient with her job training.

Still, as Avery sat in her car outside of Drat's, she couldn't help the nervous flutters in her stomach. *Flip flap, flip flap*, like bird wings against her ribs. Maybe she was going to be sick. No. She was okay. No one would kill her in a public bar.

And Weston was in there. And Air Ryder. And maybe Alana. Avery had known them for a week, and they hadn't tried to serial-murder her, not even once.

Because they are patient hunters.

Avery shook her head hard. That was the council talking. That was her parents and her teachers. She owed it to herself to figure out the world on her own. Maybe they were right, and maybe she would regret this deeply, but she was tired of assuming people were bad because someone had put that thought into her head.

She wanted to make up her own mind.

She wanted to be strong like Weston.

With a steadying breath, Avery pushed open the door to her home-on-wheels and stood on the cracked concrete parking lot. She smoothed her sundress over her thighs. This was the only thing she'd brought with her to dress up in. She fidgeted with the straps and shouldered her purse, checked that the present she'd bought was inside, then strode across the lot, her sandals clacking loudly with each step.

There was a man sitting on a bench by the door. His elbows rested on his knees, and he had the heels of his hands pressed against his eyes as one of his legs shook in quick succession. His jet black hair fell forward over his face.

"Are you okay?" she asked.

The man slid a pair of sunglasses over his face without looking up and nodded. "I'm fine."

But he didn't sound fine. His voice trembled too hard.

Avery looked longingly at the door, eager to see Weston, but she couldn't just leave this man out here on his own if he was having a shitty night. She knew all about those.

"I'm Avery," she said, sitting down beside him.

"Kane," he said gruffly, offering her his hand. His lips twitched into a smile for an instant when he shook her hand too damn hard for her comfort. Her bones nearly ground to dust. Rough man. She scented the air delicately, but he didn't smell of fur.

"What are you doing out here?" she asked.

"Just nervous to go in. There's nothing else to do around here, though, and I don't want to spend another night alone at home. Sorry." He shook his head and angled his face down at his clasped hands between his knees. "I'm just being a pussy."

"I never understood why men say that."

"What, being a pussy?"

"Yeah." Her cheeks heated with her thought process, but she pressed on. "Pussies seem pretty strong to me. They can take a pummeling. Nuts on the other hand…"

Kane huffed a laugh and nodded his head. "Fine. I'm being a big pair of wimpy nuts."

With a frown, she studied his bulging muscles and his tattoos down one arm. "I can't see why you would be afraid of anything, but if it makes you feel any better, I'm terrified of going in there right now, too."

"Why?"

"Because there are people much more powerful than me in that bar."

Kane jerked his attention to her, and she could see her polite smile in his sunglasses. "Right." His nostrils flared slightly. "Are you a shifter?"

"Are you anti-shifter?"

"Nope. I'm all for them."

"Then yes. But I'm one of those…what did you call it? 'Big pair of wimpy nuts' shifters. And that," she added, surprised at herself, "is the first time I've openly admitted my animal to a stranger. We like to stay hidden."

Kane adjusted his sunglasses farther up his nose and murmured, "I like to stay hidden, too. Come on, Avery. I'll buy your first drink."

"Oh." She smiled brightly because she had been planning on drinking free water and maybe a lemon if she got lucky. But an actual alcoholic beverage sounded awesome. She hadn't eaten much today, so she'd probably be drunk on one. "Thanks so much!"

Kane chuckled softly and opened the door for her, waited for her to pass, and followed her in. Loud music drifted through the bar from an old Jukebox in the corner, and the place was full, standing room only. She was bumped immediately, but Kane shoved the stumbling man away from her and guided her through the crowd up to the bar.

And there he was—Weston Novak. He wore a

genuine smile, his fist around the neck of a beer bottle, his camouflage baseball cap low over his dancing eyes. His teeth were bright white and straight, and the dimple was there, just faintly. He still hadn't shaved and looked like a rough ol' country boy. He'd changed into a black T-shirt and an open blue flannel shirt over holey jeans and clunky work boots.

But when she followed his smiling gaze, the grin fell from her lips. He was talking to a blond-haired woman. She was tall and leggy in a short skirt and sipped on a cosmopolitan. Weston rested his hand on her waist, and the woman ran her silver painted nails down his arm seductively. Slowly, the woman leaned in and whispered something against his ear, and damn everything, Weston was leaning into her. They were definitely going to kiss. Avery couldn't do this, couldn't watch him hook up with another woman. Envy blasted through her, stealing her breath. When she ripped her gaze away, Kane was looking at her, and without a second of hesitation, he bolted forward, dragging her with him. He shoved his way between Weston and Silver Claws and told the bartender, "Can I get a drink for my girl?"

"Hey!" Silver Claws exclaimed.

Weston looked pissed, up until the point he arched his gaze to Avery and froze. Slowly, he dragged his attention down her throat to her chest, waist, hips, legs, and then back up. How had he done that? How had he made her feel like he was touching her with just a look?

His eyes went hard again when he looked at Kane, who was ordering a couple of shots of whiskey. Whiskey? She was more of a panty-dropper fruity-frou-frou drink kinda gal herself.

"And a Sex On the Beach," Kane added. Good man.

"H-happy birthday," she murmured to Weston over the noise of the crowd.

Behind Weston, Ryder and Alana and some other giant people she didn't recognize whooped and lifted their drinks.

"She said it!" Ryder crowed. "Drink up!"

"What did I say?"

Weston took a long swig of his drink and set it down too hard for her taste. "Birthday. Maybe keep that quiet so our livers can stay intact tonight."

"Fuck you, man, she didn't know," Kane gritted

out. He handed Avery a full shot glass.

"I haven't done this before," she said over the music.

Kane's grin transformed his face, and instantly, his nervousness from earlier seemed to fade away. "You've never shot whiskey?"

"I've never shot anything."

"To a night of firsts," he said, tinking his glass against hers, then he turned and bumped the bottom of the glass on the table before he threw his head back and finished it in one gulp.

Okay then. Avery bumped the glass on the counter and drank it like Kane had done. And oh, it burned all the way down. She coughed and grimaced, her knuckles against her lips.

Ryder cheered from a few bar stools over while Avery chased the shot with the Sex On the Beach. Kane threw a few bills onto the counter for the bartender.

"Thanks for buying me these."

Silver Claws had moseyed around Kane and was now hanging around Weston's neck like a trampy necklace. Avery wanted to peck her eyes out, but at least Weston looked uncomfortable and was trying to pry her off him. She wasn't deterred, though, and when the woman leaned forward and whispered something in Weston's ear, green fury snaked through Avery's veins.

"You aren't an oyster," Avery gritted out.

"Excuse me?" the woman asked, her baby blues sparking with anger.

Well, now she was in it. The Bloodrunners had gone quiet, and Weston was looking at her like she'd lost her mind. She had. She hated the way Weston was trying to get rid of this woman, but Silver Claws was pushing him. Avery cleared her throat and clenched her hands around the strap of her purse to steady them. "You aren't an oyster, and he ain't your pearl, so let him go."

Silver Claws narrowed her eyes to feral little slits. Kane snorted from behind her. Weston was frozen in place holding the woman's wrists so she wouldn't molest him further. Ryder giggled and asked, "How do you spell oyster? I'm live tweeting this shit."

Silver Claws wrenched her wrists out of Weston's grip and stomped past Avery, bumping her hard in the shoulder as she did. It hurt, but at least she wasn't touching Wes anymore.

Wes? When had she gone from thinking of him as the Novak Raven to Wes?

"What are you doing here?" he asked Avery, leaning in close.

"It's your birth—" She cleared her throat and said, "I'm here to celebrate your big day."

His lips thinned into a somber line, much different from the striking smile Silver Claws had been able to draw out of him. "I think you should go."

"Why are you being so fucking rude right now?" A dark-headed woman with two oddly-colored eyes said from behind them. "Retract the talons, Wes. It's a bar, not a private party." She held out her hand for a shake. "I'm Harper."

Avery choked on her drink. "The Bloodrunner Dragon?" she rasped out.

"Yep," Harper said with a friendly smile. That's why the air felt so damn heavy in here.

Avery shook her hand fast, on account of being terrified of the monster in her middle. That and Harper's skin felt like hot embers. Kane handed her another shot of whiskey.

"Slow down, man," Wes gritted out.

Pissed, Avery ground out, "You don't control me." And then she took another shot with Kane and chased it with her Sex on the Beach.

"Yeah," Ryder said, typing away on his phone. "She's a grown-ass woman."

"That's right." Whoo, she felt brave right now. Definitely tipsy, but mostly brave. "I *am* a grown-ass woman."

Harper giggled and said, "I like you. Let me introduce you to everyone. That's Lexi." She gestured to a smiling woman with dark hair and bright green eyes that matched her camouflage tank top. "You clearly know Ryder, and over there is Aaron and Alana." She gestured to a tall, muscular, blond man with piercings in his ears and tattoos all over him. Alana she knew, and since the shots were making her feel invincible, she waved to the woman with the dark eyes and the scar on her lip, and this time, her raven didn't want to fly away, cawing in terror.

"And this," Harper said, "is my man, my future baby daddy, my everything, Wyatt." She wrapped her arms around a titan with bright blue eyes and spiked up brown hair.

Avery arched her neck all the way back and

grinned. At least she thought she grinned. Her lips were numb right now. "You're big, and you smell like a bear."

Wyatt laughed and said, "I am a bear, actually. What are you? And don't tell me human because you gave yourself away with your sense of smell."

Crap. Avery stood frozen in place, her lips searching for her straw. She stalled, sucking her drink and blinking slowly as though she hadn't heard the question.

"Go ahead, Avery," Wes said, his eyes cold. "Tell them what you are."

"Wait, what's happening?" Ryder asked, dragging his attention from his phone.

"Tell them," Wes demanded.

"Why are you being like this?" she asked. It wasn't cool to out her animal.

Weston turned and addressed the Bloodrunners. "Avery is a raven shifter."

The crew stilled, and none of them spoke a word. Avery couldn't lift her gaze from the ground if she tried. Angry and tipsy as hell, Avery clutched her empty glass and said, "You've been really mean to me, and it's really fucked up, Weston."

"Is it? Is it as fucked up as what you did?"

She dared a look at him because he was wrong. Wrong in whatever he thought about her. "You hurt me so badly. So *badly*! You dropped me like I was nothing, you pompous asshole. You left me with no outlet, no friends, left me to compare everyone to you. You left me with an empty life and no explanation, and you think you have a right to treat me like this?" She shoved him as hard as she could in the shoulder. He didn't budge, the monster. "Outing my animal is a fucked up move, Novak. You're not the boy I knew." Cheeks on fire, she looked around at the Bloodrunners. "It was nice to meet all of you," she said quietly before she bolted for the exit.

There were too many people in here, and Ryder was yelling something behind her, but screw it. She was done with the games. Done hoping that Weston would magically think she was good enough to be nice to. In her escape, she bounced around like a pinball as she ran into a man with a biker vest and a lady in high heels.

She shouldn't have come here to Bryson City. She shouldn't have gone hunting for a life that could never be hers. Weston had embarrassed her. He'd shamed her in front of the Bloodrunners, and for what reason? She'd already been nervous coming in here tonight, and now this? For a minute—for one single, glorious minute—she'd almost felt normal. She'd almost felt accepted, and then Weston had taken that away. Again!

Twin tears stained her cheeks as she shoved open the door, but she angrily wiped the moisture away. That man didn't deserve the emotion. He didn't deserve her hurt.

"Avery!" Weston called, jogging across the concrete behind her.

"Fuck off." Whoa, she couldn't believe she'd just told the Novak Raven that. Whiskey was liquid courage.

"Avery, wait!" He grabbed her arm, but she yanked it out of his grip.

"Don't touch me." Stupid tears wouldn't quit falling.

"What did you mean back there?" he asked as she fumbled for her keys. "What did you mean I left you with no outlet?"

"I mean you were awful when we met in Saratoga. You were rude to me. You would barely look at me, and stupid me, I'd been counting down the days until I got to meet you. I loved you! I know I was nothing to you, but for me, you meant everything. You were mine, and I was finally going to get to meet you and touch you. I was finally going to hear you say that everything would be okay instead of writing it in letters." She let off a sob and yanked open the door to her Civic. "You treated me like I was invisible instead, just like everyone else in my life, and I went home feeling like my heart had been ripped out of my chest. I wrote you after and waited for a response, but you never gave one. And I get it. I wasn't pretty enough, so your feelings changed when you saw me. I understand it, but it still doesn't change how much it hurt."

"Wait, wait, wait!" he barked, as she slammed the door beside her.

Weston reached for the handle, but she was faster. She locked it in a rush.

"I'm not taking your shit anymore, Weston. Maybe that was the girl I used to be, but I'm not her anymore."

Avery pulled out of the parking spot and gassed it onto Main Street. When she dared one look in the rearview mirror, Weston was standing there with his hands out, his eyes wide and shocked as if he didn't know what just happened. *Welcome to the fucking club, Novak.*

Tears blurred her vision, and she squeezed her eyes to clear them as she gripped the steering wheel. She didn't know what she would do, but she couldn't stay here and keep her pride.

And right now, pride was all she had left.

SEVEN

What the fuck just happened?

Either Avery was very good at twisting things, or he'd been completely wrong about what had actually gone down when they were fifteen. Weston debated bolting for his truck, but Ryder was yelling at him again as he stomped out of Drat's.

"What the fuck, man?" Ryder yelled. "You know her? And you didn't tell me?"

"We were pen pals," Weston gritted out as the other Bloodrunners filed out of the bar.

Ryder's face was as red as his hair right now. "You had a fucking pen pal? Dude, we grew up together. We told each other everything. Why would you keep that from me?"

"Because she was mine! She was just for me. I didn't want any of you giving me shit over her because I was having a hard enough time figuring out what she was to me. My mom and Avery's mom decided we would be good pen pals. I could learn about raven culture, and she could have someone outside of their community to talk to. Something was wrong with Avery. Something big, but no one ever told me. Her mom just said she needed something outside of Raven's Hollow to hold onto. And that was me. But then…"

"Then what?" Harper asked softly.

Weston shook his head for a long time, stared off in the direction Avery had gone. "I don't know. I thought she betrayed me."

"Didn't sound that way to me, man," Aaron said, his arm around Alana's shoulders. "She didn't sound like she was lying at all when she was telling you off."

"You should go after her," Harper said quietly.

"Yep," Weston said grimly, jogging for his truck. He didn't know where she lived, but there were only a few main streets, and if he drove reckless enough, he might be able to catch her before she turned off onto a side road.

He slammed the door beside him and sped out onto Main Street. The needle on his speedometer was gracing sixty before he even hit the edge of town. This place was a speed trap, and he was definitely running the risk of being pulled over, but screw it. He had this overwhelming urge to right whatever wrong he'd just done to Avery.

Bathed in darkness, the Smoky Mountain woods blurred past. A mountain jutted straight up on his right, and a winding river was on his left, which didn't leave much place to pull over. He squinted his eyes and scanned the dark road up ahead, hoping for the soft glow of taillights, but there was nothing. He was alone out here. Shit. She was probably going sixty to get away from him.

He connected a call back home and hoped Mom and Dad were still up. They'd always been night owls.

"Hello?" Mom said in that sweet voice of hers.

"I didn't wake you, did I?"

"No, what's wrong? You sound upset. Do you want me to get your father on the line?"

"No, no, I called for you. Remember that pen pal I had when I was a kid?"

Mom went quiet. After a few breaths, she

murmured, "Avery Foley."

"Yeah, her. She found me."

"Oh, Weston…" She already sounded like she pitied him, so he pushed on.

"Ma, I remember meeting her when we were freshmen in high school, but right before that, everything had gone wrong. Right? Her mom told you about the council?"

Mom sighed. "Weston, it was too complicated to explain it in a way you would understand. You got the condensed version."

"But I'm not a kid anymore, Ma. Tell me. Tell me everything because I've been really angry at this girl for a long time, and then she shows up and she's acting hurt by my rejection. It makes no damned sense. What happened? I want to know everything." He remembered the hurt on Avery's face. "I *need* to know everything."

The shutting of a door echoed through the phone, and his Dad murmured, "Is that my raven boy?" in the background.

Static blasted across the line as though Mom was covering the phone, but Wes could still hear them. "Yes. Avery found him."

His father didn't respond. Or perhaps he did, but just silently. Weston could imagine him, dark eyebrows arched in surprise, inhumanly bright green eyes wide, mouth set in a grim line. Dad had never liked the idea of Weston being pulled into raven culture, and Avery had done just that.

Weston gripped the steering wheel tighter as he hugged a curve. "Ma, tell me."

"I used to be friends with Avery's mom, Hannah, back before I left my people to find your Da. I kept in touch with her because it was nice to have a friend who was like me. You have to understand I left everything I knew, my culture, my family, everything, just on the off-chance that Beaston would be the man I hoped he'd grown into. I was in a crew of predator shifters, and ravens are naturally timid. It was hard, feeling stretched between both worlds, and I didn't want you so immersed in Damon's Mountains that you didn't know where I'd come from. Where *you*...came from. You were going to grow up a raven, a flight shifter, in a crew of bears and dragons, and I didn't want you feeling alone. When Avery's mom got pregnant after I did, it felt so good to go through that with a friend who understood my raven side. And hearing stories of Avery as she grew up, I thought more and more that maybe she could be a comfort to you someday if you ever grew unhappy with being different in the Gray Backs."

"But I wasn't different. No one ever treated me differently." Sure, his friends teased him about being a flight shifter, but that's what friends did. They gave each other shit.

"But you were. You were quiet like your dad, and you came to me one day, wondering about ravens. And Avery's mom had mentioned letting you two be pen pals for years before you questioned your heritage. So it felt like the right time. For you, and also for Avery."

"What do you mean?"

"Something was wrong with her raven. Not...wrong to a Gray Back, but wrong for Raven's Hollow. She is dominant, Weston."

Dominant? She didn't feel dominant, but maybe she was for a raven. Maybe that's why she could talk well on the phone and converse so easily with customers. Maybe that was why she was able to tell Shelly to get off him tonight. "Why would dominance be a bad thing?"

"Dominant ravens aren't supposed to exist, especially in a female. They like the flock as steady as possible, but Avery shook up everything. She was a late Changer, and soon after her raven emerged for the first time, her parents were stripped of their rank. In an effort to make Avery's animal more submissive, the council required the community to…"

"To what?"

"Weston, I don't know all the details, and that's something Avery will have to explain to you. It doesn't feel right talking about her like this."

"But when I was a kid, you told me she was untrustworthy. That she had betrayed me. You told me she was willing bait to take me away from the Gray Backs. From you and Da. She doesn't sound like bait, though, Ma. She sounds like a victim."

"Wes, her mother went to the council about our friendship, told them everything about me. Every discussion, every admission, ever insecurity I had leaving our people. And when I got pregnant, they implored Hannah to get pregnant, too. They hoped for a girl."

"What?" Weston's thoughts were churning. He hadn't known this part. "What are you saying?"

"Avery was conceived in the hopes that she would be a female who could seduce you back to Raven's Hollow. And I know them. They would've sequestered you away from Damon's Mountains, brainwashed you, turned you into one of them. I want you to live the life you choose. Not one someone chooses for you."

Wes scrubbed his hand down his face and stared blankly ahead at the road winding under his tires. Why him? Why go to such effort to draw him back to a culture he didn't connect with? "When I was a kid, you told me her mom had betrayed us to the council for all those years. You told me the council had been reading my letters to Avery, picking them apart, using them to manipulate our friendship. But if the council hates dominant ravens, why the fuck would they even want me there? What's the point of all the manipulation?"

"I don't know," his mother said helplessly. "Hannah let it slip one day while they were planning their trip to Saratoga to let you two meet for the first time. She mentioned the council was allowing her to come unchaperoned, and I was confused about what they had to do with anything. She said it as a joke, but when I pushed, she clammed up. And then two days before they came to Saratoga, she broke down crying on the phone and told me everything. She told me how she'd told the council everything about me, and how they'd guided her conversations. About how they'd pushed for you and Avery to have contact. I felt played. I felt stupid. I'd put you, my only boy, my only raven, in the sights of the council, one I had worked so hard to escape myself. Over and over I asked why they wanted you, but Hannah wouldn't tell me. Or maybe couldn't, I don't know."

"If you were so angry, why did you let us meet? Why did you still go through with it?"

"Because you asked me to. Don't you remember, Weston? You are so loyal, but you give few chances. You said you wanted to look her in the face and ask her why she'd played games. Why she let the council read your letters. Why she pretended to care so deeply for you. You wanted to see her eyes when you asked her why she hurt you."

"But I didn't. I remember sitting at the restaurant, and she was smiling like she didn't even know she was doing anything wrong, and I was so angry I couldn't speak. I thought I would cuss her out in front of everyone." None of this made any damn sense. Clearly, the council had played a big part in Weston and Avery's relationship growing up, but how much? "Ma?"

"Yeah?"

"Is it possible that Avery didn't know she was bait for me?"

The sigh she gave off said she didn't think so, but she allowed, "If she didn't know, there was a huge amount of manipulation she missed. It would mean there was a mountain of secrets she was sitting right on top of, unaware."

"But there's a chance?"

Silence.

"Ma."

"Yes, there is a chance she was unaware. Weston, I have to tell you something."

"Tell me."

"I don't know if I should."

There were brake lights up ahead, but they were at an angle. And as Weston slowed and pulled behind the beat-up old car, it was apparent why. Avery had pulled over onto the side of a steep embankment, and her driver's side door was shoved open. There was her little white sundress, soaking on the ground in the mud. Weston leaned forward, scanning the trees branches in the dark woods. She must've got desperate and Changed in there. Shit.

"Mom, tell me quick. I think I found her."

"I don't want to tell you to trust her because I don't know her. I don't know her intentions, but you've always been good at reading people. If you think she's a victim, she might be really and truly trying to break away from Raven's Hollow. And if that's the case, she'll need help. A lot of it. They make it really hard for raven shifters to leave the flock, especially females. Do you understand what I'm saying to you?"

Weston threw his truck in park and leaned back against the headrest. "I understand."

If Avery really was here with good intentions, she was in trouble from her people.

EIGHT

She couldn't do it. Why couldn't she Change? The raven was right there, scratching at her skin, cawing to be released, but Avery's body wasn't working. Maybe it was the alcohol, or that she was so angry and hurt.

Sobbing, she drew her knees up to her chest as the water drops that made it through the thick tree canopy *drip-dripped* onto her legs and head. Of course it would start raining right now.

She'd been so fucking hopeful. So determined to make things work here so she wouldn't have to return to Raven's Hollow with her tail feathers tucked between her legs. She'd wanted to live outside of that awful place and make a life for herself that she could be proud of, but tonight was the night. It was the night she had to take stock of where she really was, and that was in a muddy hole, chin deep and still sinking.

She was out of money, sleeping in her car, fucking hungry, and Weston hated her. She hadn't had a decent balanced meal in way too long. And to top it all off, her damn car broke down. It just puttered and sputtered until the gas pedal wouldn't work anymore and her muddy hole had finally swallowed her up completely.

"Avery?"

She gasped and startled hard. She hadn't even heard Weston approach through the spattering of raindrops on leaves. "Don't look at me!"

She had heightened night vision, and right now, Weston's eyes were green like forest moss. Concern flitted across his face. Instead of turning away, he pulled her up out of the mud and asked, "Did you already Change, darlin'?"

She was shaking now, from cold, adrenaline, and something more. Darlin'? She liked the way that word rolled off his tongue. Weston's gaze was locked on hers, and for the first time since she'd come here, they weren't full of hatred. Her white cotton sundress was mud-splattered but draped over his arm, and without a word, he knelt down and held her panties out, waiting for her to step into them.

Mortified, she dipped her feet into them quickly, but he was slow and methodical as he gently pulled them up her legs, the knuckles of his thumbs brushing her bare thighs. When he stood, his attention dipped to her breasts and held there for a few seconds before he forced his darkening eyes back to hers and rushed to pull her dress over her head. Slowly, he spun her and zipped the back, dragging his fingertip up her spine as he went, sending a delicious shiver up her body.

He released her too soon, and she stumbled forward slightly without his strong hands on her. Not ready to face the mess that was her car, Avery sank back down to the forest floor and rested her back against the rough bark of a tree. "How did you find me?" She wasn't exactly right off the road. She'd run for a while to get here.

"Uuuh," Weston drawled, taking a seat next to her—*right* next to her! "My dad was a tracker."

"Beaston?" she asked quietly.

"Yeah."

"He terrifies me."

"You've never met him."

"He terrifies all ravens."

"Yeah, well he terrifies most predator shifters, too," Weston said with a soft chuckle. "Not me, though. He was just Da to me. He taught me to track. And not only through woods. I can find people who don't want to be found."

"You should've been a private investigator."

"Tracking down cheating housewives doesn't exactly call to me," he said grimly.

"Right." Avery's voice was hitching with those uncontrollable breaths that came after a good cry.

"I have to ask you something," Weston said low. "I'll only ask this one time, and whatever you tell me, I'll try my best to understand. Please, just…tell me the truth."

"How could I tell you anything else? You can hear lies."

Weston smiled sadly at her in the dim light. "Did you know?"

Avery's breath hitched again on the inhale. "Did I know what?"

"Did you know the council was using you to get to me?"

Avery searched his face to make sure he was being serious, but the hardness was back in his eyes. "Why would the council try to get to you?"

"Avery, I know. I know everything. I know about why you were born."

"Why I was…? Weston, tell me what you're talking about."

"The council encouraged your mom to get pregnant when my mom was. They were friends, and the council wanted you to lure me to Raven's Hollow. Did you know about that?"

"No," she whispered, horrified.

"Did you know the council was reading the letters I sent you?"

Avery shook her head slowly. This wasn't real. "Of course not. I hid them behind a loose brick in the fireplace in my room. Those were my letters, not for anyone else. I even brought them here with me so that no one would ever find them."

Weston's chest was heaving now with every inhale. "Avery, yes or no. I can't… Did you know you were bait for me? Please."

"No! No, no, no," she murmured, her face crumpling. Was the moisture on her cheeks rain or tears? She didn't know, nor did she care. He was being mean again. The council had nothing to do with her feelings for Weston. Nothing at all. She was born to bait him? Avery covered her face with her hands to hide from him because now she knew why he was staring at her. He was trying to gauge if she was putting on a show, and she hated this. She wanted to tell him to fuck off again. She wanted to spit in his face or maybe slap him with her fingers clawed.

But something horrifying was happening in her chest right now. Such a sick feeling of rightness slid over her as she really considered what he'd just said.

Did her mother have her to be a lure for Weston? Was that the reason for her existence? Her father hadn't ever given a single, solitary shit about her, especially when her broken raven had got him stripped of his rank. But mom was different. She loved her. She had her because she wanted a baby to care for...right?

"Can I borrow your phone?" she asked, her voice trembling like the raindrop-battered leaves around them.

Without a word, Weston pulled his phone out of his back pocket and laid it in her outstretched palm. She dialed home from memory and waited the three rings it took Mom to pick up.

"Hello?" It was hard to hear because there was so much talking in the background—men's murmured voices.

"Mom, it's me."

Immediately, Mom's voice dipped to a whisper. "Avery, this isn't a good time."

"Is the council at your house?"

"What?" A beat of silence, then, "How did you know? Are you back in The Hollow?" Mom was probably at the window, peeking through the blinds.

"I need to ask you something."

"I can't really talk right now. Your father, he's... I can't talk."

"That's fine, then just answer my question yes or no, okay?"

Mom didn't answer, but that was fine.

"Am I bait for the Novak Raven?"

More silence.

"Mom? You owe me this. Just tell me. Am I bait for the Novak Raven?"

"Y-yes," Mom stuttered out. Her voice had gone all soft.

In that moment, Avery's heart broke. She'd thought this thing with Weston, this innate instinct to be close to him, was her own doing. It was her heart latching onto a man she cared for, but it wasn't just her in this. How much of her feelings were from manipulation from the people who were supposed to protect her? From the people who were supposed to love her?

"How long?" she whispered.

Mom's breath was hitching, as though she was about to sob.

"Please tell me," Avery begged, *needing* to know. "How long have I been the lure?"

"For always."

Avery gasped and hung up the phone, handed it to Weston in a rush so she didn't have to touch the damn thing anymore. This couldn't be happening. But then, a hundred things made sense at once. Dad always taking secret meetings. Mom's relieved smile whenever Avery had brought up Weston's name throughout the years. The constant encouragement to rekindle a relationship with him. The council asking her questions about the Novak Raven when she was younger. So many meetings to interview her. The feeling that she didn't belong, like she was just an object. So many times she'd been pulled from school, or from her life, for meetings with the council. She'd thought it was because of her broken raven, so they could make sure she was progressing like she was supposed to, but now that she looked back, it was so obvious. Her meetings always ended with discussions about the Novak Raven. And she'd answered because she'd trusted her people. She'd trusted them to have her best interest in mind, and honestly, it felt good to openly talk about how much she liked Weston. How much she respected him. Bond, bond, bond. She'd grown up thinking she'd bonded to him just through letters, but maybe that was just what the council had told her. Perhaps they'd convinced her she belonged to the Novak Raven. That her fate was to be with him. Maybe her feelings weren't real at all.

Bait.

Avery fell forward on her hands and knees and retched. Weston's hand was gentle on her back, right between her shoulder blades, but she didn't want the comfort. Didn't deserve it. "Don't touch me," she said, wincing away from him.

"Avery," he murmured softly.

She bolted upright to escape him. "No wonder you hated me. No wonder!" Her shoulders shook with her weeping, but who cared if she embarrassed herself now? He hadn't ever been hers to begin with...and could never be because she was nothing. She was born to betray him.

Weston stood slowly, his hands out like he was settling a wild horse. "I didn't ever hate you. I was hurt, and I lashed out the only way I knew how."

"By ignoring me, and that's fine. You had every right to pretend I was invisible because that's what I am." Her breath hitched. "I'm nothing."

He was to her in an instant. His arms crushed her as she struggled to escape his embrace. She fought and fought, but he was so strong—so much stronger than her.

When her muscles were fatigued and twitching and she was too weary to fight anymore... When she was completely defeated, she sagged against him and let off a long, heartbroken sound and whispered again, "I'm nothing."

"You aren't. I swear you aren't, Avery. I see you."

She clutched onto his damp shirt and squeezed her eyes tightly because it felt so damn good to hear someone say that. And not just someone, but *the* someone. *Her* someone.

"I'm in a riptide, Weston. I've been pulled under for so long, and I'm being thrashed by the waves and dragged down by the current, but I'm still swimming, you know? I'm watching these bubbles racing to the surface, and if I can just follow them, maybe I'll breathe again. Maybe I'll be okay. But it's been too long. I can't breathe, and it's been too long."

The rasp of Weston's jaw felt good against her face as he lowered his lips to her ear. "Fuck the council, and fuck everyone who has hurt you, Ave. Someday, you're gonna rise up from the ashes like a fucking phoenix. Everything is going to be okay. I promise."

Like a phoenix? Her? No way. She was weak, and the mud she'd been wallowing in was too heavy on her wings. She couldn't rise up. Not her. "My whole life has been a lie. I'm all alone with nothing." She let off a long, shuttering breath and admitted how screwed she was. "My car broke down."

"I'll fix it." His voice sounded so determined. So

sure.

And dammit, here was her shot to unload all her burdens on a strong man who could shoulder them. "I don't have any money, and I haven't been able to afford much food."

"I'll feed you."

Her eyes prickled and burned because no one had ever been this kind to her. But there was an even bigger shame, and right now, she wanted to tell him everything. "I've been sleeping in my car."

"I know." Weston eased back and cupped her cheeks, his calloused hands rough against her skin. His eyes were dark under the brim of his hat. "I saw the pillow and the blanket in your back seat. I have a place for you to stay. Somewhere dry and warm where you can be alone and safe, and no one will bother you."

"I don't want your charity."

"Then we won't call it charity. Call it me making up for leaving you alone when you needed a friend."

"Friend." She *hated* the sound of that, but that's all they could ever be. She'd been born to betray him after all.

Weston's jaw clenched as he pressed his body

gently against hers. His hands drifted from her cheeks to her neck, and a strange intensity sparked in his eyes. "I want to kiss you right now, but it doesn't feel right."

Avery froze. "Okay, I understand. Wait, no I don't. Why doesn't it feel right to kiss me?" Because she really wanted him to kiss her right now.

"Because you are dealing with a lot right now, finding out about the council and your car, and the—"

Avery pushed up on her tiptoes and kissed him. Way too hard. She basically bit him. Mortified, she lurched away, ducked her gaze, and apologized.

Weston rubbed his bottom lip like it hurt, but his mouth was stretching into a smile. He was laughing at her again, and she wanted to crawl into a hole and hide for the rest of her life.

But instead of making fun, he squared up to her, rested his hands on her waist, and dragged her body to his. And slowly, so slowly, he leaned down and pressed his lips onto hers. Fireworks were going off in her belly as she slid her arms around his neck and parted her lips for his searching tongue. He stayed gentle, drawing out the kiss as his mouth moved smoothly against hers in rhythmic strokes that turned the fireworks to an erupting volcano. This was it—the best kiss she'd ever had, and it was with the Novak Raven. It was with her Weston. Her inner raven was practically crowing with happiness inside of her.

The rain was falling harder, soaking her hair and clothes, but she didn't care about that. She didn't care about anything but how Weston was gripping the fabric of her dress as if he wanted more. And the way his lips were turning urgent against hers, the way his body felt, the way his erection pressed onto her belly, she'd done that—drawn this reaction from him. Her, the broken raven.

Weston thrust his tongue into her mouth one last time, then jerked away. "I'm sorry. This is… It's just I saw your tits, and I really like your tits, and your other parts, too, but your tits are fuckin' phenomenal. Just…" He held his cupped hands out over her chest. "Perfect."

Clearly, Weston was a boob-man.

He cleared his throat and frowned. "And also you're nice, sweet, and pretty."

But boobs had topped his list. Despite the gravity of her dire situation, she laughed. It wasn't a soft polite one either, but a surprised, from-the-core bellowing laugh that drew her up short. She covered her mouth with her hand to hide her giggles. She should not be laughing right now, not with all the bad shit she'd just found out about her life, but Weston was chuckling, too, and all that did was make her laugh harder.

Eyes dancing and dimple deep in his cheek, Weston took his camouflage baseball cap off and put it on backward. He twisted around and looked through the woods in the direction of the road. "I feel..." He inhaled deeply and sighed. "I feel too damn much right now, honestly, but I need to get you warm and dry and fed, okay?"

"Wes, I'm not your responsibility."

"No, but it would make me feel...good...to take care of you." His smile slipped into a frown. Looking confused as hell, he rested his hands on his hips. "Right. You don't have a bra on, and I can see through your dress. Your nipples are perfect, and we should go." In a rush he pulled off his long-sleeve flannel shirt and wadded it up into a ball, then handed it to her, his eyes averted.

Stunned, Avery took it gently from his offered

hand and cradled it to her chest. It smelled like his cologne.

With a quick dick adjustment, he spun on his heel and strode off through the wilderness, leaving Avery to stare down in surprise at her chest. Sure enough, her nipples were drawn up against the soaking white fabric of her cotton dress.

She'd just found out her entire life was a complete lie, and in the same five minutes got the kiss she'd always dreamed about from the man who had stolen her heart all those years ago with nothing more than written words on a page. Maybe the council had something to do with her feelings, she didn't know. But they didn't have everything to do with them. This right here—this moment they'd shared together—was important.

Shaking her head at the strange turn her life had taken, Avery followed Weston's receding figure through the woods and to her car.

She'd never seen Weston stammer or struggle for words, but he had just had the cutest man-freak-out she'd ever witnessed, and all caused by her.

She had no idea why, but she, Avery Foley—relative nobody, bait, and broken raven—had somehow managed to fluster Weston Novak.

NINE

By the time Avery reached the road, Weston had the hood of her car popped open and resting on the prop. He was talking low into his phone, shielding the little device from the rain by using the hood as an umbrella. His black T-shirt was plastered to him like a second skin, and his back muscles rippled as he poked and prodded around the innards of her car.

It was raining in earnest now. Avery didn't normally like the feel of chilled skin and damp clothes, but standing here on the side of the road, watching Weston try to save her, was kind of beautiful.

Weston's dark eyebrows were lowered in concentration, and his lips were so sensual as he spoke into the cell. His baseball cap was wet, there was a constant *drip-drip* of rainwater falling from the bill to trickle down his back, and his boots were covered in mud.

He'd come for her.

He'd left his birthday celebration and followed her, tracked her through the woods, and without a single plea from her, was taking the reins of her chaotic life for a minute so she could rest her weary mind. And damn, it felt so good not to have to worry about anything for tonight, because every instinct in her said Weston would take care of her. Perhaps not for always, and perhaps only as friends, but that was better than nothing.

His triceps flexed as he pushed on something inside of her car, and when he muttered a curse, she asked, "Can I do anything?"

"Nah, and neither can I tonight. Your battery is older than dinosaur shit, your belt is shot, and your engine didn't even try to turn over for me. Maybe it's just the battery, but I don't like how it died mid-ride on you."

"Oh." She wrung her hands and tried to imagine how much all of this would cost to repair at an auto shop. How discouraging that her first paycheck and probably more would already be blown.

"I can get it running again, but I need parts and can't get them until tomorrow. I'll call the police station and tell them we'll tow it to Harper's Mountains in the morning so they won't give you a ticket tonight. You can ride with me."

"But you have tours tomorrow," she said. "Weston, I appreciate you helping me, but I won't risk your new business for this."

Weston jerked his gaze to hers, and a flash of surprise was there in his eyes. Then they softened, and he let off a slight smile just before he gave his attention back to lowering the hood of her car. "You don't have to worry about that. I'll take care of it after the tours are done for the day."

"Okay." She wanted to say so much more than that. She wanted to tell him how much this all meant to her, how relieved she was that he wasn't mad at her anymore. She wanted to tell him if he ever needed anything—anything at all—she would gladly do it. But he was locked onto her with his gaze again, and her words got all caught up in her throat. His eyes were the pitch black that hers turned when her raven was riled up, and his lips were pursed, as though he was trying to figure her out.

He looked beautiful here in the soft glow of the streetlight behind him. Beautiful? That was an impossible word for a man who was strapped with muscles and covered in tattoos, but he was. He was her beautiful raven man. This moment right here felt like she was falling. Not sinking in the mud that had taken over her life, but the feeling she got when she dove from a great height and spread her wings at the last minute, when her stomach dipped to the ground and made her want to laugh and yell with happiness. She had always been intrigued and a little intimidated by Weston Novak, but now she was falling hard for him.

Instead of telling him all of her mushy thoughts, she parted her lips and said, "Thank you."

"For what?" he asked, a slight frown furrowing his brows.

For the kiss and for coming after me. For holding me when I found out my life was a lie. For telling me everything will be okay. For all the letters that saved me when I was a kid. For being you.

He wouldn't appreciate the sentiment, though, so

instead she said the only other words that felt right. "Thank you for everything."

When one corner of his lip turned up, her breath stuttered in her chest. So damn stunning.

Weston jerked his chin toward his truck parked at an angle on the side of the deserted road. "Get in and turn on the heat. I'll grab your stuff."

"Okay," she murmured, her legs and arms feeling numb with what had transpired in the woods. She'd thought her life was over, thought the darkness was swallowing her up, but Weston had come in and, like a beacon of light, absorbed the darkness and took the impossible weight off her heart.

And now the rough, quiet, dangerous Novak Raven was being so tender with her. Avery made her way through the mud to the passenger's side of his truck and climbed in. It had been lifted a few inches and sat on fat mud tires, so she had to use the rails and scramble a bit to reach the seat, but when she was finally in, she turned on the car to get the heat going, as much for her as for Weston, so he could be comfortable when he got inside.

She canted her head and watched him pull her bedding and her suitcase from her car. He even slung her purse over his massive shoulder and made his way to her with long, confident strides. Something had changed in him. And when she looked down to turn the radio dial, the word *Home* was running across the screen with a phone number underneath, like he'd just ended the call. Home. His home? He must've called his father.

She frowned. No. He must've called his mother, Aviana Novak, because she was the one who would know the most about Avery. Chills rippled up her skin. She'd grown up idolizing Aviana, and whatever her heroine had said to Weston had made a difference in his opinion of her.

She'd never talked to Aviana except for the one meeting they had when she was young, and she remembered she wasn't like the raven women she'd imagined. Aviana had sat straight and proud and had been angry, with her mother perhaps. Made sense now if Aviana had found out about the council's treachery. Avery hated the idea that the council had read Weston's letters. What must it have been like for Aviana to realize her own people were after her son? Avery felt sick just thinking about being a part of the council's plan—whatever it was.

Weston shoved her things in the back seat and jogged around the front of the truck. Raindrops fell in a constant downpour in the high beams, and his ripped torso was illuminated as he passed through. When he climbed into his truck and pulled the belt over his lap, she asked him before she lost her nerve. "Did your mother change your mind about me?"

"No," he said in that deep, rich voice of his. "*I* changed my mind about you." He cast her a quick glance and smiled sadly. "I think we both got played. I think we both got hurt, and that shit ends now. Fuck the council, fuck the ravens, and fuck your parents. You'll show them."

Weston gunned it onto the asphalt, one hand draped easily over the steering wheel, one elbow resting on the console, the epitome of relaxed and confident male. Weston knew his place in this world. He was a raven shifter who had somehow clawed his way to the top of the food chain.

The last thing he said bothered her, though. *You'll show them.* She was a fraud. "Do you know about the woman's role in raven culture? Did your mother explain?"

Weston's lips pursed into a thin line. "She told

me a little."

"Females aren't allowed to have jobs. Not after your mom left. They didn't want the flock scattering into the wind, so the rules changed. The goal is to keep females completely financially dependent on the males. They keep us so desperate for the things we need to survive that we'll stay submissive and agree to marriage contracts."

"Out of desperation." Weston's words were tainted with the hard edge of disgust.

"Out of desperation," she agreed. "It's hard to leave because we're taught we can't make it out in the real world without our mighty men to provide for us. We're taught that our one duty, our one reason for existence, is to provide heirs and secure our place and rank in the community." Ashamed, she lowered her voice. "So you see, I didn't show them anything. I failed. I couldn't provide for myself, and now you are coming to my rescue, a male raven, just like they said I needed."

"Bullshit," he drawled. "I didn't give you the job, Avery. You fought for it. You earned it. Hell, I didn't even want to give it to you, and you got it by being a stubborn pain in the ass. And you've worked hard and caught on quickly, and in a week, you'll have that first paycheck and be on your way. Bullshit, you aren't showing them. I'm calling it in two months. You'll be on your own two feet creating a life despite your fucked-up peoples' horse-shittery."

"Our."

"What?"

"Our people."

"Oooh no." Weston shook his head hard. "Ravens aren't my people. The Gray Backs are my people. The Bloodrunners are my people. Your animal doesn't matter, Avery."

"She does."

"She doesn't! You know that saying, blood is thicker than water? That works for some people, but you can't choose your blood family. Some people just get dealt a shitty hand and are born into families who aren't good people. You can make your own family, though. You can surround yourself with good people. And you will. I know you will."

Shocked, Avery whispered, "You seem so certain. That makes one of us."

Weston's smile was crooked and easy when he took his eyes off the road just long enough to look at her. "You'll be fine. You have a badass brawler raven inside of you, woman."

Avery blinked hard in surprise. Aviana must've told him that little gem. "A brawler raven that never served me any good in Raven's Hollow."

"Screw Raven's Hollow, Ave. Your raven will serve you well enough out here."

The nickname made her sit straight up against the fabric seat. She'd never had a nickname before. Well, one that wasn't a cuss word. "How do you know?"

Weston's smile grew wicked. "Because you went to a bar tonight and held your own with dragons and grizzlies."

Avery gulped. "Dragons plural?" she squeaked out.

Weston shot her an incredulous look. "Yeah, Harper and Kane."

"Kane's a dragon?" she said too loudly.

Weston chuckled. "He's the last Blackwing Dragon. We call him Dark Kane. I shit you not, I watched that man almost kill Ryder's asshole dad with his bare hands in front of an entire bar of people. He's not a shifter you fuck with…" Weston's voice darkened as he added, "But he seemed to like you just fine."

She remembered how nervous Kane had seemed outside of the bar and how he'd told her he liked to hide, too. So even big, lethal, terrifying shifters had insecurities. The last Blackwing Dragon had bought her drinks and been nice to her. Come to think of it, the Bloodrunners had all been nice to her. Sure, they could rip her from limb to limb with zero effort, but not once had they given into the urge to put a smaller shifter in its place. Not once had they treated her like she was less-than. The more time she spent with shifters outside of Raven's Hollow, the more she thought the council was expertly manipulating all the ravens who lived in their community just to create fear. But why? To keep the ravens in line? To keep them too scared to ask questions? To keep the females dependent?

They were wrong about so much.

Avery gave her attention to the thick greenery blurring by her window, just on the edge of the headlight illumination. "I think you were lucky to be raised in the Gray Backs." She couldn't even imagine Weston as one of the chauvinistic jerks in Raven's

Hollow. Instead, he'd been raised by a strong woman, while surrounded by other strong women. Hell, Weston's alpha was a woman. Before Harper established the Bloodrunners, Avery had never met a female alpha. They existed, and she'd heard stories of them, but she'd never seen that dynamic for herself.

The road wound through the Smoky Mountains, edged by a river on one side and jutting cliffs covered in blankets of ivy on the other. In some places, long vines hung from the towering trees like green snakes. Some vines were even long enough to brush the top of the truck.

Mom lied.

Avery winced away from the thought she'd been avoiding. From the betrayal. She just wanted to look at the scenery, really see how beautiful this place was, instead of give into all the dark truths of her life scratching at her heart. Crossing her arms over her chest like armor, she tried and failed to keep the stupid wisps of disappointment at bay. She was born to tempt the Novak Raven? That was insane. And horrible. Her parents had raised her not as a person, but as a means to an end. As a weapon. As a harpoon, aimed straight for the shifter they wanted to drag in close.

And for what? Maybe the flock was getting low on genetics. A lot of the marriage contracts looked at that now. Benjamin had to get the council's approval on her lineage before he was allowed to submit a marriage contract to her father. Maybe that was it. Maybe they needed a new genetic line in Raven's Hollow. Maybe they wanted the son of Beaston and Aviana to start a new line of War Birds, or perhaps they would get him there and pair him with a submissive female and breed the dominance out of the Novak line. Whatever their reasons, she hated them. Weston had been lucky to live a life outside of The Hollow, and they had tried to use her to draw him close. She felt fiercely protective over his freedom, as she was of her own.

Like Weston could hear her dreary thoughts, he slid his hand comfortingly over her leg and squeezed it.

"I'm really sorry," she murmured. "I didn't know. I thought I hid your letters well, but maybe my parents gave them to the council while I was at school or…I don't know. My dad is desperate to raise his rank, and he's been talking about gunning for a council seat for years, but I had no idea I was a part of any of that. I just thought I was allowed to have a friend to talk to outside of Raven's Hollow. I thought you were just for me, but apparently I was wrong. Every time I think of you being hurt in all of this, I get this awful feeling in the pit of my stomach."

"Avery, it's okay—"

"I kept writing to you," she blurted out before she could change her mind.

"What?" His frown was back, and his eyes sparked with confusion.

"It felt good to write everything going on in my life down on paper, and when we parted ways, I still craved that connection. I still wanted to feel like I had a friend, so I wrote to you like nothing ever happened. Like the meeting went well. I know it's stupid, I do, and I never intended to send them. It just"—she shrugged her shoulders up to her ears—"felt good to not be alone."

"Fuck." Weston shook his head for a long time.

"I'm sorry," she whispered, afraid she'd offended him.

"Don't apologize to me anymore, okay? I don't want you saying sorry. You didn't do anything wrong.

I fucked up. I should've trusted you over what I was being told—"

"You were just a kid—"

"I was old enough, Avery! I was old enough to question what people were telling me. Yeah, my mom was right, and the council had bad motives, but you didn't have anything to do with that. I'd been writing to you for years, I'd built up trust with you, and the second someone told me you betrayed me, I believed them. Just like that." Weston looked sick in the dim light. "I used to give Ryder so much hell for how loyal he was. I did. But I should've tried to be more like him instead. I was the wrong one. I was the one who should've stuck with you. I'm the one who should be apologizing, so don't say that word anymore to me, Avery, okay? You don't have to say sorry anymore."

But it wasn't that easy. She'd been trained to duck her head and apologize for everything. She was twenty-four years old and likely that habit would be one she carried until the day she died. Why? Because she'd been methodically convinced that she was only as good as her ability to secure a high-ranking mate. "Can I ask you a strange question?"

"Sure."

"What would it mean to you to be the highest ranking man in Raven's Hollow?"

"Nothing," he said decisively. "I would rather be the lowest ranking member of the Bloodrunners than the highest ranking member anywhere else."

A smile stretched her lips. That right there told her so much about Weston. He wasn't about power, or what others thought about him. He was a decent man who was happy with a simple existence. Who was happy growing his business and taking care of his friends instead of chasing ranks.

"I'm sorry, Avery," he said suddenly. "Do you forgive me?"

"There's nothing to forgive." Silly man. She was the one created to hurt him. He'd only reacted to her assumed betrayal like anyone would.

"Can you just say it out loud?" he asked so softly she almost missed it over the roar of his truck engine.

Avery slipped her hand over his on top of her leg and squeezed it gently. "Weston Novak, I forgive you." She leaned her head back on the seat and gave a private smile to the woods outside her window. He was the first man who had ever apologized to her, but he had been forgiven from the day they'd met all those years ago. Why? Because he'd been so kind to her in the letters. He'd saved her when she was a kid in so many more ways than he would ever understand. When the loneliness of Raven's Hollow had threatened to swallow her up, she'd read his letters and imagined herself in Damon's Mountains with him. Weston didn't know it, but he had always been her beautiful escape.

Using his words and giving him the same sanctuary he'd offered her, Avery murmured, "And now you don't have to say sorry anymore either."

TEN

Weston's heartrate was kicked up too high. He inhaled sharply to try to ease the tension in his chest and turned up the volume on the radio a couple notches so she wouldn't hear him freaking out. Avery was in his truck, smelling like that fucking delicious cherry lip gloss and some floral shampoo she'd used on her hair. Even her skin smelled good and so…Avery.

She'd been driving him wild for a straight week as she'd worked quietly at Big Flight. He'd been watching her. Why? Because he couldn't help himself. She was beautiful, and already so different from the first day she'd come in for an interview in that ugly sweater. At first, he'd convinced himself she just looked different because Ryder had peer-pressured her into wearing a tank top and shorts with her sneakers. How wrong he'd been.

Avery had been broken by her people.

Each day, she'd gained confidence. She'd stopped wearing her hair in a tight bun and let it flow down her back in soft waves. She smiled more and met customers' direct gazes. She'd stopped dropping that pretty chin of hers around Ryder, but she'd kept the habit around Weston. That was his fault.

Ma was right. Weston could feel it in the air. Avery did have a more dominant raven inside of her, but her people had cowed her. They'd bent her and pushed her until she'd gone to her knees and forgot how to stand back up. And damn, there was something so rewarding about getting a front row seat to watch her learn to stand again.

He would have to be careful not to coddle her. It wouldn't help a woman like Avery if he just came to her rescue like his inner animal was crowing to do. She needed to gain confidence on her own that she was a capable woman.

Already, Weston admired her so much just from what he'd learned tonight. She'd left Raven's Hollow, and he had a feeling it had been much harder to do than she was letting on.

Weston squeezed her thigh again just to reassure himself she was still here, still solid under his palm. Fuck, he loved touching her. He was gonna keep that to himself, though, because the rest of the crew wouldn't understand the history here. They wouldn't understand how much Avery had meant to Weston growing up. How she'd been a first in so many ways. First friend outside of Damon's Mountains, first crush, first lo— Weston shook his head hard because he couldn't afford to go there again. That word had dragged him to his knees, too, and he wanted to remember how to stand up along with Avery.

There was a reason he hadn't wanted a serious girlfriend over the years. There was a reason he slept with girls and ended relationships after three dates. There was a reason he'd been terrified of giving his heart to someone else. Because Avery had taken up so much real estate in his chest at fourteen and fifteen, she'd left a mountain-sized hole when they'd parted ways. She'd been a grenade, and no normal woman stood a chance of filling that void. It was too deep and too wide, and Weston didn't give trust easily. He never had.

And now she was back, her fingers linking with his, and he needed to figure out what this meant. What she meant. What it meant to feel this good just touching her leg. What it meant that his heart was pounding so hard, and why his dick had been at full-blown boner-status since the day she'd walked into Big Flight. He'd have to figure out what it meant that every instinct in his body wanted to go to Raven's Hollow and throttle everyone who had ever hurt her. The urge for violence to avenge her pain was dizzying.

Avery Foley was big. She was crawl-in-his-heart-and-make-a-home-there-for-always big. That kiss out in the woods had done something to his chest—something terrifying and elating all at once. She'd warmed him. More than that, it was like he'd been struck by lightning the second she'd leaned in and kissed him hard. Her lips had set him on fire from his toes up.

And if he went at this full-speed-ahead like his raven wanted, it wouldn't be like when they were kids. He was a man who had watched the Bloodrunners settle down with mates, one-by-one.

And somewhere along the way, he'd begun to want that, too. He'd begun to crave something more than his solitary existence. His raven was ready for more.

And now, Avery had come in right when he was softening to the idea of taking a mate. Was this the Fates toying with him?

"You're still a quiet man, like when you were a boy," Avery said.

Weston cast her a quick glance as he turned onto the gravel road that led to Harper's Mountains. "You only met me once, and that wasn't the best impression to go by. How do you know I'm quiet?"

She was resting her cheek on the back of the seat, her full lips curved up just for him, her eyes so bright nestled in all those dark lashes. Like a psychopath, he wanted to trace her freckles with the tip of his finger.

"I could tell from the way you wrote. You didn't give me extra words. Not ever. You only wrote the important stuff. I could always hear your voice when I read your letters."

"You remembered my voice?"

Avery giggled a pretty sound, like a bell. He wanted to kiss her now, just to taste her happiness.

"We weren't great at talking on the phone."

Weston chuckled and shook his head. "No, we weren't. I still don't like talking on the phone for long."

"And I was awkward. I didn't know how to talk to males. Letters were easiest."

Weston ticked his tongue against his teeth and grimaced. "I don't like when you call me a male. I'm not like your people."

"What should I call you?"

"A friend." He wanted more, but that would have to do for now. Avery was at the beginning of a long road to healing. The last thing she needed right now was a relationship. She needed to focus on herself first.

When he looked over at her again, the smile had faded from her lips. "I missed you," she whispered, and her eyes were suddenly full of emotion. It was as if he could see her heart right there. Without thinking, Weston drew her hand to his lips and let his kiss linger on her knuckles. It felt so fucking right to touch her like this. To comfort her like this.

She dragged the back of her index finger down his jaw and giggled softly.

"You want me to shave?" he asked. Her answer mattered. Did she like beards or not? He wanted to know everything about her.

"No. I like you all manly and gruff. Tattoos and pierced nipples and muscles. You turned out differently than I imagined. The whiskers suit you. And they tickled when…" Avery ducked her gaze to her lap. "You know."

Weston bit his bottom lip to hide the smile there. She was so fucking cute when she got random bouts of shyness. "When we kissed?"

"Yes, that," she said breathily. "We kissed. In the woods. In the rain."

"Technically, you kissed me."

"But you kissed me back! I thought I made you bleed. I kissed you like a wolverine."

Weston laughed. "You were very aggressive." He shot her a smile and slowed down through the front gate to Harper's Mountains. He pulled up the muddy, winding road and stopped in front of 1010, the old cabin he was convinced held magic. Avery could use some of that.

When he looked over at Avery again, her cheeks were bright red, and she wouldn't give him more than her profile.

"I liked your kiss, Ave. I liked that you made the first move. I didn't have to question what you wanted. I didn't have to feel like I was pushing us too fast."

Avery's stomach growled. "I'm so sorry," she whispered, wrapping her arms around her middle.

"Don't say that," Weston murmured. He hated that she'd gone hungry. He hated that she'd been dealing with this all alone, sleeping in her car and worrying over where her next meal would come from. She was a lot stronger than she gave herself credit for. She'd said she was nothing, but she'd gotten herself a job and was digging out. She hadn't even asked him for an advance on her paycheck. She was just one of those tough souls who wanted to face the storm alone. No more of that, though. Not when he could make sure she was safe and okay.

Weston moved to get out, but changed his mind. Fast, before he turned chicken-shit, he leaned back over the console and cupped the back of her neck, pulled her close. He kissed her and reveled in her taste, the softness of her lips. He basked in the quiet, helpless sound in her throat as she melted against him. Her clothes were still damp and she was shivering from cold, or adrenaline, or both maybe. As much as he wanted to, Weston couldn't spend all night in the cab of his truck making out with her. His raven wouldn't let him. His instincts were telling him to take care of her. Make her comfortable so she'd stay with them. So he could keep her.

Weston pecked her lips once, twice, and smiled when she sat there, lips pursed and her eyes still closed as though he'd kissed her into shock. He liked the way she smelled when he kissed her—like pheromones and happiness. He wanted to touch her. Wanted to run his hand down her neck to her tits and see if they were as soft and perfect as they'd looked out in the woods. He wanted to cup her sex and make her writhe against his hand. She was probably so wet right now. Would feel so good gripping his dick. Would feel so good pulsing around him as he made her come. Fuck, he wanted to bury himself inside her, but logic drifted through his muddled mind like a thin fog.

Feed her. Get her in dry clothes. Get her warm. Make her feel safe.

There was no room for *fuck her* on the list of immediate needs right now.

Reluctantly, he pulled away. "Avery?"

She arched her eyebrows, opened her eyes, and gave him a slow, half-drunk smile. "Hmm?"

"I missed you, too."

ELEVEN

He had missed her, too? Avery's stomach erupted in a fluttering sensation like she'd never felt before, like the tips of her wings were beating against her, tickling her until warmth pooled low in her belly and spread outward.

"Really?" she whispered. She couldn't believe a big, strong, immoveable man like Weston had given her a single thought after they'd met in Saratoga. She'd assumed she wasn't pretty enough, or he didn't like her personality outside of the letters, but now she understood why he'd cut his heart away from her. But still…he'd missed her?

"You're surprised?"

"You just have so many friends."

Weston angled his chin in denial and leveled her with a look. "I have a lot of acquaintances, but few friends. I don't give my trust easily. The friends I let in mean everything to me. You meant a lot to me. I got to know you over those years, looked forward to getting each letter. In a way, we grew up together. You were someone outside of Damon's Mountains I could tell anything to. I got your last letter, and it was so fucking hard not to write you back. I debated for a full year, but the thought of the council reading my words put me off. I missed your letters. I missed hearing about your life. I missed checking the mail and finding an envelope in there with your return address. Of course, I missed you, Avery." Weston gave her one last soft peck on the lips, his short beard rasping against her chin. "Wait there, and I'll get your door."

"Okay," she whispered, stunned.

Weston got out and jogged around the back of his truck, then yanked open the door. The rain was still pouring down, but he was smiling and, for a moment, she sat frozen, trapped in the easiness of the curve of his lips. One side of his mouth lifted higher than the other. Selfishly, she hoped she was the only one in the world who had noticed that.

Weston reached over her lap and unclicked her seatbelt, then held his hand out to help her down out of his monster truck. Avery swallowed hard. When she slipped her palm into his, electricity zinged from his touch through her body and landed in her chest. She jerked away at the shock, and when she dragged her attention back to Weston's face, his smile had dipped slightly, and under the bill of his hat, confusion furrowed his dark brows. He squeezed his fist a couple times and ducked his gaze, stepped back to give her room to get out on her own.

"Run on inside, and I'll bring in your stuff."

The inside he spoke of was a cabin on the edge of the trees, lit from the inside out with the soft glow of lights. A porch sat invitingly off the front, and the rustic windows were bracketed by dark-colored shutters. Where the warmth had consumed her a moment ago, now chills blasted across her skin for reasons she couldn't fathom.

This was the raven haven Weston had found for her. This cabin would be her safety. It would mean warmth and a comfortable bed. She wanted to cry, but refused to let loose any tears right now in front of

Weston. She would do that later when she was alone in the dark.

Avery climbed out of the truck, splashed unfortunately into a mud puddle, and moved to pass Weston. But she stopped suddenly and, as a silent thank you, wrapped her arms around his waist as tight as she could. She pressed her lips against the left side of his chest, right over his heart, and then like a coward, ran to the porch before he could respond.

When she dared a glance behind her, he was standing in the rain, in the soft glow from the cabin windows, his green eyes nearly glowing with intensity as he watched her. A slow smile transformed his face in the moment before he gave his attention to shutting the passenger door, and oh, what that man did to her insides. Over the past week, she'd wanted desperately to be the one who drew a smile from the Novak Raven, and now he was giving them to her freely.

That man required the people he cared about to prove themselves before he would trust them, and little by little, he was softening to her. Without words, he was complimenting her. He was telling her she was worthy of trust, and for some reason, her heart felt like it was raw and open. As though tonight she was going through a metamorphosis. She wasn't as scared or intimidated by him. She wasn't as intimidated by anything. Here she stood, in the middle of the Bloodrunner Dragon's territory, and instead of being terrified like she would've been a week ago, she was okay. She was happy even, and now her eyes were really burning. Happy? Was that what this warm feeling in her chest was?

She couldn't do this—couldn't dwell on these thoughts too long or she would fall apart, and she didn't want Weston to see that side of her. She wanted him to like her. She wanted him to keep her.

Avery kicked off her muddy shoes and pulled Weston's flannel shirt tighter around her soaking dress, then rested her hand on the doorknob of the cabin. The metal house numbers glinted in the porchlight. Sure, the numbers were crooked, and barely hanging on, but this cabin's address was 1010. In one of his letters, Weston had mentioned an old magic singlewide trailer in Damon's Mountains where he'd grown up. He'd called the trailer 1010. Gooseflesh raised all over her arms. Shaking her head at the strange coincidence, Avery shoved open the door and stepped her bare feet onto the uneven wooden floorboards inside. The living room led straight into an open kitchen, and a woman with black hair cascading down her back stood at the stove.

"Oh!" Avery exclaimed. "I'm sorry!" Wrong house.

She went to close the door, but the woman turned. It was Lexi, Ryder's mate, who she'd met at the bar.

"Come on in," Lexi said. "Weston called and asked if I had any leftovers for you to eat, but that didn't seem big enough for your first meal in ten-ten. I'm pan searing steaks, and I have asparagus cooking, too. Are you okay?"

Avery pushed off the wall where she'd pressed her back and nodded. "I'm okay, just...embarrassed. Did Weston tell you why I need leftovers?"

"A little." Her bright green eyes softened. "There's no shame in needing help, though."

Weston strode through the front door, his boots echoing loudly on the floors. "Hey Lexi. Smells good in here."

"It smells really good!" Avery exclaimed,

remembering her manners. "Thanks so much for doing this for me."

Lexi giggled and turned back to the steaks, flipped a pair of them in the pan, and explained, "I'm a personal chef for a cabin rental company near here. This is no problem and is the fastest meal to make. Plus, I'll be up late waiting on my mate to come home."

"Where is Ryder?" Weston asked, his tone troubled.

Lexi's shoulders lifted with a deep inhale. "I don't know. He left earlier with a couple cans of white spray paint, so I'm waiting on a call either from him or the police."

"Shit," Weston muttered. "You want me to go find him?"

"No," Lexi murmured. "I think he needs to work some stuff out on his own right now."

Weston scrubbed his hand down his face and nodded at the back of Lexi's head, as if she could see him. He bumped Avery on the shoulder and said low, "I'll put your things in the bedroom. You can get into dry clothes if you want before dinner."

Avery looked down at her dress, dripping on the

wood floors. She would probably make perfect footprint puddles when she walked. She nodded jerkily and followed him into a bedroom with a bathroom door on the opposite wall. The queen-sized bed looked warm and inviting, and the lamp on the bedside table had been turned on. It smelled like cleaner in here, and she hoped Lexi hadn't gone through too much trouble. Anything was better than the back seat of her car.

Her stomach gurgled again, reinvigorated by the scent of seasoned meat and vegetables. Heat flashed up her neck and landed in her cheeks as she covered her stomach with her forearms in a pathetic attempt to make it stop growling.

"It's okay," Weston whispered, setting her bags on the antique white bench at the foot of the bed. He approached her slowly, his boots scuffing the floors where her mortified gaze stayed. Gently, he hooked a finger under her chin and lifted until she met his eyes. And then, with determination written all over his face, he promised, "I'll never let you get hungry like this again."

When her eyes filled from that beautiful oath, she wanted to hide from him. She wanted to look away, to bury her face against his chest until she gained control of herself again, but he wasn't having it. His finger stayed under her chin, and when the first tear fell, he cocked his head sharply, like her raven people did when they were confused. Weston brushed a knuckle across her cheek and wiped away the moisture.

A soft, accidental sob broke through, and she leaned into him, pulled his palm against her cheek, and nuzzled it. He rocked them back and forth as she broke down as quietly as she could, his hand still cupped against one cheek, his heart pounding against the other. He smelled so good and felt so warm, so strong, so immoveable and invincible, and she believed him. He wouldn't let her go hungry again. Even if they were just friends, Weston took care of his people, and he'd just declared she was now under his outstretched wing.

"I'll never, ever do anything to betray you," she forced past her tight throat. Because he should know where her loyalty lay, and it had always been with him. Always.

"Truth," he murmured, a smile in his voice. "Come on, Ave. Get dressed, and then we'll eat until we pop."

"We?"

He eased away and nodded. "Unless you want me to leave."

"No!" she said too fast and too loud. Avery cleared her throat and lowered her voice. "I mean, that's all right. I would like you to stay."

Weston chuckled a deep, reverberating sound that vibrated over her skin and made her feel like the whiskey had. And then he left her alone to dress and wonder how the hell she'd gotten so lucky.

TWELVE

Weston shot her yet another secret smile, and for the hundredth time tonight, Avery's cheeks lit on fire. She rinsed the soap suds off the plate and handed it to him to dry. "You know, male ravens at the Hollow don't do dishes."

"Well, male ravens of the Gray Backs did lots of dishes. Ma would've kicked my ass if I foisted the chore off onto my sisters."

"I like your mom."

Weston snorted. "You would."

"No really," Avery murmured, scrubbing another dish. "She was my hero growing up."

"My mom?" Weston gave her a baffled look and turned to put the dry plate into a cabinet.

"Yeah. She was a badass. She escaped our people and married Beaston despite what it did to her family's rank. She was female, but she'd taken her life into her own hands and shot two middle fingers at the council and lived her life the way she wanted to. My mom had this picture of her and Aviana taken right before your mom left our people. I kept it in a box under my bed with my favorite trinkets. I brought it with me to Saratoga with plans on asking your mom to sign it for me, but she was angry with me when we arrived. I didn't know why at the time, but it makes sense now. She thought I was hurting her boy."

"I'll explain it to her," Weston murmured. "She'll understand." He let the silence linger for a bit while he dried a plate and a pot. "The box of trinkets you had under your bed. Did you bring it with you? I didn't see it in your things."

"Swear not to make fun of me."

"I swear."

"I brought it, but I dumped all my trinkets."

His eyebrows jacked up high, a look of shock on his face. Slowly he took his baseball cap off and put it on backward. "I have trinkets, too, that I find as a raven. Did you do the same?"

"Yes," she said on a breath. "They were like my little treasures. Shiny baubles that had caught my eye. I would bring them back after a Change and add them to my collection. I had quite the hoard when I got rid of them."

"Why the hell would you get rid of them? Doesn't that go against your instincts? My raven wouldn't let me get rid of a single one of mine."

"I got rid of them the day I left the Hollow to come here. I didn't really want to drag all of the things that tethered me to that place. Those were my past."

"But you brought the box."

"Mmm hmm," she said with a nod.

Weston put up another dish and turned to her, locked his arm against the counter. "Ave, what's in the box?"

She smiled down at the sudsy water she was swishing around as she washed the silverware. "You know."

"I have an idea, but I want you to tell me."

"I didn't want to drag my history with Raven's Hollow here, so I dumped the trinkets and filled the box with your letters, and with the ones I never sent you."

"Because you thought we would talk about them when you got here?"

"No," she said quietly. "I never intended on talking to you. I came here because the council leaves me alone if they think I'm near you. If they think I'm under the protection of your crew. I brought them just for me."

"Why?" His eyes were so raw, so earnest. "Tell me what they mean to you."

"Those old letters you sent me are more important than my trinkets ever were. I didn't feel so alone when I read them." She dared a look up at him. "They were my happiness. I brought them because I knew it would be hard out here in the real world. Because I knew I would be all alone, and it didn't feel as scary if I had a piece of you with me. The letters made me braver." She shrugged one shoulder up to her ear. "*You* made me braver."

"Will you ever let me read the letters you never sent me?"

"No," she said in an immediate response. "Those I wrote knowing you wouldn't read them. They were my safe place."

Weston's eyes hardened in the instant before he turned away. The muscles of his back flexed when he gripped the edge of the counter. He shook his head. "I should've been your safe place. Not your fault. Mine."

Avery slipped her arms around his waist and rested her cheek along his spine. "We're okay now."

"Are you?" he asked in a hard voice. "My mom said your people punished you for your raven being too dominant."

Avery flinched in shock and froze against him. "It wasn't punishment."

"What was it then?"

"It was rehabilitation." That's what the council had called it.

"Bullshit."

When Weston went rigid under her, she held on tighter, clenched his shirt in her hands. "It wasn't so bad."

"Would it have been easier if I was still sending you letters?"

She didn't answer. She couldn't because powerful waves of dominance wafted from Weston, pulsing through her body until her lungs didn't want to draw in air. She was standing too damn close to him right now, but for the life of her, she couldn't figure out how to convince her arms to release him.

"Tell me what happened. What did rehabilitation include."

"I don't want to talk about this."

"Why not?" He sounded pissed now, but he had no right to pry this from her.

"Because you're taking away my happy moment!" Avery pushed off him and retreated to the bedroom. His loud boots echoed behind her, but when she went to slam the door, he caught it, and the look on his face broke her heart. He looked ill and angry, but not with her. With himself. "Please."

She crossed her arms over her chest and shook her head over and over. It wasn't fair. It wasn't! Tonight had been perfect, and now he was scratching at shit that needed to be left alone.

"Please, Ave. Tell me why a dominant raven acts as timid as a mouse. Tell me why you always look at the ground and why you hunch your shoulders like you're trying to be smaller. Like you're trying to be invisible. Tell me why you always say sorry for every little thing."

She wished she could Change and fly away from him as fast as she could. She wished she could catch the air currents under her wings and avoid admitting how weak she really was. If he saw her—really saw her—he would leave, and she didn't want to go back to being alone. But he wasn't letting her out of this. He wasn't backing down.

Resentful at being pushed, she gritted out, "Because I'm broken, Weston. Is that what you want to hear? I was born with a broken shifter, and my people are ashamed of me. Ashamed that I exist. Do you know what rank is based on in Raven's Hollow? The best ravens are the ones who conform to the idea of what the perfect raven shifter is—easy going, submissive, non-combative, doesn't question anything. But I wasn't like that. I didn't Change until I was five. Strike one. And then I was a natural leader. I wanted to organize games at school, I wanted to run for class politics with the human kids. Strike two. I questioned every. Single. Thing. And when I Changed, the other ravens my age cowered away from me because their instincts told them I was a monster. I was bigger, more dominant, and I didn't believe in all the goddamned rules. Strike three. By middle school,

I was being bullied. Not by the human kids, but by the raven kids, but I didn't take it lying down like a good submissive female was supposed to. I pushed back. And when it got bad enough, and my raven was crawling out of my skin to stand up for myself, I beat the shit out of this little snot boy who wouldn't stop calling me The Great Mistake, like his parents did. I just...lost my mind and beat him until his face was bloody. Until he stopped moving. Until the teachers pulled me off his limp body. The council called for an official shunning by noon the next day."

"A shunning?"

"Yeah. A community-wide shunning. People talked about me as I passed, but not *to* me. My parents could talk to me to raise me, but no extras were allowed. Affection was a 'hell no,' and my parents didn't fight the order at all because they were good little ravens, too. I learned real quick to submit and pretend my raven didn't want to attack everyone around me for what they were doing. And the more I pretended to be submissive, the smaller my raven became. The sadder she was. I looked at the ground, ducked my gaze and spoke softly, and apologized for everything until the shunning was lifted. And it took two fucking years, Weston. Two years desperate to be seen. To fit in. I hated myself, hated my raven. I just wanted to be like everyone else, so I became like everyone else." Her face crumpled, but she blinked hard, refusing to cry again. "The shunning was lifted, but I would forget myself sometimes, and my dad would bring me to the council for every little thing I did wrong, and they would put me in The Box."

Weston was leaning heavily against the wall, legs locked, shaking his head in disgust. He asked in a hoarse voice, "What's The Box?"

"It was a tiny white room under the Council House with a bucket to piss in and nothing else. And I would go crazy in there, stuck in my own fucking mind, unable to see sunlight, feeling like I'd been buried alive, praying to God someone remembered to let me out. I memorized your letters. I would recite them when I thought I would go mad, just so I wouldn't feel alone."

"Fuck, Ave," he uttered in a heart-wrenching tone. His eyes were black now and as deep as wells. He'd locked his giant hands on his knees like he would retch right here on the bedroom floor.

"So you see, Weston, I hunch my shoulders, say

sorry, and look at the ground because I've been trained to crave invisibility. Invisibility hurts less." She approached him slowly, and he straightened his spine, allowing her to place herself between his legs. She rested her palms against his stony chest, and in a ragged whisper she said, "Now don't make me talk about this stuff anymore. It doesn't make me feel better to say it out loud. It makes me feel weak all over again."

Weston nodded, eyes locked on hers. "Okay, Ave. I won't ask anymore."

She smiled sadly and left him there. Remembering made her raven want to rip out of her body. It had always been like that. The pain of the Change was her animal's punishment for what she'd done to her feathered side. This wasn't like earlier in the woods when she hadn't been able to shift. Right now, power was pulsing against her middle, making her want to double over with the bone-deep ache of resisting the Change until she made it outside the cabin.

The Great Mistake. Weak, weak, weak. Avery gritted her teeth and pulled her T-shirt over her head, left it in a pile on the porch as she strode for the yard.

Her bra was next, but fuck her pants. They would slide off during the Change.

"Ave," Weston said from behind her.

She turned just in time for his lips to collide against hers. This kiss was urgent and desperate, unlike their others. It was numbing. It was sucking darkness away from her and filling her with something else. Something better.

He bit her lip, drawing a moan from her, then Weston disengaged and rested his forehead against hers. His eyes were tightly closed, his breath shaking hard. "You don't have to be invisible here." And then he eased back by inches, just far enough to pull off his shirt.

Without another word, he jerked his chin toward the woods. His eyes were dark as night, probably the same color as hers, and damn it felt good not to hide from him. He wanted to Change with her. She had kept her Changes private, because she hated the way other ravens cowered away from her, but Weston was strong, dominant, and he didn't care that she was powerful, too.

When Avery's lip trembled, she bit it hard. There was no room for falling apart again in the night shadows of Harper's Mountains. She turned and bolted for the tree line, closed her eyes, stretched her arms out, and then gave her body to the raven.

As she soared up and up, she could hear him, the Novak Raven, beating his powerful wings behind her, and then eventually beside her.

Her raven was huge, but Weston's was even bigger.

If she could smile in this form, she would.

Their monsters matched.

Rain-dampened black feathers covered his body, and his dark eye was on her as they coasted above the canopy. Always on her.

Lightning flashed behind him, and he opened his glossy beak and let off an echoing, "Caw!" as the thunder boomed.

She answered because it felt right to use her voice around him. Only him. Below them, Harper's Mountains were illuminated by the storm, and she was taken with this moment. She was here, in the lair of the dragon, with the man she never thought she would talk to again. And he was pushing Avery to own her shit, own her past, unlike the men of The Hollow.

She'd been wrong to question whether the council had anything to do with her feelings for Weston Novak. She wasn't nothing. The council was. This deep, warm emotion pooling in her chest had nothing to do with their manipulation. It was her choosing to love the man, as she'd loved the boy. She'd told Weston his letters had been her happiness, but that wasn't the whole truth.

Weston was her happiness.

In a way, he always had been.

THIRTEEN

This had been the most exhilarating Change Avery ever had. It was the middle of the night, and she should've been exhausted, but she'd stretched her wings and pushed her endurance for an hour, or maybe more. She'd had the big meal Lexi had made and felt so energized that she had kept up with Weston, whose wingspan was wider.

Flashes of lightning illuminated the Smoky Mountains, but nothing below looked familiar anymore. She would've panicked except that Weston was here with her, and she knew without a shadow of a doubt he could find 1010 again.

Beak open and panting, she landed on the thick lower branch of a White Pine for a rest. Weston landed beside her and sidestepped closer and closer until his wing touched hers. Turning his head, he preened his rain-glossed feathers, then shockingly, gave her feathers the same attention. He cleaned her, rubbed both sides of his beak against hers like he was sharpening a knife, and then went back to taking care of her wet feathers.

Huh. The Novak Raven was affectionate in his animal form.

Tentatively, at first, Avery cleaned him as he was doing for her. And eventually, when she got used to his bigger feathers, she closed her eyes and went off feel, memorizing his body by touch. This right here was magic.

Suddenly, Weston dove off the branch and stretched out his wings, talons angled for the ground. He shifted to his human form in an instant. Is that what she looked like? Probably not. She wasn't that graceful, but she tried.

Avery mis-timed her shift and stumbled, but Weston was there, strong arms around her before she hit the mossy earth.

She giggled and straightened up to her full height, no hunching. "You're so tall, and your shoulders are so wide. And your nipple piercings are staring me right in the face. I want to kiss them. Everything is awesome." Her excitement and relief over that Change had apparently made her lose control of her words.

Her cheeks flushed under the soft rain, but Weston only laughed. Not at her either. It was that echoing laughter that said he was as elated as she was right now. He slid his arms around her shoulders and hugged her against his bare chest. Avery inhaled deeply to commit his scent to memory. He smelled differently right after a Change—another thing she selfishly hoped she was the only one to ever notice about him.

"Why did you Change back?" she asked. "We aren't to the cabin yet."

"Because I wanted to hug you," he murmured against her ear.

Avery closed her eyes with how good that felt and squeezed his waist harder. Weston's thick erection was pressing hard onto her belly. Her breasts tingled, and her nipples drew up against him. Heart fluttering in her chest, she braved a look up at him. Should she tell him?

Weston leaned down and kissed her, pushed his tongue past her lips, and stroked into her mouth slowly, rhythmically. She should definitely tell him. But what if he freaked out? She didn't want him to back off her and make excuses to slow down. Not when she wanted this, right here, right now, with him.

She'd waited so long for this moment.

Weston's fingertips trailed from her waist up her arm to her neck, where he cupped the back and dragged her closer. He plunged his tongue deeper into her mouth and, holy heaven, her lady parts were revving up like an engine. A needy sound came from her, and she would've been embarrassed except Weston reacted immediately by pressing his hips forward. And then he was kissing down her neck and down, down until he reached her breast. The second his lips encircled her nipple, she was gone. She moaned and gripped his hair, rolled her head back and closed her eyes against the rain. His mouth was so warm on her sensitive skin, his tongue so perfect as he lapped and sucked.

What if he figured out she hadn't done this before because she was bad at it?

Stop it. Don't think too hard. Just enjoy this moment. Weston will take care of you.

When Weston sucked hard, drawing her nipple up against his tongue, she gasped at how good it felt. He eased to the other and gave it the same attention as he massaged the first in his oversize hand. She'd been too curvy for the boys in The Hollow, too unappealing. They liked normal ravens who were pin-thin and fine-boned, but she had boobs and a butt and right now, Weston was laying waste to her insecurities.

"You like the way I look?"

Weston chuckled against her skin and bit her rib cage playfully. "Woman, you're perfect." He cupped her breasts and mushed them together, and she laughed at the look of pure adulterated bliss on his face. Wes and tits went together like chocolate and strawberries.

"I'm gonna fuck these," he growled out.

Wait, what? Was that physically possible? She stared down at her cleavage. She was going to have to do some research on that, but maybe for her first time… "Can we keep it simple right now?"

Weston stood, and his lips collided with hers.

One of his arms slid around her back, and one down her belly, lower, lower. Her stomach quivered when he touched her sex. Weston wasn't shy about it either. He cupped her and dragged his finger along her entrance. He smiled against her lips. "So fucking wet."

Okay, that part she knew about from the romance books she'd been reading. Wet was good. *Way to go, body!*

Weston's grip on her waist tightened as he eased her backward. Her shoulder blades hit the rough bark of a tree, and at that exact moment, Weston pushed his finger inside of her. "If you don't want this to go further, tell me now," he murmured in that sexy, rich voice that vibrated against her skin. His short beard rasped against her neck as he sucked her skin hard there. Avery writhed against his hand as he pushed his finger deeper into her and hit something sensitive. Oh, that was fucking great!

"Ave," he rasped, rolling his hips. "Yes or no."

"W-what?"

"How far do you want to take this tonight. I'm good with whatever you want."

Consent, yes. He was asking for consent. Sweet

mate. Mate? His finger slid into her again, and the pressure was already so bright. "Yes," she cried out.

Weston froze. "Yes, stop?"

"No! Keep going. God, Weston, keep going. Everything, I want everything."

His teeth were on her, biting her neck, as he pulled his finger out. Weston picked her up roughly and pressed her up against the tree, wrapped his arms around her waist, and pushed into her.

She gasped at the pain and panicked. "Too big!"

Weston pulled out of her immediately, his face looking pained to disconnect, but shit-and-balls, that wasn't going to work. In a rush, he set her on her feet and gripped her hips. He searched her eyes. "Are you okay?"

She wanted to cry in mortification. "I'm bad at this."

"What?"

She covered her face with her hands so he wouldn't see her shame when she admitted, "I haven't ever…you know."

"This is your first time?" he asked too loud.

"Shhh!"

Weston yanked her hands away from her face.

"Woman, who the fuck is going to hear you out here? Shit!" Weston pushed off the tree behind her and paced away, then back, running his hands through his hair. "I'm not the right one for your first time."

"I disagree."

"I'm not gentle, Ave!"

"You can be with me. I know you can."

Wes was freaking out. His eyes were huge, and he kept shaking his head. When he paced back the other way, he went farther away from her.

A drop of warmth trickled down the inside of her thigh. When Avery looked down, a drop of crimson raced down her rain-soaked legs. Ashamed, she covered herself with her hands and hung her head.

"We should go back," Wes said.

"I don't want to go back yet," she whispered.

"Well, we can't stay out here all night."

"That's not what I mean. I want to finish this. With you. I'm on birth control, and we're both consenting adults."

"Fuck, Ave! I shouldn't be anyone's first."

Eyes burning, she moved her hands and let him see the red. "Technically speaking, you already were."

Weston approached silently and knelt in front of

her, traced the smear down her leg. "Did it hurt. I mean...did I hurt you?"

"I'm fine, Weston. I don't really want my first time to end like that, though. It's not like I meant to reach age twenty-four with my virginity still intact. The men in Raven's Hollow just didn't want me like that, and my..."

"Your what?" he asked quietly, dragging his jet black gaze up to hers.

She heaved a sigh. "My heart was stuck on you."

The hard edges faded from Weston's face, and slowly, he leaned forward and kissed her thigh, right where the red had disappeared into the rain water. And then he kissed her hip bones, one at a time. He stood and hugged her close, didn't say a word as the rain pattered against the leaves above them. He just stood there for a while, holding her, rubbing small circles against her spine with the tip of his finger.

"Ave, do you want me to be your first?" he finally asked against her ear.

"Yes," she whispered. She wanted him to be her only.

Weston leaned in and pressed his lips to hers, much softer than she expected. His hands went from steel to silk as he moved against her gently. He held the back of her neck, touched her breasts, dragged his finger along her collar bone. He pulled her hair gently, angling her face back so he could dip his lips to her neck and nibble her skin there. Her insides had flared up with fire again despite the slower pace. He cupped between her legs, rubbed her gently until her legs began to go numb. She clung to him, breath coming in short pants. And when she was close—so close—he laid her down on a bed of moss and eased her legs apart. Weston settled between her thighs, so close she could feel the head of his cock at her entrance. This was it. This is what she'd waited so long for.

Weston was propped up on his arms, his muscles flexing as he looked down at her like she was the most beautiful woman he'd ever seen. How could he do that with just a glance? How could he make her feel so pretty and worthy?

He was hesitating, so she leaned forward and sucked on his nipple. The metal of his piercing was cold against her tongue. So perfect. Weston bucked shallowly into her, then pulled out again. Avery relaxed back and smiled up at him. "I knew you could be gentle."

"Ha!" Weston huffed out, his abs flexing with the breath. "This is torture. I want to be buried inside of you so bad right now."

He pushed in again, a little farther before he eased out. Lowering himself to her, Weston kissed her, sucked her bottom lip and ran his hand down her ribs to her hip. Curving his body, he pushed into her again in slow torture, stretching her little by little. Weston rested his forehead against hers and clenched his teeth hard. "You feel so fuckin' good," he ground out.

And so did he. Weston was hitting that sensitive spot again, shooting sparks of pleasure through her. Avery clutched onto his back and rolled her hips to meet him on the next stroke. Weston cupped the back of her head and sucked on her neck as he slid into her again and again. He groaned and bucked harder, but it didn't hurt. Not anymore. Now it felt amazing. Way better than touching herself.

"Weston," she gasped out, pulling on his lower back.

He held her tighter, let all his body weight rest on her as he stroked into her harder and faster. "Tell me you're close. God, Ave, tell me you're coming soon."

At the sexy rasp of desperation in his voice, release exploded through her body in hard, quick pulses. She cried out and buried her face against his neck.

Weston slammed into her and froze, and she could feel it—that first pulse of his own release. How fucking sexy that she'd caused him to do this. He reared back and slammed into her again as his heat flowed into her. Her aftershocks lasted so long, spurred on by his own release. And when he hovered over her, twitching, chest heaving, eyes hooded and on her, and that sexy smile ghosting his lips, she giggled. She couldn't help herself.

"Oh, sex with me is funny?" Weston teased.

Avery ran the back of her hand across the roughness of his jaw. "I'm relieved."

"That it's done?"

"No. That you're my first. It always felt like I was waiting on something, and now I know what. I was waiting on you. On this moment, so it could be this special."

Weston grinned and looked around the woods.

"Woman, this ain't exactly a bed and breakfast and a warm bed. We just fucked in the dirt."

Avery shrugged and followed his glance to the greenery around them. "Yeah, but it's soooo…you. And it'll be memorable."

"Oh, yeah?"

"Mmm hmm. I have moss in my crack."

Weston dropped his forehead to her chest and laughed so hard his shoulders shook. "I swear I'll make it more special next time."

"Oh, next time? You're already planning on round two?"

"Uh, yeah. That was awesome. My dick is your biggest fan. Plus," he murmured, giving two hard sucks to her nipples. "I've been thinking about your tits all week."

She gasped teasingly. "Weston Novak, did you jack off to me?"

He snorted. "Did I *jack off* to you? I didn't want to because I was still pissed at you, but yeah, I anger-banged my fist a few times thinking about you in that little tank top and short-shorts number you keep wearing at the shop."

"I read romance books," she admitted. "The dirty

ones. I'm practically a pro at sex."

"I believe it," he murmured, but his glazed-over attention was back on her boobs, and he was jiggling one rhythmically.

Avery swatted his hand. "Don't make them look weird."

"They're so big. I thought raven shifters were flat-chested, mousey little things, but you have these big ol' bouncy titties and a round ass." He squeezed her behind for emphasis and ground his hips against her. "I fucking love you naked."

I fucking love you, period. She wished she could say it, but Weston wouldn't be ready. He'd only just found out she wasn't the bad guy, and she wanted to cling onto moments like these before he decided to run.

"Well, I like your tattoos and piercings and muscles. And your smile."

The smile dipped from his face. "And what else?"

"And the way you know how to do everything, fix everything. And the way you're quiet unless you have something important to say. And the way you make up your own mind on things." She ran her fingertip across his full bottom lip. "And the way you taste when you kiss me, and the way you smile when I tease you."

"I see things," he said suddenly.

Avery frowned at the seriousness of his tone. "What kinds of things?"

Weston looked like he regretted saying anything at all and pulled out of her. When he rolled them both to the side and cradled her against his chest, he stared off into the woods and murmured, "I see future things. Things that haven't happened yet. Awful things."

Avery propped up on her elbow to better see his face, but he didn't seem to be joking. "Like you are a psychic?"

"No, I don't read people's minds or anything like that. I see people's future."

"Whose? Mine?"

"No," he said too fast and too sternly. "Not yours. Don't say that anymore."

"Okay." Troubled, Avery brushed his short, dark hair to the side. "Whose then?"

"Harper's first. Alana and Lexi, too, but mostly I see strangers now. I see them dying or getting hurt. Sometimes the visions are good, but most of the time they aren't."

"How often do you have them?"

Weston rolled his head and locked his dark gaze on hers when he said, "Every day."

Gooseflesh blasted across her skin. "That's awful."

"I hate sleeping now. I put it off so I won't have dreams, but sometimes I even have them during the day now while I'm awake. The world goes away, and I get dumped into this scene. Faraway places with strangers hurting. I tried to stop a couple. I drove to meet a woman in Woodfin and saved her from a car accident. But two days later, she stepped into a busy street and was hit by a car. And it was so much worse than what I'd saved her from. Her kid witnessed it. I thought I could change her fate, but I couldn't. And now that kid will always have that awful memory, that awful scar, because of me." Weston pulled her against his side and stared up at the thick branches of the forest canopy. "My dad had the sight, so did his mom, and I used to pray that I wouldn't get it. I saw how the crews depended on my dad to tell their futures. To reassure them, and sometimes he didn't have good news. And I saw the toll it took on him. I heard the conversations he had with my mom late at night after bad visions and saw that hollow look in his eyes the morning after. I didn't want that to be me, but when I came to Harper's Mountains, something shifted. The visions started, and now I already feel like I'm losing my mind. You said you were a broken raven, but you aren't." Weston swallowed hard. "I am."

"This doesn't scare me away."

"It should. You haven't seen the bad parts yet. I can't spend the night or fall asleep beside you. It's getting worse and worse, and you'll be hurt by it."

"I won't."

"You will. I watched my mom fuss over my dad my whole life. I want better for you."

But Weston was wrong. There was no one better for her. "I don't think you're broken," she whispered, hugging him so tightly her arms shook. "I think you're perfect."

"I'm not—"

"You are for me! I get to decide what I want and don't want, Weston. Me. My choices were taken away my whole life, but my eyes are wide open on this. I care for you. Always have. Before the sight, after the sight, doesn't matter to me. You're telling me this thinking you'll scare me away, but it won't work. You letting me in only makes me care for you more." Avery scrambled on top of him and straddled his hips. Then she leaned toward his left pec, her mouth open. He was too sad and too serious right now and she wanted to distract him.

"Whoa, what are you doing?" Weston asked, sitting up and nearly dumping her on her ass.

When he held her wrists, she stretched her neck forward and chomped her teeth, missing his pec by an inch. "I'm biting you. What does it look like I'm doing?"

"Biting me for what?"

"To claim you. The bears do it."

"Good God, we aren't bears, Ave. Stop!"

She stretched forward again and barely missed his shoulder when she snapped her teeth this time. Good grief, he was annoyingly strong.

"Ave, quit!"

"Okay, fine, you're right. You bite me first."

Weston's eyebrows were nearly to his hairline now. "Have you lost your mind, woman? That shit's permanent. You really want my mark on you after one night with me?"

"No. I want your mark on me after being friends for…" She counted quickly in her head. "Fourteen years." *Chomp.* "And now official diddle buddies. You wanted to fuck my titties, Novak. We're committed."

Weston was trying and failing to hide a smile now as he struggled to keep her teeth away from his skin. "We weren't friends for most of those fourteen years."

"That's just a technicality, Novak." *Chomp.* Whoo, that one was close.

"God, you would make a relentless and terrifying zombie."

Avery peeled into a fit of giggles and fell over, clutching her stomach. "You should see your face right now." She kicked her legs and cackled. "You're freaking out."

"Joking about claiming marks isn't funny." But she could see his pursed-lip smile from here, and this was definitely funny.

She spread out like a star on the mossy blanket and heaved a sigh. "Weston?" she asked, staring up at the sky.

"What?"

"Someday you're going to want to bite me like the bears do."

"Oh, yeah? You have the sight now, too?"

"No, I just know in my bones that you will. I'm gonna make you fall in love with me."

You already have. He didn't say that last part, but she could see it there, in his dancing eyes. He liked her in the way she liked him, and someday, someway, he was going to choose her completely.

"I was made for you, Weston, remember? I was supposed to betray you, but I failed. I adored you instead. Before I even laid eyes on you, before I knew the man you would become, I started growing a bond just from words you wrote on a paper. We're fated, you and I, and you said it yourself."

Weston cocked his head in a very raven-like gesture and brushed a strand of hair from her face. "Said what?"

She leaned her cheek into his palm and whispered, "You can't stop someone's destiny."

FOURTEEN

You can't stop someone's destiny. Weston had replayed her words over and over in his head. Was that what this feeling was? Was destiny to credit for the heat in his chest that pulled him toward Avery just to get relief? Was fate the reason she felt so right in his life now?

He'd never given a single thought to destiny before the visions, but how could he see the future and not believe? He'd tried to stop events from happening, but they always found a way. Fate was a stubborn bitch, but maybe she was finally working in his favor with Avery.

The chair creaked under him as he leaned forward and rested his elbows on his knees. Thank

God for good night vision. He could see every beautiful angle of Avery's face as she slept in the bed of 1010.

She'd asked him to stay the night and sleep beside her, but he was too smart for that. He woke up from visions violently sometimes, and he wouldn't risk hurting her. He wouldn't risk showing her the dark side of his life. Telling her about it was one thing, but if she saw how fucked up he was, she would change her mind. She would break her promise to make him fall in love with her, and he didn't want her to do that. He wanted her to try. He wanted her to come into her own and break him apart. He wanted her to force his heart open and claim him. It had already been tempting to let her bite him tonight, even if she was just teasing. So tempting to bind her to him like the bears did. So tempting to secure a mate and make sure he didn't wander through his life alone. But Avery had just found out her life was full of lies, and she was on the tail end of hard times.

She needed to become stronger before she took on a bond with him.

The sound of a truck engine rattled the house,

and headlights flashed through the window. Four in the morning and Ryder was finally home from whatever vandalism he'd done in the name of anger. Weston's best friend, his blood brother, would lose his shit if he admitted how much Avery already meant to him. He was already going to have hell to pay for keeping her a secret so long.

Avery hugged her pillow closer and made the cutest fucking sleep sound Weston had ever heard in his life. He wouldn't tell her he'd come back after he left so he could watch her sleep. He didn't want to scare her, but he'd gone back to his cabin, avoided the hell out of sleep—or more specifically, visions—and snuck back into 1010 just to be close to her again.

He felt less volatile around her, which made no damn sense. He'd spent so many years angry at her, just *pissed* that she'd betrayed him. She'd been his first and only great betrayal, but finding out she hadn't been a part of her peoples' treachery had nuked the walls he'd put up. And now, instead of that slow build-up, he was completely overwhelmed with his feelings for her. This wasn't how it was supposed to be. Not for flight shifters. Their bond wasn't like the bears, right? But thinking back on Ma and Da's relationship, he began to see things in a different light. His dad had bitten his mom, claimed her, and even though her raven didn't necessarily need that, Beaston and Aviana Novak's love story had always been one for the books. So many in Damon's Mountains had looked up to them, or gone mushy in the face when they saw them hugging, kissing, or talking low, as if they were the only ones in the world.

Was that because Da was a bear shifter and capable of giving that bond?

Or was there some slim chance Weston could have that with Avery, despite them both being flight shifters?

He'd thought it was silly when Ryder had fallen so hard for Lexi. He'd thought his best friend was just falling head-over-heels again, and the bond was just some mythical thing for shifters like him and Ryder. But now he watched Ryder and Lexi, who was utterly human, and he could almost see the bond between them. He could sense it. He could tell when Ryder went too long without seeing Lexi, or touching her, because he went dimmer somehow.

In her sleep, Avery sighed a contented sound and

smiled. "Save me," she whispered.

Weston frowned and leaned closer. He waited, thinking he'd imagined it, but she parted her soft lips and said it again. "Save me, Weston."

The walls of the cabin melted like burning metal, fading and exposing sterile, white walls behind them.

"No." Weston pushed the heels of his hands against his eyes and then looked up again.

The floor melted into dingy, cracked white tiles, and the bed disappeared under Avery. She slammed to the ground but didn't flinch at any pain. She lay in the middle of the empty room in a threadbare nightgown, her knees pulled up to her chest as she shivered uncontrollably. Her bare feet were dirty, and gooseflesh covered her body. She was frail and thin, her collar bones sticking out harshly under the neck of her gown. Mascara was smudged on her cheeks, and her eyes stared at him blankly. Her lips moved constantly.

"Avery?"

She gasped and began reciting words again.

Weston looked at the door. Maybe he could open it for her. Maybe he could let her out. There was no handle on this side, but there was something else.

Something that chilled his blood to ice. Long claw marks were slashed deeply into the sheetrock on either side of the door. Some of them were bloody, and when he looked back at her hands, her nails were nothing but stubs.

He bolted for her, tried to cover her with his body, tried to keep her warm, tried to comfort her, but he couldn't feel her. "Avery," he repeated more frantically. "It's okay, I'm right here."

It was so fucking cold in here. He'd never felt cold in his visions before, but it was uncomfortable in this one. Her lips were still moving, and her words were louder now, audible.

"I played shortstop in the baseball game on Thursday, and we won. It was our first win of the season, which is sad since most of the team is shifters and we were playing mostly human kids. Mason and Clinton took us out for pizza afterward. We all got suicides. Do you know what a suicide is? It's a mix of all the different soft drinks in one cup. Clinton put whiskey in his when Mason wasn't looking."

Oh, God. He remembered this. He'd written this letter to her when he was twelve, maybe thirteen. She was reciting his words.

"Ryder ran away from home on Monday. He said he was tired of being grounded, but he only made it to the gas station right outside of Damon's Mountains before he ran out of beef jerky. He didn't even pack any underwear, and Mason was so mad he grounded him for another month. It's really hard not to laugh at Ryder when he complains about it. So dumb. Dumb, dumb, dumb," she said, hiccupping on the word. A tear slid out of the corner of her eye and made a shallow splat on the tile under her cheek. "I can't wait to get to meet you someday. I can't wait to give you a hug and finally get to hear your voice in person. Avery, I think you are my second best friend. Friend, friend." Her voice hitched. "Best friend."

The floor shook, and the walls began to crack and crumble. No, he wasn't ready. Wasn't ready for the vision to end. He wanted to stay here and be near her. He didn't want her to be alone. The bloody claw marks split open on the wall, and deep cracks blasted down to the floor and through the tiles toward him.

"Avery, it's going to be okay," he said. Desperately, he tried to hug her to his body, but his hands went right through her.

And just as the bedroom of 1010 showed from

behind the clawed, bloody walls, Avery lifted her hollow gaze to him with a heartbroken sadness etched into her beautiful face. "I miss you."

He blinked back the emotion in his eyes, and the room was gone. He was back in 1010, and Avery was sleeping peacefully, her face completely relaxed and happy looking.

What the fuck?

Gripping the back of his hair, Weston stood and paced the room. That hadn't been the future. She'd kept the darkness of her past to herself. Cut him out of that pain. He wasn't supposed to see the past, right? He was a future-teller.

God, he could still feel the chill of the white room, could still here the soft echo of her whispered words, but it wasn't real. Not anymore. How was she okay? If that's how it had been for her, how was she still upright, still fighting? How was she still kind to people? No wonder she would rather be homeless than go back to Raven's Hollow. He wanted to kill them all. He wanted to annihilate the entire fucking flock for what they'd done to Avery. His Avery. He hadn't been there to protect her, and still, she'd clung to him. To his letters. To his words. In the vision, she hadn't looked that much younger than she did now. That had to be recent, and she was still holding his letters in her heart to get through the bad stuff. Shit.

He had to get out of here before he woke her. He was shaking with his need for violence and vengeance, and it would scare her. And goddammit, she'd been scared enough in her life.

He bolted from 1010, strode up the winding dirt road to his house. He couldn't sleep or risk another vision. For fuck's sake, they even came to him while he was awake now!

"You look like two-week-old shit," Ryder said grumpily from the front porch of their attached cabin.

Probably. He'd just watched the woman he cared about in a moment of torture. In a moment of breaking. He wasn't okay at all. Heart banging against his chest, Weston ignored him and yanked the tackle box and one of the fishing poles from the side of his porch.

"We're fishing?" Ryder said, standing with hope in his eyes.

But Weston couldn't fish with Ryder this morning. He couldn't stomach laughing at Ryder's jokes when he'd seen Avery in The Box. Weston needed an hour, two hours, fuck, and entire day if he could manage it. He needed time to wrap his mind around the fact that he could now see the fucking *past*. Avery's past. He wanted to puke just thinking about the empty hopelessness in her eyes.

"Not today. I need some time alone," he muttered as he strode down the porch stairs. Like a coward, he kept his gaze diverted away from Ryder because he couldn't shoulder hurting yet another person he cared about. He'd unknowingly helped destroy Avery by leaving her alone with the shitstorm of her life, and now he was disappointing Ryder. It was all too much.

His best friend didn't say anything as Weston tossed his gear in the back of his truck. Thank God for small blessings because his head couldn't handle anything extra right now. The fucking past! Like the sight wasn't bad enough already!

When Weston looked in the rearview mirror as he skidded out of his front yard, Ryder was standing there, looking pissed, with his arms across his chest. He felt bad for falling apart right now, he did, but Weston couldn't deal with the amount of shit Ryder was going to give him. He couldn't deal with apologizing and mending fences when he was reeling like this.

He would make it up to Ryder, but right now, he needed to get as far away from here, and away from that vision, as possible.

FIFTEEN

"Eh hem!"

Avery scrunched up her face at the grating sound of someone clearing their throat loudly. When she eased her eyes open, Ryder was sitting in the chair he'd pulled up next to the bed. He was petting long strokes down the back of a tiny cream Chihuahua he had cradled across his arm. Ryder's bright gold eyes were narrowed to pissed-off little slits as he glared at her. The Chihuahua's glare at her matched.

"What are you doing here?" she asked in a groggy voice.

Ryder snorted an offended sound. "What am I doing here? What am *I* doing here? I live here. I'll ask the questions, thank you very much."

"Ryder," a small voice came across from a cell phone resting on the arm of Ryder's chair. "Be nice."

Ryder gritted his teeth and petted the tiny dog in his arms again. "This is Sprinkles, my princess, my hairy snuggler, the warmer of my toes." He jerked his head toward the phone. "This is Sexy Lexi, my mate, the stroker of my boner, the keeper of my seed—"

"Ryder, she'd already met me," Lexi said.

"—the future mother of my dozen owl babies—"

"Three max. Focus, Ryder."

"—the human of my heart, with the perfect toes, and the perfect ears, and the perfect nubbins—"

"Wait, what are nubbins?" Avery asked, utterly confused.

Ryder's eyes went wide like she had the brain of a one-celled amoeba. "They're nipples, Avery Foley. *Nipples.*"

Lexi sighed so loudly into the phone, static blasted across the speaker.

Ryder petted Sprinkles again with the flat of his palm. "Lexi is at work but insisted on being here for this, *to curb my rage*."

"Okay," Avery said, sitting up in bed to better face him. "What can I do to make you less...enraged?"

"I have interview questions."

"But I already work at Big Flight."

"You aren't interviewing for a job, Avery, come *on*. You're interviewing for my twelfth best friend."

"Twelfth?" It was the crack of dawn and Ryder was being really confusing.

"Yes, twelfth. Weston, Alana, Lexi, Dark Kane, Sprinkles, Harper, Wyatt, Aaron, Sammy Scrotum, Maximus Red Balls, Bart, and then waaaay at the end, you."

Okay, she knew most of those people, and the name of the mouse that lived in 1010 had already been explained by Weston. "Who is Maximus Red Balls?"

Lexi answered for him in a tired voice. "That's what he named one of the tomato plants in my vegetable garden."

Great, Avery ranked lower than a tomato plant. "And Bart?"

Ryder lifted his red-bearded chin primly. "A cat crapped on our porch last week, and in that pile of smelly poo wiggled a little white worm. I named him Bart."

Fantastic.

"I apologize for anything that happens after this," Lexi said. "He's had a special morning."

"Damn straight, it's been a special morning," Ryder exclaimed. "Do you know what today is, Avery Foley?"

"Weston's birthday?" Avery squeaked out.

"Yes, and do you know where he is instead of sitting across from me on our annual birthday bro-date eating a plateful of pancakes and taking selfies? Hmm?"

"Not...on your bro-thing with the pancakes?"

"He's fishing without me! Fishing! Without me!"

"Rein it in, Ryder," Lexi said.

Ryder composed his face, but his neck was still as red as his hair, and he stroked Sprinkles so vigorously she growled at him.

"Interview question number one. How long have you known Weston?"

"Um, our moms let us start writing to each other when we were ten years old."

Ryder arched a ruddy eyebrow. "Well, I saw him on the first day he changed, and his dad told me we were going to be best friends and blood brothers, and we are."

"Next question, Ryder," Lexi urged.

"Did you always plan on stealing him away from me?"

"What?"

Sprinkles growled again at the rough petting, but he told Avery it was because, "Sprinkles can sense evil."

Dear lord, she wanted to go back to sleep. "I don't want to steal him away from anyone. I just really like him and want to be in his life."

"Why didn't you tell me you knew him when you interviewed for Big Flight?" Ryder asked, and now his face was going red again.

"I didn't mean to conceal anything from you, but I was scared of the Bloodrunners, including you, including Weston. Ravens aren't the bravest shifters, and then Weston didn't seem to recognize me, so it was awkward blurting out who I was. I didn't mean to hurt you or anyone else. And I really don't want to put a wedge between you and Weston. He used to write about you when we were growing up. I already felt like I kind of knew you, and then working with you over the past week has been really fun. Normal. I don't really want to lose that."

Ryder lifted his chin higher and narrowed his eyes suspiciously. "Good answer, Avery Foley." He stood to his full, imposing height and told Lexi, "I'm going to put you in my pocket now, right next to my pecker."

"I'm hanging up now," Lexi said. "Sorry, Avery. I'll see you later." The line went dead before Ryder could finagle the cell phone into his front pocket.

"Air Ryder approved," he said magnanimously. "You have earned the coveted spot of twelfth best friend for a probationary period. I'll make the announcement on my social media accounts today."

"Wait, I don't really want to be on your social media…"

Cradling Sprinkles, Ryder ignored her and walked out of the room. The front door banged closed, and Avery plopped back onto the mattress. Well, that was weird.

And now she needed to make sure she didn't cause tension between Weston and the Bloodrunner Crew. Maybe she should talk to Harper. Or all of them? Maybe she should just come clean and tell them everything so they didn't think she was here for the wrong reasons. But the thought of talking to the notoriously badass Bloodrunners was intimidating and made her want to shrink into the mattress and hide.

But she wanted to give Weston another relationship, not take other relationships away from him. He'd already given her so much, and she wanted him to feel as happy as he made her feel. She could be brave and talk to the Bloodrunners if it meant Weston would give more easy smiles.

Weston was my first.

The thought drew her up short. Avery squealed and kicked her legs, then covered her flushed cheeks with the blanket to hide her massive grin. It had felt so good! Better than she'd imagined. And they joked afterward. On television, sex was so serious and passionate, and there had been that, but after, it had been fun, and she'd laughed hard, for the first time since she could remember. The big belly laughs that made her feel all warm and fuzzy inside.

She'd lost her virginity to the Novak Raven. It was finally done, and she didn't have to worry about what it would be like anymore. Sure, she wasn't a professional yet, but she would catch up. She would go back and pay more attention to the smutty scenes in her favorite romance novels, and maybe she would order one of those sex-position books with some of her first paycheck.

He was the perfect first. He was the perfect always.

Oh, she was losing her heart fast. She rolled out of bed and padded into the bathroom. The first tour for Big Flight wasn't until noon today, and it was still early, but she needed to get ready and get moving. Why? Because it was Weston's birthday, and she had a plan to make his life easier.

Avery didn't care how long it took, or how intimidated she felt.

She was going to win over the Bloodrunners.

****

Avery psyched herself out three times before she finally approached the women talking and laughing in the shade. Alana was standing on a picnic table in a gorgeous, sparkling white gown, while the dark-headed alpha of the Bloodrunners pinned the hem of her dress. Lexi had come back sometime while Avery was getting ready for the day, and now she sat on the edge of the table, reading from a list.

"H-hi," Avery stammered as she approached. She

thought they would clam up and stop having fun, but Lexi and Alana waved and smiled brighter.

"Hey, girl," Alana greeted her. "What do you think? Honest opinions please. I bought two dresses, and this one has the fullest skirt. The other one is one of those mermaid dresses with no train, but it fits too damn tight."

Her dark skin practically glowed against the white princess dress. "It's beautiful," Avery murmured. "I've never seen a prettier dress than that one. Are you getting married?" Avery shook her head at her stupid question. "Of course you're getting married."

"Two more weeks," Alana said easily. "I'm already nervous."

"About getting married?" Harper asked around the row of pins hanging from between her lips.

"No, I can't wait to marry Aaron. I just get nervous about everything coming together. I always wanted a big wedding. I had no idea how many moving parts are involved in something like this though."

Avery stood there awkwardly, wringing her hands and shifting her weight from side-to-side. She needed to borrow someone's car to run errands before work, but she hardly knew these women, and none of them had any reason to trust her with their rides. Stupid Civic for breaking down.

Lexi patted the table next to her in invitation, and while Avery gingerly took a seat beside the dark-haired beauty, Lexi continued reading off the checklist.

"Cake."

"I can pick that up the day of," Harper volunteered. "I can grab the chairs and runner from that rental place while I'm in town, too."

"Good. Flowers."

"That's on Weston and Ryder," Harper murmured as she pinned the bottom of the gown. "They already said they would pick everything up from the florist that morning. Is Aaron's fire crew coming?"

"Yes, all of them have RSVP'd with plus ones," Alana said a little breathily. "There's so many people coming now."

"Stop panicking," Harper said. "We've got this."

"You'll do really good, and you will be beautiful," Avery murmured. "And Aaron will be there waiting for you at the end of the aisle. It'll be the best day." The Bloodrunners had gone silent, and fire blazed across Avery's cheeks. "What kind of flowers are you getting?"

"Gerber daisies and roses," Alana said, sounding more excited. "Bright colors, too, since we're having it outside. Oranges and pinks."

"Oh, that sounds perfect," Avery whispered. Why couldn't she inhale? Sitting this close to Harper was doing bad things to her body. God, she was going to pass out soon.

"Breathe, girl," Harper said easily. She hadn't even looked over at Avery, so how had she known the panic attack was coming?

"You are all scary," she blurted out. "Not as scary as you used to be, but you have a freaking grizzly bear in you." She pointed at Alana and then Harper. "And you have a dragon. *A dragon*. Fire. You can *eat* people. Please don't eat me."

Harper giggled—the dragon giggled!—and said, "I promise I won't eat you. I don't much like the taste of crow." And when the alpha looked over at her and winked her blue dragon eye, Avery nearly fell off the edge of the table in shock.

Alana and Lexi laughed, and a surprised, "Ha!" belted out of Avery, too. Talking about man-eating dragons should not be funny, it really shouldn't, but this was a subject the crew was obviously comfortable with. If they even knew the terrifying stories the council told to Raven's Hollow about predator shifters, dragons in particular, the Bloodrunners would probably laugh at her people, too. Little terrified wieners, all of them.

"Um, I have a favor to ask."

"What's up?" Alana adjusted her big boobs in the wedding dress distractedly.

"I have an errand to run in town, but my car broke down last night."

"That one?" Harper asked, jamming her thumb over her shoulder.

Sure enough, Avery's beat-up old Civic sat on blocks in front of a double cabin up the hill.

"Yeah, did Weston bring that up here?"

"Yeah, he had it towed in this morning. He worked on it for a while, then said he had to clear some trails, whatever that means."

"Oh, it's where the boys take chainsaws to the trails and clear out the branches that have fallen during the night or are hanging too low," Avery explained. "It keeps the tourists safer if they can keep the lanes clear."

"Do you ride the trails, too?" Lexi asked.

"No, but I want to really bad. I've never ridden an ATV."

"And you work for an ATV tour company?" Harper asked, her dark, delicate brows arched up high.

Avery shrugged one shoulder and tried to smile. "Pretty crazy, huh?" Nope, she didn't want to explain that Weston hadn't trusted her for the first week and would've rather cut off his own nards than taken her up on a trail. Things were different now.

"You can borrow my Jeep," Lexi offered.

"Are you sure?" Avery couldn't help the hope in her voice.

"Hell yeah, I owe you."

"For what?"

"We'll just call this an apology for what my mate pulled this morning."

"What did Ryder do?" Harper asked, the joking tone gone from her voice.

"Uh, he interviewed me."

Lexi snickered and shook her head. "Avery's being too nice. He's mad about Weston keeping his pen pal a secret when they were kids. Ryder was a little monster to her first thing this morning."

"You mean Ryder was a big monster," Avery murmured. "He's got a lot of muscles. I shit you not, he had to walk sideways through the bedroom door." More heat in her cheeks when the girls laughed. She wished she had a better filter. At least they didn't seem to be laughing *at* her like the people from Raven's Hollow had done, so there was that.

Lexi handed her a set of keys with a little wooden owl dangling from them. Ryder's animal. "Thanks, Lexi," she said softly, then stood to leave.

"Do you want to come to the wedding?" Alana blurted out. "I mean, you and Weston are a thing...right?"

Avery didn't know how to answer. Yes? At least, they'd slept together last night. More heat in her cheeks, and she couldn't meet their gazes. It was still too soon to put a label on them, but... "I hope we're a thing. And yes, I would be honored to come to your wedding." Determined not to ruin the moment with her running mouth, she turned to flee to the black

Jeep Wrangler parked by her Civic.

"Avery?" Harper asked.

Avery hunched under the seriousness of her tone and turned slowly. "Yes?"

"I have a crew to protect—one that means the entire world to me. Should I expect trouble from your people?"

Avery mulled that over for a few moments. She understood Harper's desire to keep her friends safe. This place, these mountains, were a paradise, and they housed important and good people. "I don't think so. The ravens are scared of you."

Harper stood to her full height and locked her oddly-colored gaze on Avery. "Are *you* in trouble from your people?"

"No." Avery tried and failed to smile. "I don't have any people."

SIXTEEN

Ryder glared at her from the porch of Big Flight's main building and slurped hard on a swirly straw hanging from his lemonade. Or margarita?

"Please tell me you aren't drinking an hour before a tour," she said, shutting the door to Lexi's Jeep.

"Please tell me you didn't steal my lover's car."

Okay, they were starting off on the wrong foot again. "I got you a present."

He narrowed his bright blue eyes suspiciously. "Is it boudoir pictures of Lexi or beer?"

Avery frowned. "No."

Ryder blinked slowly and slurped loudly on his straw, showing his absolute disinterest in her present.

Weston came out of the front door looking like a tall drink of water in a Texas summer with his holey jeans and white T-shirt. He grinned when he saw her, but behind that smile, something was off. He looked...tired.

He jogged over to her and shocked her silly when he picked her up and squeezed her. He kissed her lips hard enough to knock their teeth together. "Who am I?" he teased.

Oh, she got it. He was making fun of her first kiss. With a firm swat on the arm, she muttered, "Stop."

"Barf," Ryder drawled. "I'm going to barf my margarita."

She *knew* he was drinking.

Ignoring Ryder like a pro, Weston said, "You're here early."

"Not as early as I wanted to be."

"I was going to come pick you up in a few minutes."

"Well, I didn't want to wait any longer to see you."

"Still barfing," Ryder called. "And now you're blocking my view of beautiful mother nature. Can you move to the right by like, seven miles?"

Unable to help herself, she cupped the scruff on his cheeks and grinned. "Happy birthday, Weston."

He buried his face against her neck and chuckled warmly. "Thank you."

"I got you a present."

"I thought you got *me* a present," Ryder called.

Avery sighed as Wes settled her on her feet, then pulled him by the hand up onto the porch. Carefully, she tugged two small, newspaper-wrapped presents from her purse and handed them to the guys.

Ryder set his empty glass down with a clunk and tore into the wrapping.

"It's not much," she warned them, suddenly feeling self-conscious. What if this had been a terrible idea, and they hated it?

Ryder reached his gift first and plucked the orange bear paw beer bottle opener from the newsprint with a frown. "What am I going to do with a keychain like—"

"Ryder," Weston murmured, holding up his shiny blue one.

"Oh my God, you got us matching beer bottle openers," Ryder said, his eyes huge. A gleeful grin took his face as he began securing the ring to his keys.

"Avery?" Weston asked. "How much money do you have left?"

She ducked her gaze in shame and refused to answer. It didn't matter. She wanted to do this for them.

"How much?" Weston asked, gentler.

With a sigh, she answered, "Ninety-eight cents."

"To your name?" Ryder asked.

She nodded once.

"And you spent money on these?" Ryder asked.

Another quick nod as Weston slid his hand around her waist and hugged her to his side.

Ryder cleared his throat loudly once, twice. He stood and hugged her and Weston in a quick, rough bear hug that nearly cracked all her ribs. In a hoarse voice, he said, "I like you more than Bart now." He jogged down the stairs and pushed his keys into his back pocket as he escaped toward the ATV garage.

Ryder liked her more than a worm in a pile of cat crap, so she'd just been promoted to eleventh best friend. She shouldn't be this touched, but her eyes went a little misty.

By the time she turned around, Weston was wearing that crooked grin she adored.

"This is the best birthday present," he murmured, hooking the shiny beer bottle opener to his keychain. "Is the bear paw cut-out because of my dad?"

"Yeah. And your crew, and the crew you grew up in. And the first day I saw you here, you were drinking a beer, so I knew you liked the stuff. You told me in a letter one time that your favorite color was blue. I picked up Ryder's this morning. I asked Lexi what his favorite color was, and they only had one orange bottle opener left." She kicked at the edge of a floor board with the tip of her hiking boot. "I don't want your relationships to be stressed because of me."

Weston shoved his keys in his front pocket and pulled her into a crushing hug and rasped his beard against her neck. "You just did more than you even know, Ave."

"It's just a keychain," she said, blushing with pleasure as she hugged his neck up tight.

"Nah, don't do that. Don't downplay it. You spent the last of your money on me and my best friend, fixing something I've been failing at all day. I can tell you just made Ryder really happy. And you made me really happy, too. The thought you put into this… I'll always think about how sweet you are when I see it on my keys."

"Good," she murmured happily. But his eyes were still off. Still a little too hollow for her liking and pitch black, like his raven was all riled up, and for what? He sounded okay. She traced the dark circles under his eyes and frowned. "What's wrong? Did you not sleep well?"

The smile drifted from his face, and he gave his gaze to the woods. Cupping his cheeks again, she brought him back to her. "You can tell me. Did you have a vision? Do you want to talk about it?"

"Yes, and no I don't want to talk about this one. Not now. Let's leave this one alone, okay?"

It must've been a bad one then. She hated this, hated that he had to endure something so awful. Hated that he couldn't get good sleep. Hated that he felt like he couldn't talk to her about it. She leaned up and pressed her lips gently to his. "When you feel like it, I'll be waiting."

"Hmm," he said against her lips. He pulled away

suddenly and said, "I got you something, too."

She let off a playful gasp and linked her hands behind his neck. "Something like what?"

She could feel the relief wafting from him at her willingness to let the last conversation go. It wasn't her way to push a man who didn't want to be pushed, and Weston seemed to be happier when their chats were lighter. So was she. Joking with him made her feel so delightfully normal.

Weston grabbed her hand and pulled her toward the shop. "Come here quick. I hear the first car of the tour coming up the road." As Weston led her inside, she could hear it, too, the faraway roar of a truck engine, or perhaps an SUV.

On the desk in the office sat a beer can vase of small-stemmed wild flowers in purples, blues, and yellows.

"Weston," she whispered as he handed it to her.

"I called my parents this morning and told them about you. Told them about the way the council used you without your knowledge, and my Da told me I should make you a knife and pick you flowers." Weston ducked his grin to the floor. "I'll work on the knife, but the flowers I can do today. I haven't ever been anyone's first, you know? I want today to be special for you."

Avery hugged the blue beer can of flowers to her chest and smelled them to hide her mushy smile. "I've never gotten flowers before. And I've never had a knife. Will you teach me how to use one?"

"Hell yeah, woman. I'll have you comfortable with a blade. We'll get you on that chainsaw as soon as you feel ready. There's this, too." He handed her a white envelope. "I've decided we're doing paychecks once a week now instead of every two weeks. I cut Ryder his first check this morning, too, just so you know I'm not giving you special treatment." Weston slipped his hand to her waist and rested his cheek against hers. "You've done really good work, Avery. I'm glad we hired you."

And then he left her there, stunned. The door up front closed, and she set the flowers down gingerly and opened the envelope. There were two pieces of paper. The first was her paycheck. She wanted to cry when she saw the numbers. Not because it was riches, or anything like that, but because this was the first paycheck she'd ever earned. She'd worked hard and earned her way, and she didn't only have a dollar to her name anymore.

She was going to be okay.

Carefully, she set the check on the desk and unfolded the other piece of paper.

Weston's handwriting was chicken-scratch, just like when he'd been a teenager, but she could read every word easily.

Ave,

I should've written to you way before now, but I dropped the ball a decade ago. Here is the first letter of many to come. I promise I won't disappear on you again. I'll be someone you can depend on, and I know it'll take a while for you to trust that again, but I can be patient. I'll earn it back. So, it's my birthday, but that isn't the best part about today. The best part is that first thing this morning, out in the woods, I got to Change with you for the first time. And then you gave me even more. I got to touch you. I got to kiss you, and be with you. I got to be your first, and it was one of the biggest moments in my entire life. Keep this in your box with my other letters. Someday, when we're old and gray, it'll be fun to go back through these and piece together our story.

Later gator,

Weston

P. S. You said you were going to make me fall in love with you.

Done.

Avery stood with her hand over her mouth, a shocked sound stuck in her throat as she read the last line.

Weston was in love with her?

He'd even signed it like he used to when they were pen pals. *Later gator*, and she would respond on hers by signing *after awhile crocodile*.

She could hear people outside now, talking and laughing with Weston and Ryder, so in a rush, she pulled a piece of computer paper from the printer and scribbled across the middle.

Weston,

I love you back. Always have.

After awhile crocodile,

Ave

She folded it in half, set it in the middle of his

desk, zipped her paycheck and his letter into her purse, and grabbed the beer can vase of flowers because she wanted to look at them all day. She set the bouquet by the cash register out front and booted up the system so she could start checking in the tour. There was a stand of tourist sunglasses on the counter, and she caught a glimpse of herself in one of the reflective lenses. She was grinning from ear-to-ear, and for a shocking moment, she didn't recognize herself. Had she ever smiled like this before?

The landline rang, the front door opened, and the chaos began. Big Flight was officially open, and she was on the clock. She was earning her own money, gaining independence by the day, and now she had the love of a good man. Real love. The kind she hadn't even dared to dream of. The kind that wasn't supposed to exist for a female raven shifter like her.

This feeling was better than flying.

SEVENTEEN

Two long back-to-back ATV tours meant Avery hadn't seen much of Weston all day. Between groups, Wes had run in to refill on bottled waters, given her a quick kiss, and ducked back out to the new riders to start their safety and mechanical lessons. Ryder hadn't even given her the evil eye or made devil horns on his head. And once, when she'd handed him a cold water bottle and the lunchbox of snacks he liked to devour between rides, he even smiled and told her, "You don't suck, woodchuck."

She pulled another hot pink Big Flight T-shirt from the box, folded it neatly, and put it with the right size on the long, multi-tiered table Weston had made. She'd asked Ryder about putting more tourist-friendly souvenirs in the shop to gain an extra stream of revenue for Big Flight, and he'd approved it. The stuff she'd ordered came in while the boys were out, and she wanted to surprise them with how good the shop looked. There were T-shirts, water bottles, post cards, jewelry from the local reservation, and on the back wall were even a few paintings from local artists.

Outside, the sound of laughter and excitement echoed as the riders shut down their engines. They would probably linger, snapping pictures near the ATVs like the other groups had done before they headed inside to fill out surveys, shop for souvenirs, and say their goodbyes.

She would get to see Weston soon. A trill of anticipation zinged through her body and landed in her chest, creating a soft fluttering sensation. Avery folded the last shirt, stacked it precisely on the pile of larges, and began to break down the cardboard box.

The door swung open so hard it banked against the wall and made her jump. "Oh, shit," Weston muttered, steadying it. His white T-shirt was damp with sweat, his camouflage baseball cap on backward, and a pair of reflective sunglasses had been shoved up to rest on his forehead. Along with his goofy grin, he looked silly and sexy. The hollowness from earlier was gone as he jogged over to her and pressed his lips against hers.

His dark whiskers were scratchy now, and she giggled when he dragged her closer. He was smiling big against her lips and, God, she loved this. She loved that he was so open with his affection. The Novak Raven surprised her. He wasn't at all like she'd imagined.

"Sweaty man," she punched out through her laughter.

Uncaring, Weston wrapped his rock-hard arms around her so she couldn't escape and wiggled his damp shirt all over her.

"Quit," she squealed. "The customers will see!"

Looking around, he released her and said, "Whoa, this place looks different."

"Good different or bad different?"

"Looks great." He fingered the edge of a purple T-shirt with the Big Flight lettering in bright pink across the front. "When did you order all this?"

"Ryder and I were working on it the first couple of days I worked here. We did rush shipping. I hope you don't mind. Ryder said it was okay and cut the check."

"No, yeah, that's fine. This is a good idea." Looking impressed, he nodded as he scanned the room. "You did good, Foley."

She snorted. "Last names now? You sleep with me and then resort to calling me by my last name?"

Weston cracked a grin and leaned down, nipped her lip, and squeezed her ass hard. "Yep." He waggled his eyebrows once and strode toward the office, his thick-soled boots echoing on the wood floors.

The letter! He was going to see her response to his letter. She hadn't given it much thought while he was out for the day, but now a wave of nervousness blasted through her.

Act busy!

Avery turned for a stand of jewelry she'd just arranged and studied her favorite piece, a shiny turquoise ring set in sterling silver. It matched her eyes, and she considered purchasing it with some of her first paycheck, on the off-chance that Weston would think it was pretty on her.

She wasn't really seeing it right now, though, as she touched the cold stone with her fingertips. She was imagining Weston's face when he read her note. *I love you back. Always have.*

She'd never said or written that to a man before.

"Avery?" Weston asked from right behind her, and she could hear it. She could hear the crinkle of the paper in his hands.

Slowly she turned around. Too scared to look in his eyes, she looked at his dusty boots instead.

"I'll keep this with my letters," he murmured in that deep, rich baritone voice of his.

"You kept my letters?" she asked.

He lifted her chin and nodded. "Yeah. I asked my Ma to send them to me. They should be here in a few days." His bright green gaze flicked to the ring on the jewelry stand over her shoulder. "You like that?"

Heat rushed up her neck and landed in her ears. Avery shrugged. "I think it's pretty."

He opened his mouth to respond, but the door swung open hard again and hit the wall.

"I'm gonna have to fix that," he murmured as Ryder led the chattering, dust-covered tour into the shop.

Avery bustled behind the counter and began handing out surveys and answering questions while

Weston charmed the masses right along with Ryder. Two of the couples handed them tips and shook their hands, and for a moment, Avery just took it all in. The clients were happy, Weston and Ryder were happy, and outside, the sun was sitting low in a cloudless sky over the vibrant green Smokey Mountains. She had her first paycheck sitting in her purse, the work day was almost done, and she would be spending the night in 1010 instead of the back of her car.

Life couldn't get any better than this!

And now she actually looked forward to going back to the heart of Harper's Mountains with Weston. Why? Because for some reason, she felt safe here, and that was a really big deal.

They said goodbye to the tour, and she closed up the shop while the boys took care of the ATVs out near the garage. When she locked the front door and readjusted her purse on her shoulder, a white diesel truck rumbled under the welcome sign. For a moment, she thought it was a late tour, but Harper was driving, and Lexi sat in the front seat. And behind that truck was a big black one on mud tires. Wyatt pulled his pickup in a wide loop around the yard as Ryder and Weston jogged up the dirt path toward them.

"What's this?" Weston called over the noise of the engines.

"Obviously, it's your birthday party," Ryder said. "Since you broke our pancake bro-date this morning with your emotional constipation, I begged Lexi to make us pancakes so we can have them for dinner."

Weston hooked an arm around Avery's shoulder and hugged her close to his side. "Are we riding out somewhere?"

"We can!" Ryder said, his eyes going wide like that was the greatest idea on the planet. "ATV's are all gassed up, we have shit for a bonfire, and enough booze to fill the Nile. We gettin' wild tonight, old man?"

Weston snorted and explained, "Ryder is five years older than me."

"Not according to maturity," Wyatt said, leaning on the back of his truck.

"He's got a point," Ryder deadpanned.

"You want to finally get on an ATV?" Weston asked.

"Me?" Avery asked. "Like…my own ATV? One I get to drive?"

Weston laughed and nodded. "I won't make you hang off the back of mine. You're wearing the right shoes for it," he said, looking down at her hiking boots. "It'll be fun."

"ATVs tonight?" Lexi asked. "Hell, yes. First, though..." She pulled down the tailgate of Wyatt's truck. "I have a birthday surprise for you."

A giant pile of water guns in all shapes and sizes sloshed forward.

"Oh. My. God. You are the perfect woman!" Ryder crowed, bolting for the arsenal. "You just gave me a boner!"

"Ryder Croy, this is Weston's birthday present," Lexi growled, tugging on a huge soaker Ryder was trying to strap to his back like Rambo. "He should get first choice."

"I...need the...biggest gun," he gritted out, struggling to pull the soaker out of her hands, "...because I have...the biggest penis!" Ryder yanked the trigger and squirted Lexi right in the face, then froze with an oh-shit look on his face. "Accident," he murmured.

And oh, when Lexi opened her eyes again, she looked mad as a hornet.

Everyone in the clearing went still for a moment, attention on what Lexi would do. Then, as if there was some unspoken, *ready, steady, go,* everyone bolted for the water guns.

Weston pulled Avery behind him and frantically began strapping himself down with the sloshing weaponry. Avery hesitated a moment, unsure of herself, but Weston said, "You better move, woman. Defend yourself!"

Well, okay then.

Avery pulled a couple straps over her shoulders, shoved two water pistols in the back of her jean shorts, and screamed when Aaron blasted her in the shoulder with a stream of cold water. Giggling uncontrollably, she pulled a couple water balloons from a neon green bucket and launched them at Aaron and Alana, who were on the run.

Wyatt stood in the back of the truck, legs locked, as he shot two water rifles in the air and battle-cried like a lunatic. Ryder was shooting Lexi's white shirt all to hell, right at her boobs, Weston was running full-speed after Aaron, the mountains were echoing with laughter, and everything was perfect.

Harper blasted her with water, and Avery

gasped at how shockingly cold it was. What had they put in these, ice water? She pulled the trigger on her biggest gun, but nothing.

"Pump it!" Weston yelled from where he, Aaron, and Alana were embroiled in a water battle.

"What?"

"Ryder, quit!" Lexi said through a peel of laughter.

Ryder was hugging his mate, pelvic thrusting against her butt. "He said *hump it.*"

"Hump it?" Avery called, confused.

"No, pump it!" Weston yelled again, pulling the mechanism under his water gun to show Avery.

Right. She did as he'd shown her and pulled the trigger on Harper right before she disappeared around the truck. Harper squealed and said, "Aaah, that's cold!"

Avery chased Harper, but Wyatt was still in the back of the truck raining down water bullets, and by the time Avery caught up to the Bloodrunner alpha, she was drenched and laughing so hard it was difficult to stay upright. She slipped and slid in the mud they were creating, her wet hair plastered to her face, and her clothes sticking to her like a second skin. Alana and Lexi appeared out from behind the truck as Avery bolted for the trees. She and Harper screamed and dodged the new jets of water, looked at each other with giant grins, then turned their guns on the other two girls. Her biggest gun was already empty, so she tossed it on the ground and grabbed the next, ducking and hiding around trees.

"Aaaah," Aaron yelled as he jumped from behind a pine. He sprayed Avery across the stomach, and she reacted by hitting him in the chest with the stream from hers.

Another splash of water hit her and another, and then Weston was there, pulling her hand toward a thick grove of trees and tossing water balloon grenades at the others as they bolted for cover.

They played and shot and ran and hid until every water gun stream was nothing but a drip. Avery was heaving breath, her arms and legs were shaking, and she was soaked to the bone, but she'd never had more fun in her life. And when her last water pistol was empty, she shot a beaming smile at Weston, who was standing beside her, his short, dark hair dripping, eyes dancing, and his grin big and white. There was that dimple. His chest was heaving with exertion, and his shirt so wet she could see every tattoo through the thin material.

And for a moment, they just stood like that, locked in each other's smiles. He felt like happiness.

Weston dropped his water gun and cupped her neck, pulled her gently to him, and dipped down to her lips. It was a soft kiss, one where his lips fit perfectly to hers. He didn't push his tongue past her lips, but instead, stood up straighter and slid an arm around her back, brought her closer to his hard body. His erection pressed against her, but still, he didn't push. He was tender as he sipped at her lips.

He disengaged, then gave her a soft peck, once, twice, then another lingering one before he rested his forehead against hers and drew her palm against his chest. "Feel." His heartbeat was fast under her hand. Weston brushed damp hair from her face and smiled. "You do that to me."

Avery pressed his hand to her lips, kissed his work-hardened palm, then rested it under her collar bone so he could feel how fast hers was racing, too. "We match," she whispered.

"Weston's touching Avery's boob," Ryder called. And then he loudly sang, "Weston and Avery sittin' in a tree, F-U-C-K-I-N—"

"Ryder!" Harper yelled.

Avery cracked up and rested her face on Weston's chest to hide the color of her cheeks. "I like your crew," she admitted. "I thought they would be terrifying and mean, but they aren't."

"Nope. Just crass and immature," Weston said, his voice tinged with amusement.

Weston bent down, and shouldered their water guns. And on the way up, he slung Avery over his shoulder.

She squealed and struggled, but Weston was much stronger than her, so she gave up quickly. He headed back for the clearing, and Avery arched her back so she could see the others. Lexi was riding Ryder piggy-back style, Alana and Aaron were picking up a pair of water pistols off the ground with lovey smiles on their faces, and Harper and Wyatt were making out by a pine tree.

Avery's face hurt from smiling so much. The shifters of Raven's Hollow didn't show affection like this. There had always been a coldness, a distance that had made her uncomfortable, but here, it was accepted to hug, kiss, and show adoration.

Up at the shop, Weston disappeared inside and brought her a dry T-shirt in the right size. Her shorts were soaking still, but they would dry soon enough. The Bloodrunners changed into dry shirts without a single care about nudity, but when Avery hesitated, Weston pulled her to the other side of the truck and told her, "It's okay, you can change over here."

Relieved, she peeled off her wet tank top and slipped her T-shirt over her head. And when she peeked through the neck hole, she snorted. Weston was staring wide-eyed at her bra-clad boobs.

Busted, he offered her a wicked grin and said, "I was staring at your heartbeat."

Avery's shoes squished with every step as she walked beside Weston toward the garage, but even though she was a little uncomfortable, nothing could ruin this moment. While the others loaded up on ATV's and strapped coolers and supplies to the backs of the biggest ones with bungie cords, Weston showed her how to turn her camo print ATV on and get it into gear. Apparently they would be riding in "high" to get where they were going.

A rush of nervousness took her, but Weston rested his hands over hers on the handlebars. "You'll do fine. Follow in my tracks. I'll take the easiest way. And look"—he jerked his chin toward Alana, who was receiving a similar lesson from Aaron—"you aren't the only first-timer."

Well, that did make her feel better.

When Ryder arced his ATV in a wide circle, the others followed. Avery hit the throttle too hard and her quad lurched forward, scaring her. She skidded to a stop with the handlebar brakes. Alana had done the same thing in front of her, except she was laughing and her mate, Aaron, was looking at her like she was the cutest thing he'd ever seen. Okay, making mistakes wasn't so serious. Not with this crew.

Avery tried again, easing her thumb onto the throttle slower this time. She moved forward at a good, smooth clip, and when Weston tossed a glance over his shoulder at her, he winked and gave her that crooked smile. And her butterflies fluttered on. Grinning, she eased her quad right after his. Harper was behind her, and any other day, it would've bothered her to no end to expose her neck to a dominant dragon shifter like this. But she and Harper had just had a water fight, had even fought together some, and she'd never made Avery feel like she was in danger. Plus, it was really hard to see Harper as a threat when the alpha was giggling and joking with Wyatt, who was pulling up the rear.

For the next fifteen minutes, all she heard was her own giggling and the roar of her ATV motor as they sped up and down trails. Sometimes they would ride along a cliff edge adorned with towering trees, and she would have to remind herself she was a flight shifter. If the ATV rolled, she could Change. Her raven made her braver, where before, her inner animal would have burrowed deep inside of her in the face of fear.

She'd done that to her animal—trained it to be frightened and hide.

Avery made a silent oath to take better care of her raven, and herself.

She wasn't as fast as the others, but Weston never pulled too far ahead, and Harper and Wyatt seemed perfectly content with the speed she kept them at, so she didn't get overwhelmed like she usually would've. Up and up they climbed the rocky trails until they reached a flat part with a wide loop of trail around a single sourwood tree. There was a rocky ledge overlooking miles of shallow hills with buildings dotting the distant green. It was beautiful, so Avery snapped a picture with her phone while the boys unloaded the backs of the four-wheelers. She would print this photo out and write the date on the back so she could always remember today. She would keep it in the box with Weston's letters.

The Bloodrunners built a fire in a pit that had obviously been used before, and Lexi heated up giant pancakes on an iron griddle over the flames. Ryder had been right about the booze being a substantial amount. Weston scooped a red plastic cup through a blue cooler full of a fragrant fruity concoction Ryder called Clinton's Trashcan Punch.

One sip, and Avery's eyes watered from the burn. "Holy moly," she choked out as the crew laughed at her. "That's potent."

"Weston pulled her down onto his lap in a bag chair and took a long drink of his own. "Look," he said, pointing up the steep hill through the trees.

"What?"

"Wait. Just watch."

A tiny blinking light flickered through the woods. Avery gasped. "Fireflies?"

Weston kissed her shoulder, bit it gently, and

nodded.

"You know," she said, relaxing back against him. "We don't have fireflies in Raven's Hollow. And when I first moved here a month and a half ago, I would see them through the woods when I drove at night, or when I was sleeping in my car." She pointed excitedly as another firefly sparked to the right.

"Mmm hmm," Weston said in a happy, deep murmur.

"Anyway, I was so stressed out about what I was going to do, where I was going to find a job, how long I would be able to make my money stretch, that I didn't really have the mental capacity left to really look around at how beautiful this place is. I get to see fireflies. And I'm on the side of a beautiful mountain overlooking the Smokies. With *you*." She leaned to the side so she could better see him. "This is amazing."

"Uh, I think you forgot to say you get to hang out with the coolest fucking crew on the planet," Ryder added from across the fire where he was dumping syrup over a plate of pancakes.

"That, too."

Ryder snorted. "*That, too*, like we're an afterthought. "You mean *that first*!" He shook his head like he was offended. "We're awesome."

"Lexi, did you hear?" Avery asked softly.

"Hear what?" she asked, handing Avery a plate of three pancakes.

"I got promoted to eleventh best friend."

Lexi handed her the butter next. "Above the worm?"

"His name is Bart," Ryder said around a giant mouthful of pancake. "He's my spirit animal."

Lexi rolled her eyes and flipped the pancakes on the griddle with a plastic spatula. "Last week he said his spirit animal was the pterodactyl."

"No," Weston drawled. "No. You can't pick an animal that is extinct."

"I didn't pick it. The pterodactyl picked me."

A chunk of pancake flew from Wyatt's general direction and hit Ryder in the face. Harper laughed when the redheaded jokester didn't miss a beat, just plucked the morsel off his lap and popped it in his mouth.

"Look at that," Alana mused, staring over the ridge at the sunset. The sky sure was putting on a show with pretty pinks and yellows. "This is what it will look like at our wedding," she said to Aaron.

"Two weeks from today, at this same time, I'll be taking your last name. Alana Keller."

"Has a ring to it, baby," the blond-haired grizzly shifter said, pulling her chair closer to his. "I can't fuckin' wait to put my name on you."

"What kind of wedding do you want, Harper?" Alana asked, her attention back to cutting the food on her paper plate.

"I know the answer to this one," Wyatt said. "Ivory dress in a big chapel, all of Damon's Mountains invited. Reception in her mountains."

"So a big wedding," Lexi said.

"Huge," Harper confirmed through a grin. "I want it to be a massive party when we finally do it. Booze, fireworks, the whole nine yards. What about you?" the alpha asked Lexi.

"Oooh, no," Lexi muttered. "Don't even get me started on weddings."

Avery giggled, "Why not?"

"Ryder already has a wedding idea book."

"Picture if you will," Ryder said theatrically. "Doves flying overhead the entire ceremony—"

"So bird shit everywhere," Wyatt murmured through a grin.

"A harpist playing our song."

"Which is?" Harper asked.

Lexi piped up, "Oh it's super romantic. It's that song about humping like they do on the discovery channel."

Weston had been mid-drink and spit his Clinton's Trashcan Punch with his laughter.

Ryder didn't look amused. He arched his red eyebrow primly. "Can I finish now?"

Lexi was trying to hide a smile, her pretty green eyes sparking with humor. "Go ahead, Groomzilla."

"Thank you. Flowers everywhere, but like, poison ivy around the cake so if any little fuckers get to eating the icing too soon and ruin my pictures, they'll swell up and itch like hell. Beef jerky fountain, balloon animals, a wild-west theme with Lexi wearing one of those tit-baring corset dresses with the lace. We ride in on a pair of pure white stallions…"

"What kind would you want?" Weston asked Avery quietly in her ear.

"Me?" she asked as Ryder droned on about how he wanted armored medieval knights jousting behind the altar.

"Yeah." It was dark enough that the flickering orange of the fire showed up across the chiseled planes of Weston's face. He sure looked handsome in the firelight glow.

Avery fed him a giant bite of pancake, then took a long drink to stall. She'd never thought about that before. The idea of marriage to any of the ravens of The Hollow had put her off imagining any romance on the big day.

"Don't think too hard about it, Ave. Just blurt it out. If you were getting married tomorrow, how would you want it to be?"

"Well tomorrow would be less than two weeks before Alana and Aaron's big day."

"So?"

"So I wouldn't want to take away from that in any way. I guess something small and intimate, with just me and..." *You.* Avery cleared her throat and dipped her gaze to the red drink cupped in her hands. "Just me and the groom, and maybe he would take me to eat after. Somewhere fancy. And I would wear a pretty dress, and he would wear a dark suit, and maybe we would stay at a bed and breakfast or something that night for a honeymoon." She laughed nervously. "Sounds lame, huh?"

"No," Weston murmured, lifting her hand to his lips. He pressed a kiss there, just between her knuckles. "Sounds perfect."

Avery smiled at him gratefully for being so nice to her and relaxed back against him, rested her cheek on his, and listened to Ryder talk about the life-sized painting of him and Lexi on a pirate ship that he wanted to commission for their engagement photo.

Weston had only asked because she was the only woman here who had been left out of the wedding conversation. He was just trying to make her feel included, but now that she thought about it, yeah—a small, intimate ceremony was the new dream.

But only if it was with him.

EIGHTEEN

Today had been the best day of Avery's life.

She cast another glance over at Weston who was laying under her car, changing the oil. He'd been working on her Civic for the last hour, telling her stories she'd missed out on in the years they hadn't written each other. Most of them were about his Gray Back Crew and how much trouble he and his friends got into when they were kids. She liked those best—the ones that included Wyatt, Ryder, Aaron, and Harper. She felt like she was getting to know them better. She enjoyed imagining she'd grown up alongside of them in Damon's Mountains with the normal childhood they'd had.

She liked knowing that, for other people, good

childhoods had existed. Maybe it should've made her jealous, but it really didn't. Instead, it made her happy.

She rolled over onto her side on the blanket he'd laid out for her beside the Civic. From here, she had a perfect view of the sexy southern half of him from the top of his abdominals down, and that man had blessed her greatly by taking off his shirt before sliding under the car.

"What was your mom like?" she asked.

"Uuuh, let's see. She was quiet, strict. She was a worrier. I was her only raven boy, and Da was so protective of me it definitely rubbed off on her. I got away with less than the other kids in the trailer park, but I didn't mind. I knew it was just because they loved me. She was really good at cooking. Still, when I go home to visit for holidays, I just eat the entire time I'm there. I've tried to make some of her recipes over the years, but my cooking can't touch hers."

Avery smiled and gave a soft laugh. "It's because she cooked with love."

"That's what Da says, too."

"I think I will pee my pants if I ever meet Beaston."

"Oh, you will meet my Da, and no, you won't pee your pants. For one, I've watched you grow tougher every day. You showed no fear around the Bloodrunners today, and I was so fucking proud of how well you fit in. You held your chin up more when you talked to them and spoke your mind when you wanted."

"The alcohol can be blamed for that."

"Bullcrap, you're coming into your own. It's pretty fuckin' awesome to watch. Two, my Da isn't that bad."

"To you. You grew up with him, and you're his son. He had no reason to maul you. I was made to betray you."

"But you didn't. You made me happy instead." When Weston twisted sideways and peeked out from under the car, the light he'd hung from the undercarriage illuminated his half-smile. "Besides, I told you, I already explained you had nothing to do with whatever the council was planning. My Da has no problem with you anymore. He told me to take good care of you."

"He did?"

"Yeah, in his own way. His exact words were, 'If

she makes sense to you, don't let nothin' ever hurt her, or it'll hurt you worse.'"

Avery propped her cheek on her elbow and fiddled with a loose thread on the blanket. She was going to write that quote down on a scrap of paper and keep it in her treasure box. "I think maybe I won't be as scared when I meet him now. Weston?"

"Yep," he gritted out, struggling to tighten something under her car.

"Will you sleep beside me tonight?"

He let off a little growl that sounded much more feral than a raven shifter should've managed and slid out from under the car. "You don't know what you're asking, Ave. Trust me when I say you don't want that."

"But that's why we're out here in the middle of the night, right? You're avoiding your visions? You're avoiding sleep? You can't just go forever without resting your body, Weston. It's not good for you."

Weston's jaw was clenched hard as he stood and wiped his filthy hands on a cloth. His eyes were black as he ghosted her a glance.

With a deep frown, Avery sat up and asked, "Why is your raven so worked up?"

"I had a vision about you last night." Weston rushed the words, as if he wanted to say them before he changed his mind.

Avery was shocked into silence. "A bad one?" she whispered.

"Yeah. No." He upended a container of oil under the hood of her car and locked his other arm against the edge while it emptied. "I was awake when it happened, and it was a vision of the past, not your future."

Dread dumped into her system, freezing her into place like an ice sculpture. "What did you see?"

"You in The Box, and you were—"

"That's enough. I don't need to know anymore."

"You didn't tell me it was that bad."

"No one ever laid a hand on me—"

"You were clawing at the fucking walls, Ave! Your nails were bleeding, and you were freezing and skinny and reciting my letters—"

"I said that's enough! Please," she begged in a whisper. "Please stop. It doesn't help me. Can't you see I'm better when I don't think about The Hollow? My raven is stronger here. I'm happy here. Let me keep my happy."

Weston tossed the empty oil container to the ground and reached for the next and unscrewed the cap slowly. "I couldn't help you, and it did something awful to me, Ave. Really consider what you are asking when you want me to sleep beside you because you would've been really upset if you dealt with me right after coming out of that vision."

And there it was. He didn't believe her strong enough to handle the darkness inside of him, and her panic over him talking about his vision had proved him right. She wasn't yet, but she really, *really* wanted to be.

Ashamed, she asked, "Will you at least lay beside me until I fall asleep?"

One corner of Weston's lip curved up, but the smile didn't reach his tired eyes. "Always," he murmured.

Always. He would always give in and lay her to sleep, but letting his body go unconscious beside her was something different. It was too much for now. It was trusting her to handle the hardest part of his life and, in this moment, she swore to herself she would work harder to own her past so she could be stronger in the future. For Weston, but also for herself.

Avery would make this easier for him. She had to because she loved him, and she wanted to help shoulder his burdens, the way he was shouldering hers. Weston knew what The Box had been like. There was no downplaying the confinement since he'd seen it with his own eyes and soul.

He'd seen her darkest moments, and someday soon, she wanted to be tough enough to see his.

Weston finished refilling her car with oil, lowered the hood, and backed her Civic off the blocks. He'd replaced the battery, did God-knows-what when he was digging around under the hood and in the steering column, and had given it a full tune-up, including new windshield wipers. Avery was officially convinced there was nothing Weston couldn't do. Her car started and idled better than it had done in years.

"I'm so attracted to you right now," she murmured as he offered her a hand up.

"Oh yeah?" he asked. "You like me sweaty and covered in dirt and oil?"

He'd tossed his baseball cap so his dark facial scruff matched those raven black eyes of his. The dimple was showing again. As she dragged her attention down his muscular throat to the tattoos and piercings that covered his ripped chest, she murmured, "Hell yeah, I like you dirty." And muscly, and tattooed, sweet, funny, quiet, and mysterious. She'd been imagining all day what they'd done in the woods. She was already wet and ready for him. Even Avery could smell the pheromones she was putting off.

And then he touched her—just a brush of his fingertips down the side of her neck. She rolled her eyes closed at how good it felt. His other hand gripped her waist, pulled her closer until her breasts pressed against his hard chest. His mouth brushed hers, and Avery angled her head, parted her lips so he could push his tongue inside. The second he deepened their kiss, she let off a happy hum. God, she loved this. Loved the taste of him, loved the way his body fit perfectly to hers, loved the way he gripped her shirt in his hands like he couldn't help himself.

He made her feel beautiful with a touch.

He made her forget all the bad stuff…with a touch.

He healed the cracks in her broken heart, fusing them together one by one…with a touch.

Avery slipped her arms around his neck and

pushed up on her tiptoes, desperate to be closer to him. Weston pulled her so hard against his body, there was no end to her, no beginning to him, but still, she wasn't close enough. This was an addiction. Weston was her drug, and she could never get enough of the high he gave her.

When she slipped her tongue shallowly past his lips, Weston let off the sexiest sound. He leaned forward, lifted the backs of her knees around his waist, and slammed her backward against the car, ground his hips onto her slowly and bit her bottom lip hard. She was gone. Weston wasn't a naturally gentle lover, and that was okay. More than okay. She loved him wild, adored his dominance. He was good at telling her what he wanted without words, and right now, he wanted her more than anything. Her inner raven drew up like a goddess.

Weston pushed his hard dick against her again and touched her sensitive clit perfectly. She'd thought her first few times would be bad, or awkward, until she learned how to use her body, but nope. No problems here. Weston was good at taking control and teaching her as they went. He didn't coddle her or question her. He just trusted her to rise up to the occasion like the damn phoenix he believed her to be.

Weston lurched backward, taking her with him, then strode up the stairs to his porch. His cabin and Ryder's shared a roof but were separated by a dog run right through the middle. He set her on her feet at the front door and kissed her for a minute longer, tongue stroking hers rhythmically, driving her body mad.

"I have to tell you something," he murmured, his voice deep and sultry.

She nipped his lip. "Tell me anything."

His dark brows drew down, and he gave a nervous glance at the door behind her. "My house... It's different."

"Is it messy? I don't care if it's messy."

"No, no. It's more like a...den. Like how I grew up. I haven't ever let anyone in here." He shrugged. "I keep my dens private."

But he was letting her see it? As he pushed the door open, her heart tethered to him even more.

Inside didn't look like inside at all. It looked like outside. Avery gasped and padded to the center of the room, spun slowly to take it in. He'd covered the walls with strips of bark and nailed young sapling trees in an overlay that stretched from the scratched wood floors to the wooden ceilings.

Weston flicked on a deer antler lamp, but the light was muted by a cloth covering the shade. The entire cabin was one big open room with a kitchen to the right of the living room and a queen-sized bed under exposed oak beams on the left. Even his bedding was brown and deep forest green, and the kitchen counters were made of gnarled wood that looked hand carved and polished.

"It looks like a treehouse," she whispered reverently. Avery ran her fingers over the smooth wood of the foot of the bed. "Did you make this?"

"I made everything in here," he said low. "I like working with wood. I like creating things. I like giving wood function." He ran his hand over his hair and gave a self-deprecating laugh. "It probably sounds dumb, but I like spending time in my shop alone. I like the sound of silence. I work through my shit better without all the…" He waved his hand over his head. "Noise."

Full of emotion, she smiled. She knew he hadn't shared this part of himself with anyone but her. "Will you show me your shop sometime?"

"Yeah," he said quickly. "Whenever you want. It's out back." Weston looked around the room, hand resting on the back of his neck. "Do you like it?"

"Come here," she murmured, heart thumping so hard at how fucking cute he was. Big, dominant, tatted-up monster, and he was worried about what she thought of his den? Weston had so many layers, and the more she learned of him, the more she loved him.

He strode closer, and she turned him slowly and pushed him down on the edge of the bed. He chuckled, and his eyes sparked with desire as she pulled her T-shirt over her head.

"I love your den so much it's ridiculous."

"Yeah?" Weston sounded distracted and was staring at her black satin bra.

"It feels homey, like the woods do." Avery shimmied out of her jean shorts, and clad in only her lingerie, she climbed up onto his lap. Straddling him, she pushed up on her knees, so she was just above eye-level. She kissed his smiling lips. His hands were rough, gripping her hips, and maybe she wouldn't have liked that with anyone else. But with him, it was just so perfect, so Weston.

She rolled her hips forward, building her own excitement because his dick was so hard, so thick under his jeans, and she remembered exactly how he felt inside of her. She was still a little sore from last night, but her arousal was bigger than that. Weston wrapped his arms around her back and crushed her to him, rocking his dick against her.

Tonight, he was hers. She wasn't nervous like their first time. She wasn't hesitating to touch him. She didn't have to. He would let her do what she wanted, so she dragged her fingertips down the strong curves of his arms. Someday she would trace every tattoo on his body, but tonight…tonight she just wanted to feel his skin. She wanted to familiarize herself with every inch of his body.

As she explored his chest and the flexing mounds of his abs, she rolled her hips against his.

"How are you this fucking sexy?" he asked breathily.

He trailed kisses down her neck, sucking hard, biting, pleasure and pain before he eased back and popped her tits out of her bra, grabbed them hard, and lowered his lips to one of her nipples. Their bodies were like water, flowing and moving as he sucked.

She could absolutely come like this, even with his pants on. He was already working her close to release, so she unsnapped the button on his jeans. Weston pulled his lips from her skin just long enough to work his pants down his thighs, and then he unfastened her bra in back with a quick snap of his fingers. Rushing now, he yanked the cups from her shoulders and threw it on the ground. His hand slid down her belly into the front of her panties as he swallowed up the gasp that rose from her throat.

A curious shiver trembled up his back and landed in his shoulders when he dragged two fingers through the wetness he'd conjured between her legs. In a smooth movement, he lifted her just enough that she hovered over the swollen head of his cock. And in an instant, he moved her panties to the side and slid her down.

"Ooooh," he groaned as she sheathed him slowly. His eyes rolled closed, and he gritted his teeth.

He filled her, stretched her, felt amazing inside of her. He was so long and thick he was almost too much, but she relaxed as much as she could and eased back up when he went too deep. And by the third stroke, the soreness had disappeared. In its place was core-deep pleasure and heat. She pressed her chest against his and hugged him tight, eased up and back down again. She was already too close. "I'm almost there," she panted. *I'm sorry!*

"Good. Come for me, Ave," he growled against her ear.

She cried out softly on the next stroke, and again on the next, her fingernails digging into the back of his neck. His kiss was rough, and his teeth grazed her lips. Punishing him, she bit him back hard.

Weston's reaction was instant. He bucked into her harder and let off a sexy sound.

Over and over, she slid onto him, and this felt better than anything ever had. Her chest was on fire, and her mind was completely fogged with the high. Slowly, she worked her biting kisses down, down until she reached the muscle right at the top of his peck. Testing, she bit him harder there and rolled her hips. But Weston didn't try to escape her like he did last time. This time, he cupped the back of her head and dragged her closer, bucked into her deep.

"Do it," he rasped.

Avery sank her teeth into his chest just as her

body exploded with ecstasy. This was happening. Her life was changing for the better, right now, in this moment. Every instinct in her body screamed to do it right. To do it hard. To scar him so he would never be able to look in the mirror without thinking about her. Inside, Avery's raven was crowing in triumph that she was claiming her mate. Avery had never heard of claiming marks for normal ravens, but she wasn't normal, and Weston sure as hell wasn't normal either. He was half grizzly shifter, raised in a crew of claiming monsters that made this moment feel so right.

Weston threw his head back and gritted out her name as his dick pulsed hard inside her. Heat flooded her in jets as he pushed into her again and again. Warmth flowed into her mouth, the taste of copper struck her tongue, and then it was done. Her mark was made.

Avery released his torn skin and writhed against him, arched her back, and closed her eyes when his lips landed on the base of her throat. The scrape of his teeth brought on another pounding aftershock from both of them. She was prepared to beg, but Weston didn't ask, didn't hesitate.

He bit down near the tip of her collar bone, right on her shoulder, and he bit to claim. It was hard, his teeth cutting straight to her bone. Pain blinded her for a moment before he relaxed his jaw and let her go. Both of their chests heaving, they hugged each other tightly, bodies crashing against each other as Weston drew every aftershock from her.

"I love you. I love you," she panted. Those were the only three words that made sense right now. Her chest was hot, as if someone had poured lighter fluid down her throat and lit a match.

And just as the sensation got to be too much, too harsh, Weston winced away hard, putting inches between them when he grabbed his chest. And just like that, the burning was gone. It was as if someone had doused her fire with a bucket of cold water. The shock remained, but not the burn.

Weston started shaking hard, staring at her with wide, dark eyes. She understood. The adrenaline in her system was doing something strange to her body, too. His gaze ducked to her bite mark, and slowly…so slowly…a smile crooked his lips.

Streams of red were racing down his chest from where she'd bitten him. Yet another way they matched. They'd chosen each other.

Weston gently ran his hands down her hips to her knees, then lifted that dark, sexy gaze to hers. "Mate," he murmured. "I love you, too."

NINETEEN

Mate.

It had been one week since Weston had called her that for the first time, but Avery still got a giddy feeling whenever she thought of that word.

She finished washing her hands in the bathroom sink of Big Flight and looked at her reflection in the mirror. She'd changed so much since she'd come here. No longer did she hunch or try to stay as small as she could. No longer did she stare at the ground or avoid gazes. No longer did her raven stay quiet and sad inside of her. Weston's encouragement to own her inner badass made her stand taller. Her growing friendships with the Bloodrunners and her observations of the other strong women in the crew made her damn proud of the animal in her middle.

Avery's skin was clear and glowing with her happiness. Her eyes were light teal and clear, her skin was tanner, and her hair lighter from working outside. Her hands were calloused, where they had been frail and easily blistered before. That was from Weston and Ryder insisting she come on some of the ATV tours to learn the trails. Even her arms were becoming more toned, and her body felt stronger, more capable of endurance. Raven's Hollow hadn't broken her like she'd thought. It had just weighed her down for a while.

No longer was she meant to stand in the shadows and look pretty. She used her body now. She was proud of it. She was even happy with her curves that had been so different from the other shifters of Raven's Hollow.

Weston and the Bloodrunners, had helped to make her proud of who she was.

And the best part of her reflection was the healed circular scar Weston had given her.

She was the mate of the Novak Raven, and no one could ever take that away from her.

She wasn't alone in the world anymore. She

wasn't invisible.

Avery adjusted the strap of her Big Flight tank top so it wouldn't cover any of the claiming mark, then she dried her hands, and left the bathroom in search of Weston. He would be back from the last tour any second now.

This was her favorite time of day. Evenings in the mountains were gorgeous, but that wasn't all of the magic here. She would get to spend the rest of the evening with her mate, riding in his truck, eating dinner—sometimes just them, sometimes with the Bloodrunners—and they would hold each other and love each other until she fell asleep in 1010. Not tonight, though. Tonight she was going to let Weston read all the letters she'd never sent him. She was ready. She was strong enough to sit beside him and answer his questions about the dark parts of Raven's Hollow. And then she would ask him again to sleep beside her the whole night because she was strong enough to shoulder his burdens along with her own.

When the roar of ATV engines brushed her ears, Avery grinned, rushing to the front door to greet the tour.

Ryder held back to gas up the quads for the busy

day tomorrow, while Weston strode toward her with the large family they'd taken out. His gaze collided with hers the second she opened the door, and his smile was breathtaking. God, she loved him.

The tour filed past her, murmuring their greetings, and Weston did what he did every time he returned from a tour. He leaned down and kissed the claiming mark he'd given her, brushed the pad of his finger over it gently, then kissed her lips. "Hey, little phoenix."

And then he squeezed her ass hard. With a laugh for her shocked expression, he followed the others in. The butt-grab was new.

The next twenty minutes was a rush of getting surveys filled out, answering a late call to book a tour for next week, and getting all the returned helmets in order on the shelves in the gear room. Out in the shop, Weston rang up the souvenirs the family wanted. She loved the routine around here. She and Weston and Ryder had grown so comfortable with each other they were running Big Flight like a well-oiled machine already.

She said her goodbyes to the last tour, her hands on her back as they exited the shop. "So I've been thinking," she said to Weston, who was closing down the cash register.

"Uh oh."

Ignoring him, she said, "I think instead of doing the safety lesson each time, we should do a video, and set up a little screening room out back where the clients can watch it. Then it cuts out the smart alecks who want to joke through the lessons, and it saves you and Ryder's voices. And you'll have more time to prepare in between those back-to-back tours while the clients are watching the safety video. We could even make it funny if you want."

Weston snorted. "Ryder would love that." He closed the cash register and took the credit card receipts and cash to the office. "I think that's a good idea. I'm tired of saying the same thing over and over."

Avery fist pumped and gave a manly grunt, then called, "Can I shoot it? I watched videos on how to make videos."

Weston laughed from the other room and said, "Sure."

Ryder shoved open the door and sighed the word, "Margarita."

She knew the drill, though, so she pointed to the counter where the frosty can of his favorite libation was waiting with a swirly straw already. "Guess what?"

"You got your period."

"No! Well...yes, but that's not what I'm talking about."

Ryder slurped his drink. "You got invited to be one of Alana's bridesmaids."

"Nope." Avery drew back. "Wait, is that going to happen?" Damn the excitement in her voice, and damn the smirk on Ryder's face when he zipped his lips and pretended to throw away the key. Narrowing her eyes at him, she said, "Weston said yes to the video."

"Oh, hell yeah," Ryder crowed, giving her a high five that made her whole hand sting. She was still new at those. Ryder drank down the rest of the margarita and raised his hand like a schoolboy. "I already wrote the script. I call lead role!"

"You can have all the roles," Weston muttered as he strode in from the office. "I don't want to be in it. You ready to go home?" he asked Avery.

"To fuuuuuuck," Ryder sang, using the tiny blue

can as a microphone and pelvic thrusting. "Y'all are loud."

"*We're* loud?" Weston asked. "I literally heard you and Lexi role-playing a saloon girl and an outlaw last night. Every word, Ryder. I'm traumatized."

"We had to hone our acting skills."

"Did you have to yell every word in the front yard? I can't get you saying, 'Lemme stick my six-shooter in your cooter' out of my brain. It's on this puke-inducing endless loop."

Ryder cocked his head like a proud rooster. "You're welcome."

Avery snickered as she made her way behind the counter to grab her purse.

She liked that the boys didn't tame down their discussions around her. It showed they were comfortable with her. That she was accepted around here. Plus, she had broadened the colorful nature of her vocabulary greatly since she'd started working, and she didn't know why that made her feel lucky, but it did.

For a moment, a shadow shielded the light from the front window.

Crap, a late tour?

But when she got a glimpse of the visitor through the other window on the porch, Avery froze in fear. It couldn't be him. Not now, and not here.

Two more figures walked in front of the window, blocking out the pretty evening sunlight. Avery stumbled backward, then inched her way toward the corner, as far away from the door as she could get.

Maybe she'd imagined them.

"What's wrong?" Weston asked, his eyes intensely trained on her. He was too close to the door. Too close to them.

The door swung wide and in stepped a man she'd never planned on seeing again.

Benjamin.

His eyes weren't the blue they usually were, but instead were pitch black, matching his dark crop of hair.

Behind him was the head council member, Caden. Her own personal demon. His thick gray hair was disheveled on top of his head, and he looked different. He'd always been able to terrify her with a look, but today his cheeks were red, and his dark eyes sparked with a fury she didn't understand. He was breathing too hard as he stared down Weston. Maybe he was sick. She couldn't muster a single ounce of concern for his well-being though. He'd never cared about hers. Behind Caden, her father pulled up the rear and closed the door with a quiet, echoing *click* behind him.

"W-what are you doing here?" Avery stammered.

"We're here to bring you back home," Benjamin answered in a cold voice.

"She is home," Weston murmured. "Who are you?"

Benjamin smiled. She'd always hated the way his face looked when he did that. He always wore an empty expression that didn't reach his eyes and looked more like a snarl. His smiles were pretend.

"I'm Avery's fiancé. Who are you?"

Weston went rigid, his back muscles freezing against his damp T-shirt. She couldn't see his face, but from the scent of fury wafting from him, it probably looked terrifying. Avery cowered, wishing she could melt into the wall completely. She knew these men well. Caden had always been the one to put her in The Box. He didn't mind breaking people. His eyes were empty, too, just like his soul, and now Dad wouldn't look her in the face. He was here to ruin her life. He *should* be ashamed.

Weston crossed his arms and canted his head. In a bland voice, he said, "I think you probably know who I am. She ain't leavin' with you unless she wants to. Avery?" He looked at her over his shoulder and, oh, his eyes roiled with fury.

"I don't want to leave here." She forced trembling words past her lips. "Remember that boy I told you about? The boy who wouldn't quit bullying me? The boy I beat up?" She dared a look at Benjamin. "That's him."

"Dude, you got your ass kicked by a girl?" Ryder asked. He laughed hard and too loud, but Avery didn't miss it. He was inching his way behind the counter, closer to her.

"The lady made her choice," Weston gritted out. "Kindly get the fuck off my property."

Ryder pulled a long, serrated machete from below the cash register and slammed it onto the counter top. With a psychotic grin, he said, "Please?"

Caden stepped forward and spoke up. "Avery was taken from our care at Raven's Hollow without permission, and the engagement between her and Benjamin was already in negotiations." His leathery gray lips rimmed with white spittle as he talked.

"I didn't sign any contract, and I'm not marrying—"

"Don't speak!" Caden yelled, his dark eyes round and furious.

Weston was on him in an instant. There was a blur, and then Caden was up against the wall, his feet kicking three feet off the ground. "I fuckin' *dare* you to speak to her like that again."

The other ravens surged toward Weston, but Ryder leapt gracefully over the counter with the machete in hand and put himself between them.

Caden wasn't protecting his neck from the stranglehold. He was hitting Weston in the face and shoulders with his closed fist, and his eyes were full of a hatred Avery didn't understand. He was turning blue, but still, he gave up his throat to try and hurt Weston.

Weston didn't seem affected by the punches. He barely even reacted to them, like they didn't hurt at all. Instead, he slammed Caden against the wall twice, hard enough that his head made sickly thuds against the logs, then he threw him in a crumpled heap and turned to the others.

"She isn't going with you assholes. I know what you've done to her. I've seen it! You'll have to pry her from my cold, lifeless talons."

"Look at her. She's terrified!" Caden choked out from the floor, his eyes flashing with rage that didn't match the concern in his words.

"Dumbass, she's scared of you," Ryder muttered, looking like he wanted to kick the shit out of Caden's ribs.

"Are you engaged to her?" Dad blurted out, eyes averted. He was holding a cell phone. He'd never cared about cell phones before. What the hell was happening?

Weston hesitated. He cast a quick glance to Avery, but she still couldn't move. Terror had seized every muscle in her body.

"Are you engaged?" Dad yelled, enunciating each word.

"No." Weston blinked slowly and stood to his full height, looked down on the others like they were nothing. "But she's mine. I'm not letting her go. Come here again, and I'll rip your intestines through your mouths and watch you choke on your own entrails. I know about The Box, you sadistic fucks. If I see you in these mountains again, if I even *feel* like you're thinking about coming back for her, I'll burn your entire fucking flock to the ground." He licked his swollen, split lip and looked like he wanted to spit. "Get out."

Ryder was grinning and bouncing on the balls of his feet as though this was the best day ever. "Yeah, what he said, mother fuckers. Get out!"

"Come on, honey," Dad said, waving Avery to him. "You don't have to stay here with this bad man."

Avery stood there panting, frozen against the corner, wishing she was braver. Wishing she understood what was happening. What the hell was he talking about? He didn't care about her. He didn't care about anyone but himself, his precious rank, and a seat on the council. "You're the bad man." Avery forced herself out of the corner and scuffled her lead shoes across the wood floors until she reached Weston. She stopped beside him, absorbed the ready rage that was pressing from Weston against her body, and used it to fuel herself. He was as much a beast as a raven shifter could be—a true War Bird—and that made her braver. Weston would keep her safe. Safe, safe, safe. She was safe under his care. The council had no power here.

"I was never yours, Benjamin." She dared a look up at him. "I am my own."

Benjamin huffed a breath and shook his head. His eyes as cold as a snake's, he said, "This isn't over."

Ryder was picking at his teeth with the pointed blade of the machete and made a loud sucking sound. "It should probably be over if A, you don't want Weston serial-killing all you assholes, and two, our alpha charring your corpses like little crispy chickens and getting her eat on. Our monsters are better than yours." He arched his red eyebrows up. "Bye."

Weston and Ryder didn't say a word as the raven shifters filed out of the shop with Caden leaning heavily on Dad.

They followed them out and watched them leave in a gunmetal gray Jeep Patriot. And when the sound of their engine disappeared completely, Avery whispered, "I'm so sorry."

"Ave, please tell me you aren't really engaged," Weston growled out.

"No! Well…kind of."

Weston ripped his hat off and threw it into the yard, strode away from her down the porch and returned looking frightful. "What do you mean you're *kind of* engaged?" His voice was dark and intimidating.

"What happened was…I told the council I was engaged to you, and they allowed me to live here to obey our customs of courtship."

Weston shook his head in shock and blinked hard. "What?"

"So, you and I are kind of technically engaged. Or we were, before you told them we weren't."

Weston stared off in the direction the Patriot had disappeared. "Ave, that makes no sense. They seemed to think you were still with Benjamin. They sure as shit didn't seem to think we're living our happily ever after!"

"I don't understand what they were talking about. I swear I'm telling you the truth. My Dad telling me I didn't have to stay with you—"

"That was your dad?"

"Yes. He was acting all concerned for me, but that's not the relationship we have, Weston. It's not! I left in the middle of the night from Raven's Hollow, sure. But my mom encouraged me to elope with you."

"But I didn't even know you were here for me.

We aren't even engaged!"

"Yeah, but the council didn't have to know that. I was just going to live here near you, near the Bloodrunners, and pretend I was under your protection so I didn't have to marry Benjamin or anyone else. Benjamin is scary. He's powerful in the community, the future head of the council, and he would give my family the rank they want. But he's the boy who was awful to me. He's always hated me, and now he wants to marry me? No. He wants to have control over me. I couldn't do it, Weston. The day after I left, my mom gave the council a letter I'd written, telling them I couldn't marry Benjamin because I was being courted by you. It was a desperate move, but I didn't see any other way they wouldn't come for me. I called her when I had been here a couple days, and she told me the council approved a courtship with you. And of course, they did. I should've wondered why they let me go so easily, but I was just so happy to be out of there, I didn't ask questions. But you're the Novak Raven! Why wouldn't they be happy that I was being courted by you? That was the game plan since birth, right?" She held her hands out helplessly. She hated the disappointment on Weston's face. "I don't know why they were here acting surprised and concerned. They aren't like that. None of them are."

"Benjamin said this isn't over," Weston murmured, a deep frown marring his striking face. "You can't go back there. What can I do to stop them from coming?"

Marry me. She wouldn't force him into that, though. If he'd told Dad that yes, they were engaged, this would be done. But that wasn't fair on Weston. He'd only just begun trusting her again.

Weston was staring at her, waiting for an answer, so she gave him what she could. "Until I'm married, I'm up for grabs. Claiming marks don't count in Raven's Hollow. I'm of breeding age and apparently Benjamin is determined."

Standing here, looking into Weston's eyes, the ones that had grown dark with his anger and disappointed at the turn of events, she hated the ravens for tainting her home here.

"What do we do?" Ryder asked grimly.

Weston didn't take his angry gaze from Avery, but he answered his best friend without a moment of hesitation. "We call a crew meeting. Avery's one of us now. If the ravens pose a threat to her, they pose a threat to the Bloodrunners."

TWENTY

"If the ravens are coming, I can't protect her," Harper said.

Anger blasted through Weston's veins. His alpha was sitting on the tailgate of her truck beside Wyatt, who looked sick.

"It's okay," Avery whispered. "I'm not one of you."

"Stop," Weston gritted out. He swung his pissed-off glare to Harper. "What the fuck, H? You'll throw down for anyone here, but when it comes to the mate I choose—"

"Don't finish that sentence, Wes," Harper gritted out, her blue dragon eye flashing brighter. "I love you like my own brother. I love all of you. Avery is one of us, sure enough. I knew it from the first time I saw you two together, but I can't physically protect us if the shit hits the fan right now."

"Why not?" Weston yelled.

"Because I can't shift! I don't have a dragon for you. I don't have fire. I don't have the fucking ability to shield you right now."

"Why the hell not?"

"Because I'm pregnant!"

Weston felt socked in the gut. All of his air whooshed out of his lungs and wouldn't return.

"Harper, you're pregnant?" Alana sounded like she was crying.

Lexi reached her first, though, hugged her up. Alana followed, and slowly, submissively, Avery padded to the tailgate and slipped under Harper's outstretched arm.

The girls were new to the crew and didn't understand though. Harper could die from this. Female dragons weren't like bear shifters or flight shifters. Harper was going to have to force herself not to Change for the next nine months until she grew weaker and sicker and likely died in childbirth.

"What the fuck man?" Weston asked Wyatt.

Wyatt gritted his teeth so hard the muscles in his jaw jumped. "You don't understand."

"I do! I understand this could kill her. *Kill her*, Wyatt!" Weston squatted down and clutched the back of his hair, so pissed he didn't know what to do. He stood and jammed a finger at Wyatt. "You were supposed to protect her!"

"Beaston said she won't die in childbirth. Not after we lost Janey."

"Beaston," Weston repeated. "Everyone relies so fucking heavily on my dad, but visions don't work like that!"

"Yours don't," Aaron murmured. "Maybe Beaston's are different."

Harper was crying, and she wouldn't meet his gaze. He was fucking this all up but, goddammit, he loved Harper. *Loved* her. She was one of the few he trusted, one of the few people in the world who was more important to Weston than air. He didn't want her to die. He didn't want to watch her wither away. "Fuck!" he yelled.

"Wes, I want a baby," Harper said in a heartbroken voice. "I felt empty after I lost Janey, and I need this. I have a lot of grizzly shifter blood in me, some black bear, too. My grandfather did the math, and I'm at about a fifty-fifty percent chance of survival, even without your dad's prediction." She released the girls and rested her hand on her still-flat stomach. Tears fell down her cheeks, and Wyatt rubbed her back. "I'm going to do this. I'll be strong enough. I know I will. We'll have a baby in the crew, and I'll be back to my fire-breathing badass self afterward, but right now, he needs me more. Do you understand?"

"He," Weston said, his eyes burning.

"Beaston called me the vessel for the next male Bloodrunner Dragon. A fire-breather like me. A brawler like Wyatt. He's seen it." Harper's voice tapered to nothing as two more tears streaked down her cheeks. "I already love him so much."

Weston scrubbed his hand down his face and strode over to her, pulled her hard against him. A sob wrenched from Harper, and she clung to him tightly, clutching his T-shirt in her fists. Wes shook his head and pulled Wyatt to him, too, cupped his dumbass head, and held him for a moment before he shoved him away. Wyatt chuckled thickly and wiped his cheek on his shoulder, sniffed once, and got pulled into a back-cracking hug from Ryder.

Avery stood near him, smiling and clearly touched as the girls wrapped themselves around Wes and Harper. Whatever came next with the ravens, the Bloodrunners were down their biggest weapon. The second the world realized Harper couldn't shift anymore to protect her child, enemies would come out of the woodwork. Vampires, wolves, ravens, unforeseen dangers. But that had to be okay. Weston would fight with his life to protect what they'd built here, to protect his alpha, to protect Avery, and the others in this crew would, too.

"Oh, Harper girl," Weston murmured, rocking his alpha slowly. "You *are* going to do this. You're so strong, of course you will. You'll give our crew a better treasure than even the mountains. Rest now, Dragon. The Bloodrunners have you."

****

"I don't think they'll attack," Avery murmured.

"Hair band," Harper said, holding out her hand. She was sitting in the rocking chair behind Avery who sat on the porch. She was French braiding Avery's hair into two long pigtails.

She handed back the black hair deal she'd been

fiddling with. "Ravens aren't made for war. I really don't think they'll come here to fight."

"Why don't you think so?" Weston asked from where his head rested on her lap. Over and over, he was throwing a baseball up to the rafters of the porch of 1010 and catching it. The Bloodrunners were all spread out over the porch, recovering from the emotional charge of Harper and Wyatt's big news.

"I don't think they'll physically wage war on us because they are scared of other shifters. Not just nervous, but terrified, of dragons and bears especially. I think that's why they visited the shop instead of confronting me in Harper's Mountains. Threatening three flight shifters I can see, but threatening the predator shifters in this crew?" Avery shook her head. "I think Benjamin was bluffing. I can't see any of our people rallying to fight. They have no fight experience, and all the females have been trained to be scared. They aren't equipped for battle, and almost all of them are submissive."

"Almost all of them?" Alana asked from where she rested her back against the porch railing beside Aaron.

"Yeah, some of the males are dominant, but

raven dominant...not fire-breathing dragon dominant. Caden is one of them."

"Caden?" Weston asked, catching the ball and sitting up.

"Yeah, the guy you smashed against the wall."

"Caden Edwards?"

Avery frowned, her head jerking back and forth with each braid Harper wove into her hair. "Yeah. Do you know him?"

Weston narrowed his eyes suspiciously. "Yeah, he was engaged to my mom for a year before she ended it and chose my dad. We'll just say he didn't handle it graciously. She had her parents' support, though, so it made it easier for her to leave Rapid City."

Avery huffed a stunned breath. She'd had no idea Caden had been engaged to Aviana Novak. How the hell had that been hidden from the flock? "Yeah, he's been an asshole for as long as I've known him. He was the council member who would put me in The Box when I needed 'rehabilitation.' Even if I struggled. I heard about the days the flock was located in Rapid City, but after Aviana left, the ravens all relocated to the Blue Ridge Mountains outside of Damascus. They named the community Raven's Hollow, and the rules became really stringent. The council, led by Caden, sequestered us off from other shifters and most humans after your mom left. The council got scared all their strong-minded ravens would pack up like Aviana had done, and our shifter species would fall apart and slowly go extinct. They made the rule that women couldn't get jobs anymore after what happened with your mom pairing up with a bear shifter. Aviana's parents were already low ranking, but when Aviana picked your dad, they were put at the very bottom of our community and shunned. When I was ten, I remember they left in the night. I didn't blame them. I wished they had taken me with them. The only interaction the ravens have with the outside world now, other than the internet, is the public school system, where we get to go to classes with human kids. Caden has been trying to get a school just for raven shifters approved, though."

"What a boner biscuit," Ryder muttered, drawing his legs up around where Lexi sat on the porch in front of him.

"Total boner biscuit," Lexi agreed, chipping away at her half-gone nail polish.

It didn't sit well with Avery that Caden had history with Weston's mother. Not when there had obviously been some long-term plot to lure him back to Raven's Hollow. She had the sick feeling they weren't just drawing him there to put some new genetics into the community anymore. She would bet her first paycheck that Caden had been behind the plan to use Avery as bait in the first place. Who else in that community would have a reason to connect so directly with Weston and Aviana? No, she didn't like this at all.

Maybe she should call her mom and see if she could get more information from her. She owed Avery.

Aaron jerked his attention to the front gate of the property and froze. Eerily, Alana and Wyatt did the same. Weston, Ryder, and Harper were next, and now Avery could hear it—the soft hum of an approaching vehicle. Dread filled her veins as she stood with the others, preparing to face whatever was coming.

Blue and red lights flashed through the trees.

"Sheeyit," Ryder muttered. "What do we do?"

"Hold steady, crew," Harper murmured. "We have no beef with the cops here, and we've done nothing wrong."

But every instinct screamed for Avery to flee. Something was wrong, and she naturally feared law enforcement. Why? Because the ravens worked very hard to keep human law out of Raven's Hollow, and it had been ingrained in her since birth to avoid flashing lights like the ones on the police cruiser bumping and bouncing through the gate of Harper's Mountains.

Weston pulled her behind him protectively, his hand gripping her hip. She ran her hand up his back, to steady herself as much as him, and every muscle was hard as a rock, tensed and ready.

"Should I Change?" she asked, panicking as two uniformed police officers got out of the vehicle.

"No," Harper said sternly. "It'll only cause more trouble if one of us runs."

A second police cruiser coasted through the gate, and now Avery couldn't breathe. They were here for her. She knew they were.

"Evening," one of them said. "We've had several calls about an Avery Foley being kept here."

"She's not being kept here. She lives here," Weston said calmly.

"That's not the story we've heard. There was a missing person's report filled out five weeks ago in Damascus."

"No, I'm not missing," Avery said, stepping in front of Weston. "I'm here because I want to be."

The officers shot each other matching frowns. "If that's true, then we'll sort through it, but we're going to need you to come down to the station and answer some questions."

"She can answer them here," Harper said. "She already told you she's here because she wants to be."

"Bloodrunner Dragon," the officer said.

"Harper, please."

He inhaled deeply and rested his hands on his hips, right near his holstered weapon. "Harper. We don't want any trouble, but we have an entire community convinced she's been taken from them and brainwashed. The calls have been relentless, and then there is a video that has caused some concern. The detective handling her case is on his way from Damascus right now, and in order to clear all this up, we have to bring her in. We don't want any trouble. We'll get to the bottom of this. Weston Novak, we'll need you to come in as well."

"What the fuck? They aren't going anywhere," Ryder exclaimed, taking a step off the porch.

"Ryder, stand down." The power in Harper's voice brushed through Avery, rocking her on her feet.

Instinctively, she hunched her shoulders and ducked her gaze, but the quieter of the two officers was watching her with a concerned frown.

"Ms. Foley, it's okay. We're here to help you."

"But I don't want to leave. I have a house and I have people, and my hair isn't done." Avery showed them her half braid. Her cheeks flushed with heat, and she stared at the ground, fiddling with the ends of the braid. "I'm tired and I want to go to sleep in ten-ten, and I want to wake up and all this be over with." Her voice crumpled to nothing, and then she began to cry.

Weston hugged her up tight, rubbed her back, and pressed his lips to the top of her head. "I can come with her?" he asked.

"Yeah," the taller police officer said. "We need you both to come in."

"No," she said. "I don't want to go anywhere."

"I know, darlin'," Weston murmured against her ear. "But I'll be right there. I won't let anything happen to you. We'll answer their questions, and then I'll bring you right back home, okay?"

"Swear?"

He chuckled like she was cute. "I swear." Easing back, he ticked his finger under her chin. "Come on, little phoenix. You've got this."

She tried to smile, but her lip trembled instead.

"Okay?" Weston asked.

She nodded and let him lead her down the steps by the hand. The quiet police officer helped her into the back of the police car, and she slid all the way over to make room for Weston. But the officer shut the door before he got in.

"Wait," she said, knocking on the window frantically. "There's been a mistake!" *Knock, knock, knock.* "He's supposed to be with me!"

But the police officers ignored her. They talked low to Weston, turned him around, handcuffed him. The Bloodrunners surged forward, angry, yelling, cursing. The quieter officer was reading him his rights, but she couldn't understand why they were guiding Weston to the police cruiser behind hers.

"Weston!" she screamed, panicking. "Something's wrong! I changed my mind. I changed my mind. I don't want to do this. Weston!" Avery was sobbing by the time the officers settled into the front of the cruiser. Through the glass, she pleaded with them. "He's mine. That man back there is mine, and you said we would go together. I don't want to go if I can't be with him. Please. Please put him beside me or let me out."

The quieter police officer turned in his seat as they drove away. "I'm Officer Ryan and this is Officer Hammond. We aren't here to hurt you. We're here to help. Everything is going to be okay, I promise. We'll have you back where you belong in no time."

Tears blurring her vision, Avery pressed herself against the window and watched the Bloodrunners and 1010 disappear. A whimper crawled up the back of her throat.

"You don't understand," she said in a small, terrified voice. "I've never belonged anywhere but here."

TWENTY-ONE

Weston shook his leg in quick succession and clenched his hands tighter. Waiting to be questioned, he was handcuffed to a chain on the table. What was taking so fucking long? If they would just ask what they needed to, he could clear this all up and get Avery back to 1010. Kiss her, hold her, tell her everything was going to be okay. He'd seen her face through the window of that cop car. She'd been terrified.

"Fuck," he gritted out. He cast another pissed-off glance over his shoulder at the two-way glass. There were people behind it watching him. He could feel them there, but all he could see from here was his angry face, shadowed by his baseball cap. His eyes were black as tar, but fuck it. They knew what he was. No point in hiding.

He could Change right now and escape the stupid fucking handcuffs, but what good would that do? It would just prolong this already spectacularly shitty night.

He had to get to Avery, make her feel safe again. She'd been holed up into herself, like a retracted turtle, ever since she'd seen the ravens at Big Flight. They were to blame for this. He didn't know what was going on completely, but every instinct in his body screamed this was the doings of the council. Fuckin' ravens. He wanted to pluck every feather from their bodies and light them on fire. Anger was his only companion right now. Weston's body hummed with it until he was uncomfortable. Squeezing his eyes closed, he rubbed his eye sockets with the heels of his palms and tried to stave off an oncoming headache.

When he opened his eyes, though, he wasn't in the interrogation room anymore. He was back in The Box. The single swinging lightbulb above swayed back and forth from the vent that blasted freezing cold air. Gooseflesh rippled across his body with the bone-deep chill. The claw marks were still in the wall, but there were more, and they were deeper. The red was gone, though. The room smelled of bleach. There was a single bucket in the corner, but other than that, there was nothing in the room.

Nothing but Avery.

She sat pressed into a corner, balled up, her knees to her chest. She looked older than the last time he'd seen her in here. She wasn't emaciated or pale looking. Her hair looked clean and cascaded down her shoulders, but her face held the same horrified, hopeless expression, and her lips moved constantly as she whispered something too low for him to hear. Her glassy aquamarine eyes stared right through him.

Weston looked behind him to see where her gaze landed, but the two-way mirror had disappeared and nothing remained but a white wall. He wasn't chained to the table anymore, but was standing. His palms were up, outstretched. They looked so solid in this vision.

Avery was panting too hard now, her words coming out jerkily. The hopelessness in her eyes tore at his chest. He couldn't save her from her past. It was done. Over. He couldn't even comfort her, but that knowledge didn't stop his instinct to try.

Weston strode over to her, his boots loud against the dingy white tiles. Louder than in any of his other visions.

He could hear her now. "Me and Ryder bought a whole box of spy stuff and put the cameras all around Willa's Wormshack. She's a Gray Back like me, and really funny. You would like her. If she caught us, she would just laugh, so that's why we picked her to spy on first, but all we got is three straight hours of video footage of her working with her worms. She sells them to bait shops and for people who make fancy gardens. She makes a stupid amount of money at it, but that's not why she does it. She loves worms. Like…she LOVES worms. We did catch funny audio of her talking to them, though. She called them her babies, and named one of them Dingleberry. And I swear she thought of kissing one when he wiggled extra cute in her hand. Ryder and me were laughing so hard." Avery's voice hitched, and another tear streamed down her face. "The spy cameras are so small we'll never get caught. Never get caught. Never. Never. So small we'll never get caught."

Avery clenched her fists to her chest behind her knees, and her shoulders shook hard. It wasn't until she ducked her chin to her chest and fell apart that Weston noticed her clothes. Jeans, instead of the nightgown from his last vision. And two thin straps of a tank top curved over her shoulders. He knew what the logo on her shirt would say if he could pry her knees away from her torso. Horror dropped him to his knees right in front of her. On the tip of her shoulder was the circular scar he'd given her the night he'd claimed her.

This wasn't a vision from the past.

This was her future.

"So small we'll never get caught," she repeated in an empty tone.

It wasn't fair. Something bad must've happened to him if she was here in The Box because he would never let her come back here if he was still breathing. "Darlin'," he whispered, his eyes burning from a fate he couldn't save her from.

"I knew you would come," she said so softly he almost missed it.

"What?"

Avery lifted her gaze and locked onto his, as if

she could see him. Her eyes were rimmed with tears, and her bottom lip trembled hard.

"You said you would be here with me, and you are." Slowly, she opened the palm of her hand, and in it sat one of the old cameras he and Ryder had bought all those years ago. It was the size of a quarter. "I'm stronger now." But she didn't look strong. Her whole body was shaking, and she looked scared.

Weston reached out and touched her hand—*touched* her. Shocked, he wrapped his fingers around her wrist. "Avery, I can save you. I can get you out of here. Look, I can touch you. Come on." He pulled, but she shook her head hard and stayed where she was, her wrist slipping from his grip. When he looked down at his hand, the tile floors showed through his palm.

"Weston," she whispered. "This is the way it's supposed to be. I can do this." Two tears dislodged and streamed down her cheeks, but Avery looked different now. Her eyes were harder, more determined, and her breathing had steadied out. "You make me stronger. Wait for me."

There was echoing power in those last three words, and Weston was catapulted backward so fast, his hands and feet flew out in front of him. He held onto the sight of Avery as long as he could.

"I love you, Ave," he rushed out, because she should know. Whatever was happening, or if he was dead, she should hear it from him one last time.

As he slammed back into the chair in the questioning room, her whispered words echoed around the room, filling his head. "I love you, too. Wait for me. Wait, wait, Weston. Wait for me."

Adrenaline and shock did something awful to his body, or maybe it was the power of that vision, but he was drenched in sweat and shaking uncontrollably. Weston dry heaved and closed his eyes tight against the blinding light from the fluorescent bulbs above.

The door to the interrogation room swung open, and in walked one of the cops who had taken Avery away from him. His nametag read *Hammond*, and after him filed a shorter man in a gray suit.

"This is Detective Sutton," Hammond said as he took a seat next to the man in the suit. "He's been the one working on the missing persons case for Avery Foley and her family."

Weston clenched his hands together in an effort to slow the shaking in his body. He was still reeling from the vision. "Missing person's report…" Weston shook his head hard, trying to rattle free some clear thoughts. "Avery isn't missing. She's where she wants to be. Or was, until you took her away in a fucking cop car like some criminal."

"Avery isn't under any suspicion," Detective Sutton said blandly, slapping a thick, beige folder onto the metal table. "You are." His hard, green eyes sliced right through Weston. "You were read your rights, yes?"

Weston nodded. What he needed to do was lawyer up and demand they bring in Harper before he said more, but then he would run the risk of them going tight-lipped about why he was here, and he needed to know what he was really doing strapped to a table in the Bryson City police station. "I'm being charged with kidnapping, but that's not what happened." Voice steady, he told them how Avery came to interview for him and work for him. Told them how he fell for her, and she fell for him. He kept his emotions to a minimum, kept the story simple, just stuck to the facts, and the more he spoke, the more Detective Sutton lost his air of pompousness. A little frown crept into his poker face, and his eyes narrowed.

"Do you feel like you love her?" Detective Sutton asked.

Weston leaned back in his chair and considered his answer. Something had made the detective see him as an obsessive stalker, and this question was a shiny lure into a deep trap.

"Do you feel like she is yours?" the detective pressed on.

Weston should call for a lawyer now. He should wait for Harper before he said more, but the thought of Avery sitting in the interrogation room next door, getting grilled, made him want to end this as fast as possible.

"I want her to be a strong woman and find herself. I want her to be happy. I want her to choose her own path, connect with people, and know how special she is. So yeah. I love her. I love her so much, but if she ever wanted out of a relationship with me, that would have to be okay, because more than I want to be happy, I want her to be happy."

Hammond looked utterly confused now. He sighed heavily, then murmured, "I'm gonna show him the video."

"No, you won't," Sutton said.

"I am! This is my precinct, and he lives in Nantahala under my jurisdiction. And to be completely honest, none of this makes a lick of sense to me. The Bloodrunners have been good members of this community since the day they moved here. One of them owns the coffee shop in town, this one just opened a tourist business, the alpha has opened a law shop right on Main Street, Aaron Keller is a respected firefighter in town. And besides all that, I rode in the car with Avery Foley, and she seemed scared shitless…" He leveled the detective with a significant look. "But not from him. She spent the whole damn ride falling apart to be in the same care as Weston Novak."

"She was falling apart?" Weston asked. "Is she okay?"

"She's being transported to Asheville on a twenty-four-hour psych hold," Hammond said.

"What? No, she's been abused by her people. She can't be strapped down or put in solitary. They can't put her in a white room." Weston stood and yanked on the chains.

"Sit back down!" Sutton yelled.

"Fuck," Weston muttered, panicked. He wanted to Change, but escaping this room as a raven would be impossible unless he could somehow break through the two-way mirror.

The door swung wide, and Harper strode in, dressed in a black power suit and looking like she was about to bring hell to earth. She jammed a nail at Weston and ground out, "Sit. Now."

Power rippled from her voice, buckling Weston's legs under him. With a pained grunt, he slammed down into the metal chair so hard the legs screeched backward by a few inches. Wincing, Weston tilted his head away from the Bloodrunner Dragon and exposed his neck to her. Goddamn, she didn't use her alpha powers often, but when she did, it sucked balls.

"Officer Hammond," Harper greeted.

"Bloodrunner Dragon," he murmured, eyes wide.

"I told you to please call me Harper." She shoved her hand out for a shake to the detective. "Harper Keller. Who are you?"

"Uuuh, Detective Sutton." The man shook her hand in a rush, then jerked away as though he'd been burned. Dragons. That was a power move if Weston had ever seen one but, fuck it all, he couldn't find it in himself to be amused. Not when he was getting a crick in his neck from her alpha dragon shit.

Harper sat down, crossed her legs primly, and set her briefcase down on the floor beside her chair with a click against the tile floors.

"A kidnapping charge? We all know that's bullshit, so what are we really doing here?"

"They took Avery to a psych ward in Asheville," Weston gritted out.

The fire in Harper's bi-colored eyes nearly buckled Weston. "Fffuuck, Harper, let me up."

After she inhaled deeply, then blew it out slowly, leveling her intent gaze back on the officers, the heaviness lifted from the air.

Weston sat up straight and sucked oxygen.

Officer Hammond hit a couple buttons on his phone and shoved it across the silver table to rest in front of Weston and Harper.

A video opened on Avery's dad's face. He was in a car and looked worried and disheveled. "That monster has my daughter. He took her from me and from our people. From her fiancé, and I'll stop at nothing to make sure she comes home safe again. I've promised my wife I will save our baby girl. I won't fail my family."

The humans in the room couldn't hear the utter bullshit lie in Mr. Foley's voice, but Harper shot Weston a disgusted look. She hadn't missed it either. Fuckin' manipulative ravens.

The scene cut to Big Flight's shop, to Avery, who was huddled against the back corner. The camera was shaking, but no one could mistake the terror in her eyes. Her long hair had fallen forward, covering her cheeks, and she was hunched badly, as though she would be attacked at any moment.

"We're here to bring you home," Benjamin said.

Weston's face was contorted with hate and rage, and his fists were clenched. "She is home," he gritted out. "Who are you?"

"I'm Avery's fiancé."

The scene was edited and jumped straight into Weston slamming Caden against the wall again and again and Ryder threatening the others with the machete. More editing, Weston dropped Caden and said, "You'll have to pry her from my cold, lifeless talons."

"Look at her, she's terrified!" Caden choked out from the floor.

"Are you engaged," Mr. Foley yelled.

The scenes were jerky, lurching from one to the next where they'd cut out dialogue.

"No." Weston blinked slowly and stood to his full height, looked directly at the camera and said, "But she's mine. I'm not letting her go. Come here again, and I'll rip your intestines through your mouths and watch you choke on your own entrails." And there was no denying from the look on his face, Weston had meant it—every word.

"Come on, honey," Mr. Foley said in a shaky voice, waving Avery to him. "You don't have to stay here with this bad man."

Avery stood in the corner, shaking, panting, tears in her eyes as she glanced at Weston and then at the camera. A single tear streaked down her cheek, and then the video faded to black.

"Wow." Weston wanted to hurl the phone at the wall and destroy that fucking lie, but he couldn't. He clapped slowly and leaned back in his seat. "That was a great fucking show, but that wasn't how it happened. And please tell me you can decipher a *heavily* edited video from the original."

"Of course, we can," Hammond said. "But this on top of a longstanding missing person's report from across state lines, calls from everyone in the entire raven community, and we have to follow this up. Caden Edwards has threatened to put this in front of every media outlet he can reach. Do you know what a field day the public would have with that? Two rival groups of shifters warring over a woman. This isn't the only copy of this video, and the public won't give a single shit about whether it's been edited or not. You look guilty as hell in this. You look like a monster. You look abusive, and Avery looks like your terrified victim. And even if you're proven innocent, the word 'kidnapping' will be synonymous with the Bloodrunner Crew forever. I don't want that. I respect you for pushing the vamps out of our area. The wolves, too, and yes we know about that. Crime rate around here is pretty damn close to *zilch*, and this is going to bring our town an avalanche of attention we don't want. So please illuminate us, Mr. Novak. What the hell is actually going on?"

Weston looked at Harper, and she nodded once.

So he did illuminate them. He told them about being pen pals with Avery, about how she was treated in Raven's Hollow. About how all the women were treated there. He told them how Avery fled an engagement to Benjamin, and the role he'd played in bullying her when she was younger. He told them every dirty secret about Raven's Hollow that Avery had shared with him because they'd pushed him to this—airing out every scrap of dirty laundry. They weren't his people, they weren't Avery's people, and now they were going to drag the Bloodrunners through the mud? For control of a woman. Fuck. That.

Detective Sutton scribbled away on his notepad as Weston spewed every sordid detail about what really went on behind the closed doors in the raven community. He told them of how much stronger Avery had grown, and how she'd made friends in the Bloodrunners, began to laugh and smile, and stand up straight again. He shook like a fucking leaf when he told them that part because he knew she was sitting in some cold psych ward room right now probably losing all the progress she'd made in Harper's Mountains.

"If you want to help Avery, let her come back to me. Let me care for her the way she deserves."

Harper spoke up somberly. "Let us all take care of her the way she deserves. She might be registered to Raven's Hollow now, but she's part of my crew. She's my friend. She deserves to be happy where she chooses, not manipulated by the people she left behind."

"If you want to help," Weston said, glare on Detective Sutton, "go look in that room under the council house and see for yourself how they break their people."

Detective Sutton huffed a humorless sound and set his pen on top of his notes, shook his head. A band of sweat beaded on his upper lip. "Tried that. Reached hard and missed. I've been on the outside for years, waiting for something, anything, that would get me an in on Raven's Hollow. I can't get a warrant without them doing something blatantly wrong, and Caden Edwards runs a tight ship."

"If you know something is wrong there, why did you come so hard at me?" Weston asked. "At Avery? She's a victim, being treated like a criminal."

"Just because I have instincts about something

doesn't mean I can ignore my job, Mr. Novak." Detective Sutton relaxed back in his chair and linked his hands behind his head. He lifted eyes to the video camera in the back of the room, the back to Weston. "Do you have any proof of The Box."

His lips had barely moved, and his words were nothing more than the barest whisper, but Weston had caught it with his heightened senses.

He leaned forward and dipped his chin so the camera wouldn't catch the shape of his lips as he whispered, "Avery is your proof. She remembers everything. She could testify against them."

Officer Hammond stood and leaned over the table between Weston and the line of sight of the camera. "Her testimony won't stand up in court. First thing the ravens will do is have her deemed an unreliable, unstable witness. She broke down in the car, Weston. Just..." He shook his head. "Rambling, repeating stories about you and Ryder when you were kids. She couldn't answer a single question we asked her. She's not fit to bring them down alone."

"You're wrong," Harper said. "She's tougher than you think she is. You just dumped her in a terrifying scenario."

"Court will be terrifying for her," Sutton whispered. "She could hurt a case against them so much more than help. But if we had proof along with her testimony. Concrete. Proof. We could get Raven's Hollow busted up and those women out of there. We could put away the people who hurt Avery. Do you understand what I'm saying to you?"

Weston swallowed hard and nodded. "You can't get the evidence. You've already tried and failed."

Sutton dipped his chin once.

"You need evidence to fall into your lap. Real, undeniable proof of abuse."

Another nod, and now Weston's vision made sense.

He'd thought his death must be imminent since that was the only way he would let Avery end up in The Box again. He'd been wrong. He was the one who would send her in there.

To save her from looking over her shoulder all her life. To save the Bloodrunner's name. To save himself from that video going straight to national news. To save the women of Raven's Hollow from further tyranny.

Weston couldn't save Avery. That wasn't his

destiny.

The vision wouldn't have happened if there was another way.

Avery was going to have to save herself and everyone else instead.

TWENTY-TWO

Avery had been wearing the same clothes in the vision that she'd been wearing tonight when the police had taken her away. What did that mean? It meant she wouldn't come home before she ended up in The Box.

Shit, think. Weston had never used a vision like this. He was more of the fight-it-and-try-to-change-fate kind of guy. That wouldn't work here and now, though. This one needed to happen.

What if something happened to her after the dream? It had cut off, and he didn't know the outcome, so what if he let her go in and something awful happened to her? Did he trust the Fates?

Fuck if he knew, but he couldn't change the

future. If he did fuck with destiny, it would just happen anyway, but worse.

Rubbing his wrists where the handcuffs had cut into him, he followed Harper out of the precinct. Times like these made him wish raven shifter healing was as good as the bear shifters. The rawness on his wrists was bothering him, taking up space in his head that should belong only to Avery right now.

Even though the police believed Weston, she'd panicked in the car and then in the precinct interrogation room. They'd transferred her to a hospital where she wouldn't get out early on good behavior. No matter how much he raged, she was on a twenty-four-hour hold, which meant they had one day to figure out how to get her straight from the psych ward to Raven's Hollow. One day where every second would feel like an hour to Avery. She was probably so scared right now.

Twenty-four hours, but it wasn't enough time, and way too much all at once.

"Who are we fucking up tonight?" Wyatt asked, hellfire in his eyes. He was standing around the back of his truck with the other Bloodrunners under the single streetlight of the precinct parking lot. The whole crew was here for him.

Aaron ran his hand through his blond hair and looked like a demon in the harsh light. "Look, Harper is out on this one, but she isn't the only dragon we know. I can call Rowan."

"Aaron, you know she won't come out of Damon's Mountains," Harper said low. "She won't leave the Gray Backs."

Aaron crossed his arms over his chest. "Okay, Dark Kane then."

Wyatt made a ticking sound behind his teeth. "Kane won't help us."

"Why not?" Aaron asked, his voice cracking across the parking lot. "Because he's a Blackwing? Fuck that. He knows us. He knows we'd help him if he needed it. And you know he's hiding a titan inside of him. We'll bring war to the ravens for what they've done to Avery, and show every other crew in the world to keep their fucking treachery to themselves. Aren't you tired of this?" Aaron looked from face to face, his lips pulled back, teeth bared, eyes blazing green-gold, looking like a battle-ready Viking warrior. "Aren't you tired of people coming for us? Vamps, wolves, ravens. We've handled everything quietly, but maybe we were wrong. Maybe we should've made a statement. Maybe we should've erected a giant fucking sign written in their blood that tells the world, 'Don't fuck with the Bloodrunners.'" He stank of fur and dominance, and he was ready. Aaron was poised for vengeance like a fiery arrow drawn back on a bow string, aimed for the heart of Raven's Hollow. But hunting the ravens wouldn't work for this one.

Weston rested his arms on the bed of the truck. "We aren't going to war, as much as I want to. Harper is out of commission and you called Kane *Dark Kane* for a reason, Aaron. He's a Blackwing and could burn the whole damn world if we let his dragon taste blood. I was there when he went after Ryder's dad. He was going to rip him limb from limb in a bar full of humans, and his eyes were completely empty. He's too big a risk, and not a weapon we want to use, trust me. This one's on us, and the ravens have numbers. Not to mention the people who live in Raven's Hollow aren't all bad. Brainwashed, sure, but they're sheltered and convinced they're right. They have a corrupt few in power, and that creates the worst situation, not only for their people, but for ours.

Ryder?" he asked the somber redhead leaning quietly against the side of Wyatt's truck. "I need our old spy kit. I need one of the cameras out of it. The smallest one."

Ryder frowned and shoved off the truck. "How did you know I brought it with me?"

"One, you're a sentimental idiot, and two, I had a vision."

His ruddy brows arched high. "I sure as hell hope it was a good vision."

"Uuuh." The memory of Avery chanting and crying shot across his mind, bringing on a sharp headache with it. "It wasn't, actually. But it has to happen."

"Well, I know you have a plan," Harper murmured. "Are you going to let us in on it?"

"Yeah. Let's load up, and I'll tell you on the way."

"On the way where?" Lexi asked softly.

"To Asheville. We're gonna have to break into a psych ward."

****

Avery couldn't breathe. The walls were creeping slowly toward her, sucking the oxygen out of the room as they approached. Soon, she would be crushed.

"Avery, we can give you medicine to calm you down," the nurse, *Patty* her nametag read, murmured from her chair in the corner.

Avery paced the length of the wall again, clutching her gown right over her heart. "I'm gonna Change."

"You can't do that in here. We already explained the rules. How did you like talking to Dr. Lancaster?"

"I didn't. I didn't. I didn't like it because I don't want to talk about this stuff. I want to forget it. Talking doesn't help, and you're making me do things I don't want to do. What have I done wrong? Why am I here? No one will explain to me. When can I leave?"

Patty was scribbling notes onto a clipboard, and Avery had to try really hard not to Change and claw her eyes out in defense of whatever damning words Patty was writing about her. It wasn't Patty's fault she was here. It was Caden's. It was Dad and Benjamin's.

She hated them.

"Because of your erratic behavior and because of how you were acting during the interview—"

"Interrogation," she gritted out. "Those police

officers grilled me like I'm some criminal."

"No, they needed to get down to the bottom of what's happened to you and what that trauma has done. My job is to make sure you don't hurt yourself and to give you a safe place while we figure out who to send you home with."

"I'm a grown woman!" Avery yelled. "I need color. Can you take me down the hall by the landscape paintings again? Or do you have a room with painted walls where we can leave the door open. Purple or blue or green or yellow. Please," she begged. "I swear I'll be good, but this room is too little, and the walls are white, and why do we have to close the door?"

"For the other patients' safety and yours. Breathe Avery, or I'll have to bring someone in to administer something to keep you calm."

"Whoo," she breathed out in a shaking voice, trying to steady herself as she paced down the wall again. The letter was clear in her imagination, ready for her to read, so she said a few lines just to feel like she could do this with Weston here. "My Da builds treehouses. He can do anything with wood. I want to be like him someday."

"What?" Patty asked, a slight frown marring her blond eyebrows. Her pen was poised right above the clipboard.

"Nothing, nothing." They would keep her here longer if she kept that up.

"Your mother is here to see you. She just arrived with your dad and your fiancé, and she wants to reassure you that everything is okay. I can't allow you to see her until you have calmed down, though."

"That's a terrible bribe. I don't want to see them. Don't want to. Tell her to go fuck herself."

Patty reared back like she'd been slapped across the cheek. "Honey, what you're going through is normal."

"I assure you it's not." More hand-wringing, and Avery paced back down the wall, careful not to touch the white paint with her elbow when she pivoted. She tried not to look at it, but the long, white wall was right there at the edge of her vision, haunting her, taunting her. "He's the best man I know. People are scared of my da, but they don't see him like I do."

"Why do you keep repeating lyrics? Is it a song?" Patty asked.

Avery swallowed the comforting words, recited

them silently, moving her lips just enough to connect with Weston's letter. Weston's eleven-year-old self was saving her now.

She closed her eyes and imagined his face. The way his lips looked when he smiled, and how his eyes had sparked that striking green color over the bottle of his beer when she'd first seen him at Big Flight. The feel of his skin under her hands. His tattoos, a mash-up of flowing organic shapes and mechanical renderings etched into his skin, covering his chest and both arms. She had those memorized now, could recall them in perfect detail. The way his muscles moved when he reached for her, how hard and strong his body felt when he held her. The way he smelled, and the way his facial scruff scratched against her soft cheek. She remembered the sting of his claiming mark. She was his, and he was hers. She just needed to get back to him.

"When can I go home?" she asked again.

"You've been ordered here for a twenty-four-hour hold."

A whole day? She wanted to leave now! "H-how long have I been here?"

"Six hours."

Avery turned and strode down the wall again, but all she wanted to do at that news was slide down the wall and fall to pieces. "Can we just open the door?"

"No, that's against the rules here."

"Please! I don't like tight spaces and white rooms, and this room is only making everything harder for me."

A trill of hope blasted through her when Patty reached over and opened the door, but she held her clipboard up to stop Avery from rushing it. "Can we get her something to calm her down?" Patty asked to someone in the hallway.

Shit.

"No, no, no, I'll be good, please. I'll be good. You can change your mind. You can tell them I don't need it. Please, please, Patty, *please*!"

Patty closed the door again and crossed her legs. "Honey, I don't know what to tell you. If you would just settle down, you could talk to your family."

Avery opened her mouth to argue, but Patty held up her finger and gave her a warning look. "Dr. Lancaster already explained this. I know he did, but sometimes victims like you can grow an unhealthy attachment to their kidnappers. You have become susceptible to what they've said about your family, but I've met your parents, Avery. They are worried sick about you. Your mom wouldn't stop crying, and your dad looks gutted about what you've been through. Your next therapy session is an important one. Listen to Dr. Lancaster. Really absorb what he tells you. Share what you have actually been through, and he can help you. Or…he can order you to stay here for longer." Patty stood and walked out, but before she shut the door behind her, she said, "Carl is going to come in here in a few minutes and give you something to make you more comfortable. Don't throw a fit, don't Change, don't make him have to call a bunch of nurses in here to hold you down. Don't make us use straps. I'm trying to help you with actual advice. That kind of behavior will get time added to your stay here. If you want to be rewarded, you have to mind the rules." Patty sounded like a raven.

As the door clicked closed behind the nurse, Avery let off a long, keening whimper and searched frantically through her memories for that letter that had been keeping her calm enough not to Change.

Some son-of-a-goblin had designed this room

with no windows and, other than the door, there was only a bed screwed to the floor, topped with a white, sterile mattress and no covers. At least it wasn't frigid cold in here, and that helped to anchor her in the here-and-now. This wasn't The Box, just something way too fucking close to it.

Eighteen more hours in this hell, and then she could go home to 1010, to Weston, to the Bloodrunners—not with the ravens pretending they cared in some waiting room of the hospital. Just thinking of them this close to Harper's Mountains angered her all over again. They were ruining everything.

She'd been happy. Why the hell couldn't they just let her be happy? Parents should want that. Normal parents anyway. When she had babies with Weston, she was going to love them so much. She would breathe for their happiness, like her heart beat for Weston's. She would be a good mother for his children because he deserved that, and so did they. A sob wrenched from her throat, and she gave herself to the fantasy just to escape the stupid room.

Weston hadn't mentioned wanting kids, but he would be a great daddy. He was so patient and funny with the kids that he took on ATV tours. He always had the best rapport with them. Maybe it was from being around Ryder all the time, who was basically a giant child, or perhaps it was natural for him to speak so well to kids. And he was so understanding with what she'd been through. She could just imagine him sitting next to her, one hand on her leg, one arm curved under their little sleeping baby. A boy. No…a girl, with rosy, plump little cheeks, who smiled in her sleep because Weston was talking to her in that rich, deep tone of his. And he would rock her back and forth, back and forth, tell her she was going to be a fearsome little raven someday, just like her momma. She liked that part a lot—Fantasy Weston thinking her strong. Avery was sitting on the edge of the mattress crying and weak, but in her imagination, Weston thought she was braver. And that made her feel braver. Avery wiped her damp cheeks and smiled at the next thought—the one of Weston holding a little, black, fluffy baby raven, newly Changed and peeping cutely from the bowl Weston made with his big hands.

If he wanted kids someday, Avery swore to herself she was going to give him the best, happiest nest she could. Even if she had no tools, or any idea how to do that because she hadn't grown up in a normal household, she was going to ask the other women in the Bloodrunners. She'd watched Harper, Alana, and Lexi draw infinite smiles from their mates. So, fuck her past. Avery had strong women to look up to now. She wiped her eyes again, drying her cheeks completely.

Someday, she was going to be a strong woman, too. She was going to earn her place in the Bloodrunners, and she was going to be so fucking proud of the work she put in to get there.

"Hey!" Someone yelled right outside of her room. "How did you get in here? Don't take that! Stop!"

The small window on Avery's door shadowed with nurses running down the hall to the right. What the hell? She padded over to the door and stood on her tiptoes, craned her neck, and looked as far down the hallway as she could see. A flash of red hair bolted away from the nurses, and Ryder's most psychotic laugh echoed through the thick door.

Weston's face appeared in front of her window, scaring her nearly to death. He cast a glance over his shoulder at the grand chase Ryder was leading the hospital staff on. Through the remaining sliver of window Avery could see out of, Ryder was flapping his arms and squawking like a total nutcase.

"Move back quick," Weston murmured over the jingle of keys.

As she backed away, the lock clicked, and the door swung open. Weston rushed inside and closed the door behind him.

Stunned, she stood there frozen while he checked the window down the hall both ways. But when he turned around, looking like a million bucks in his black T-shirt, backward hat, and big old muscles poking out everywhere, her body loosened right up.

"Weston!" She launched herself at him and clung to him like a flying squirrel catching a tree trunk. God, the relief she felt when he crushed her to him was insane.

"Ave, we don't have much time."

"Are you breaking me out of here?" she asked, hope nearly choking her.

He eased back and cupped her cheeks, but his eyes were hard and worried. That and they were black as night. Something was wrong. "This is where you have to make a choice. A detective has been working on getting a warrant to search Raven's Hollow, but he has no evidence of anything illegal to get one. If I break you out of here, it'll cause trouble, not only for you, but it'll make us look guilty."

"Us. You mean the Bloodrunners? But you didn't kidnap me!"

"Ave, they sliced up a video of when they came in the shop yesterday. It looks bad. I look bad. You look like a victim, and the ravens have threatened to go to the media."

"No," she whispered, horrified. "They can't do that. This is all a lie. I want to be with you!"

"Shhhh," Weston said, stroking his thumb across her cheek. "And we will be together. No matter what, we will. But the ravens are after us, for revenge on my mom or on shifters outside of their community, or maybe on me, I don't know. They will haunt us if we don't put a stop to their manipulation."

"What can I do? Weston, should I leave? I can't have the Bloodrunners under attack from the public. I can't! I love them. I love you. Do I run? Hide? Maybe they'll forget about me if I just disappear for a while."

Weston shook his head slowly, eyes locked on

hers. "Avery, I don't think you're a runner, and I don't think you'll be happy with that decision."

"Then what? How do I protect you? How do I protect the Bloodrunners?"

Weston swallowed hard, and his skin paled. Slowly, he eased something small and brown out of his pocket. "Remember the spy cameras I told you about in that letter? The ones Ryder and I used to spy on Willa's Wormshack?"

She took it gingerly between her finger and thumb. It was so much tinier than she'd imagined. "Yeah."

"Ave, the detective needs evidence. Concrete, undeniable evidence that you've been mistreated. Evidence that can get Caden and the rest of the council taken out of power so the ravens can recover and rebuild, if they want. Evidence that will take Caden and whatever game he's playing out of our lives forever."

"Evidence of what?" Oh, she already knew the answer. The two words were already scratching against the back of her mind like nails on a chalkboard, but she needed to hear it. She needed to know exactly what Weston was asking her to do.

"He needs evidence of The Box."

There was yelling outside, and a couple nurses rushed by again, so Weston pulled her to the side of the door so they couldn't see him.

The Box? She wanted to fall apart just thinking about going back there. She wanted to cry, hold onto her memorized letters, and curl up in a ball on the floor. Willingly go back into The Box?

But the vision of her fantasy, of Weston telling their child someday that she would be a fierce lady raven like Avery, drifted across her mind. If this were Lexi, Harper, or Alana being called to help the crew, they would do it. Without a shadow of a doubt, Avery knew they would.

And she wanted to be strong like that. She wanted to earn her place in the Bloodrunners at Weston's side. She wanted to protect them. If the ravens stripped the crew down in the media and ruined their names, their good reputation, and Avery did nothing to stop it, she would never be able to forgive herself.

This was her chance to be the heroine of her own story.

This was a chance to feel like she matched

Weston because, if she could do this, if she could pull this off and pluck Caden from power, she was rising up like a phoenix, just like Weston believed she could.

She couldn't depend on Weston to go into the heart of Raven's Hollow and break into The Box. The council had put a lot of effort into luring him to The Hollow, and instinct said it was for dark reasons. She couldn't lose Weston. Couldn't risk him getting hurt, or worse. She didn't want him inside the gates, gathering evidence that she could do on her own.

She forced the words out. "I'll do it."

More yelling. A nurse shouted from outside the room that she was going to check on patients. Their time was up. Avery closed her fist around the camera and nodded at Weston's questioning glance. In a determined whisper, she said, "I can do this. Wait for me outside the gates of Raven's Hollow. Don't come in, no matter what. I can do it as long as I know you're close, but if I think you'll risk yourself or the crew, I'll screw this up. Promise me you'll wait."

The blood drained from Weston's face, and he stood straighter. "I promise I'll wait. I know you can do this, Avery." He gripped her shoulders tightly and leaned down to her eye level. "I can't explain how right now, but I'll be there with you."

And she understood. He would be there with her. He would be in her mind, in the letters he'd written as a boy. In the words she would recite when The Box swallowed her up. And she loved him even more for it.

"Go now," she murmured. "I'll go home with my parents. I'll get the evidence you need."

Weston straightened, lifted his chin, and smiled proudly at her. "Push the button on the back of the camera. The green light on the side will flash twice to tell you it's working. It'll store three hours of video and will pick up the audio. As soon as you have enough, get out of there. Come to the gate. Come to me, and I'll take you home, and everything will be okay."

Everything will be okay. Oh, what a beautiful promise that was.

Her voice would shake if she used it, and she wanted to be strong for Weston, so she nodded once.

His lips crashed against hers, and he plunged his tongue past her lips. A soft whimper escaped her because she understood the desperation in this connection. If something went wrong... No, she couldn't think like that. This wasn't it. She didn't go her whole life in darkness only to reach the light and then fall. Her time with Weston wasn't done. Her time in Harper's Mountains wasn't done. She just needed to tie up the loose ends with the people who had hurt her. She had work to do. And when it was through, she would claw and fight to get back to her Weston, her mate, her life, her love.

Weston pulled away abruptly at a knock on the door. Ryder shoved open the cracked door. "We have to go now." He looked panicked, but still took a moment to look at Avery. "I like your dress."

Avery looked down at her thin hospital gown. It was nearly see-through, hung crooked, and fit like a burlap sack. "Um...thanks?"

"You're welcome." Ryder yanked Weston's arm, and they bolted out the door. And just before it swung closed behind them, Weston shot her one last look that said so many things without the use of a single word. *Be careful. I'll wait for you. You can do this. I love you.*

She ran to the door as it clicked shut and watched him and Ryder bolt down the empty hallway. The panic was flaring in her chest at being in a white room with the door closed, but this was just the warm-up. Soon, things would be so much worse.

Patty was coming down the hall from the opposite end, checking doors, so Avery ran to the bed, sat down, and pulled up the hem of her dress. There was a thick stitching at the bottom, but she ripped the thread viciously for an inch until there was a little pocket right near her left ankle. She secured the camera inside and settled the fabric over her lap as the door lock turned.

"Are you okay?" Patty asked.

Avery nodded her head jerkily. "I've had time to think."

"Okay." Patty looked flushed and distracted and glanced down the hallway in the direction Weston and Ryder had disappeared. "What did you think about?"

Avery blew out a steadying breath. This was the point of no return. This was her making the decision officially to volunteer for The Box. *Be brave, little phoenix.*

"I want to see my parents. I'm ready to go home."

TWENTY-THREE

"This wasn't how it was supposed to be for you," Dad said.

Mom had been angry, crying intermittently, but she hadn't said a word since Avery had been released from the hospital. It was shocking that Dad was the one who broke the silence.

"You mean I wasn't born to bring the Novak Raven here?" Avery asked sarcastically.

"You've lost your damn mind if you think you're going to talk to me like that, Avery Marie Foley. You've spent too much time out there with those animals—"

"I'm an animal—"

"You're a civilized shifter—"

"I'm just like them!" Avery barked out. How had she said "Yes, sir" to all the bullshit he'd spewed over the years? Everything was different now. Everything. The way she felt about herself, the way she felt about other shifters and humans. The way she saw the world.

The ravens of The Hollow were jaded. The men were so domineering, the women so demure, and no one had challenged them enough. So here they were, a community cut off from the world, treating women like shit. Fucking barbarians.

"You will have to change your clothes before we enter the gates," Dad said.

"Hard pass, these are comfortable."

"Shorts up your ass and your chest hanging out for everyone to see. That's not how the mate of a future council member should dress."

"Stan," Mom warned in a soft voice.

"Oh don't you fuckin' argue with me, too—"

"Don't talk to her like that," Avery said, resting her forehead against the back window.

Mom was crying again in the passenger seat, her shoulders shaking with silent sobbing. Avery had forgotten what it was like for a little while, but now seeing Dad put Mom in her place made her sick. Weston would never, ever treat her like that.

Mom had lied and betrayed Aviana, betrayed Avery, but she didn't have any control over her life, and there was something incredibly tragic about that.

"You will change your clothes, or you'll go in The Box."

Avery closed her eyes against the fear in those two words. She blew a breath onto the window and drew a little raven in the condensation just to feel closer to Weston.

Voice trembling, Avery told him, "I'm coming home, but I won't be cowering anymore. You will just have to get used to me."

"The hell I will!"

"You will!" she yelled. "You should've a long time ago. You should've loved my raven, not trained her to be nothing. To be invisible. Mom, stop crying. Stop it. Dad's a shit. He always has been. Leave his ass. Leave him. Why did you marry him in the first place? And don't tell me for love because I've never seen him say a single supportive thing to you."

Dad gripped the steering wheel so hard it creaked, and his profile turned beat red.

"I married him for the same reasons you have to marry Benjamin."

"I'm not marrying that douchebag. I would literally rather sit my bare vagina on a cactus than walk down any isle to that prick."

"What's wrong with you?" Dad bellowed. "He can provide for you."

"He'll hurt me."

"So what? *So what*? If you weren't such a mouthy woman, he wouldn't want to. You have no one to blame but yourself. No one."

She opened her mouth to tell him to go fuck himself, but ahead, the gates to Raven's Hollow lumbered, heavy and made of wrought iron. Two giant decorative ravens faced each other in the center, like great warriors guarding something precious. But raven shifters had never been warriors. None of them had but Aviana Novak, and her son, the Novak Raven. Everyone else had gotten so messed up and just dug deeper and deeper until they didn't remember how to be okay anymore.

The gates opened, and Avery's gaze followed the two men who stood somberly beside it, ready to close the iron barrier back against the outside world.

"Why am I here?" she asked softly, tears burning her eyes. "Why did you work so hard, lie so much, and put my friends in danger to bring me back to this place?"

"Because," Dad said hoarsely. "The Novak Raven can't lift our rank anymore. Only Benjamin can. He is in line to take Caden's place. He has no heir. Any revenge he wanted on his mate will pass down to Benjamin."

"Caden had a mate?" Avery asked, confused. First she'd found out Caden had been engaged to Aviana, but now he'd bonded to a mate? He'd always seemed to hate the fairer sex.

"Aviana was his mate," Dad gritted out. "She's the fucking queen of our people, but she's been sitting on the throne of the Gray Back Crew this whole goddamn time, completely unreachable. Protected from Caden's wrath by Damon, by Beaston, by the shifters of those mountains. She had a duty to Caden. She should've bore a son for him, not for some fucking grizzly. Weston should've been Caden's heir, but because of the actions of his mother, his bloodline is tainted. She failed as a mother and a mate."

"She was a great mother, and she was never

Caden's mate," Avery ground out. Romance-less marriage contracts didn't a mate make. That was like calling Mom Dad's mate. If she was, he wouldn't be able to treat her like he did.

And oh, she could see it now. She could imagine how Caden had obsessed over Aviana Novak over the years, waiting on a chance to exact revenge on the woman he felt like he *owned*. Benjamin saw Avery the same way. That they had to have the women who didn't want them back was a sure sign of their monstrous egos. Something was seriously wrong with the men in this community.

Dad drove up the winding mountain road, past the houses that were dimly lit. It all looked so eerie in the dark. This wasn't home anymore.

"Caw!"

Avery lifted her gaze to the tree branches above the road.

"Caw! Caw! Caw!" The branches were heavy with ravens welcoming her back to Hell.

Chills rose all over Avery's body. The whole town seemed to be Changed. What if Weston got too close to the gates? What if he was seen? His raven was massive, much bigger than any raven here. He would be recognizable.

Weston knew how to take care of himself. She'd never seen him falter, never seen him hesitate. Even last night, he'd broken into the hospital within six hours of her being there and gotten away with it. She'd heard the nurses talking about how the redheaded man had gotten away. They hadn't even mentioned Weston.

He could be a ghost when he wanted to.

Dad didn't even bother to take her home to change her clothes. Instead, he stopped directly in front of the council house and got out.

Avery clenched her shaking hands. Her palms were sweating just thinking about what waited for her inside.

Dad opened her door and murmured, "I'm sorry, Avery, but you will have to be reconditioned to accept life here." The apologies of an asshole.

She stood slowly, her legs and arms heavy as lead. Mom was staring at Dad like he was a monster, and she had the right of it. He was so deep in his belief The Box was okay because it wasn't physically hurting her that he'd lost his sense of right and wrong. Or maybe he'd never had it in the first place.

Avery hugged her mom. She wished she could hang onto her anger, but Mom had tried to save her in her own way. She'd encouraged her to go out in the real world and grow roots near the Novak Raven. Maybe that was all part of some fucked-up revenge plan on Aviana, but Avery was clinging to the thought that Mom also wanted to protect her from the life she hated. She clung to the idea that Mom wanted better for her.

Mom hugged her shoulders tight and didn't let go until Dad pried them apart. "People are watching," he muttered, tugging her hand hard.

"Where is Caden?" she asked. Usually he was the one to do the honors.

"He'll be here any minute. He and Benjamin gave an extra statement at the station before they began their drive."

Avery was panicking. With every step through the sprawling entryway, down the hall, down the basement stairs, her heart felt like it was going to beat out of her chest.

Dad stopped in front of the door of The Box. Inside, the single hanging lightbulb was already turned on, swinging gently in the frigid air from the vent above.

The tendrils of frosty air stretched into the hallway and surrounded her, beckoning her inside as if the room had missed her warmth. "How long do I have to stay down here?" Avery whispered meekly. She wished her voice was stronger.

Dad looked like the grim reaper in the swaying, harsh light. "As long as it takes."

TWENTY-FOUR

"Me and Ryder bought a whole box of spy stuff and put the cameras all around Willa's Wormshack. She's a Gray Back like me, and really funny. You would like her. If she caught us, she would just laugh, so that's why we picked her to spy on first, but all we got is three straight hours of video footage of her working with her worms. She sells them to bait shops and for people who make fancy gardens. She makes a stupid amount of money at it, but that's not why she does it. She loves worms. Like…she LOVES worms. We did catch funny audio of her talking to them, though. She called them her babies, and named one of them Dingleberry. And I swear she thought of kissing one when he wiggled extra cute in her hand. Ryder and me were laughing so hard." Avery's voice hitched with emotion, and another tear streamed down her face. It was so cold in here, chilling her blood, freezing her bones. She wanted to be out of here, but she was supposed to stick to the plan. Only she couldn't do this without Weston here. She needed his letters. "The spy cameras are so small we'll never get caught. Never get caught. Never. Never. So small, we'll never get caught."

She'd drawn her knees up to conserve warmth and was clutching the spy camera like a life-line. When the time came, she needed to be ready. Ready to let the letter go, ready to accept that she was in The Box again, ready to move. *Come on, Avery. You can do this.*

She dropped her chin to her chest and sobbed because the letters weren't keeping the walls from closing in. Not like they used to. She'd had the real Weston, and now the letters had lost their potency.

"So small, we'll never get caught," she whimpered.

"Darlin'."

Avery's sob froze in her throat. That had sounded like Weston. It was just the whisp of a word, but it was his voice. She smiled as another tear dripped off her chin and onto her Big Flight tank top. Weston was here, and even if it was just in her imagination, it counted. He'd come when the letters stopped working. "I knew you would come."

"What?" The breathy voice was so faint, so soft, but she would know it anywhere. Her mate. Her Weston. Her Novak Raven had kept his promise.

And when she looked up, she sighed in relief. He was there, barely, on his knees right in front of her. His body flickered and wavered, and the air around him seemed to move, but his eyes held hers. Black like his raven's and full of emotion. He was so handsome, even in the harsh light, but he looked confused. Strange. His confusion made no sense because this was all part of the plan.

"You said you would be here with me, and you are." She opened her hand and showed him the spy camera so he would remember, and recognition flickered through his troubled gaze. "I'm stronger now," she reassured him. And she was. She hadn't lost her mind or clawed at the walls. She hadn't gotten so lost in the letters that she'd forgotten her job here—to protect the ones she loved. She was scared and shaking, but she could *do* this.

He reached out, and she gasped as his fingertips warmed her skin. He seemed so real. So solid. Weston grabbed her wrist and pulled. "Avery, I can save you. I can get you out of here. Look, I can touch you. Come on."

But that wouldn't work. She'd already gotten video of the room, the claw marks, and the bucket in the corner, and the lightbulb swaying in the frigid draft, but she needed concrete evidence against Caden. Against his abuse of power and control over an entire race of shifters. As tempting as it was to try and let Weston save her, Avery's job wasn't done. Not yet.

"Weston," she whispered. "This is the way it's supposed to be. I can do this." The two tears dislodged and streamed down her cheeks, but those were the last two she would allow since he'd come just as he'd promised. He was here with her. "You make me stronger." She smiled because she knew that somehow, someway, she was going to see him soon. "Wait for me."

Weston flickered out of existence, but his rushed words remained, filling her head and her heart. "I love you, Ave."

"I love you, too. Wait for me."

Footsteps sounded on the basement stairs, and Avery rushed to hit the button on the camera, hiding it in the shadows right between her drawn up legs, like she was huddled up and scared.

She wasn't scared, though. Not of Caden or Benjamin or anyone else. Not anymore.

Now, she was angry. Such raw fury roiled inside of her, she felt as if she could breathe fire like the Bloodrunner Dragon herself. Inside of her, Avery's raven was ready to blast out of her skin and make an escape. She was ready for battle. Ready to get hurt, ready to fly, ready to succeed, ready to leave this place and never look back.

The door swung open and Benjamin entered. He left it open a crack. So tempting to flee now, but she had to wait. *Not yet, raven. Not yet.*

She was shaking still from nerves, from anger, from seeing Weston. Benjamin smirked. "Scared Avery. You aren't so cocky now that you're back where you belong, are you?"

Where she belonged? The Box? No, this puckered asshole was mistaken. She belonged with the

Bloodrunners.

"I don't want to marry you."

Benjamin leaned against the opposite wall and crossed his arms over his chest. He was tall and lanky. If Weston stood like that, his muscles would bulge out. He could squish Benjamin like a blood-filled tick.

"You will want to marry me eventually, Avery. I'm a patient man. If it takes six fucking months down here, you'll come around."

"Why do you want me?" she asked, trying to hold the tiny camera steady between her shaking fingers.

"You know why."

"Because I beat you up when we were kids?"

"You *humiliated* me." Benjamin's blue eyes flashed with disdain as he twitched his head to shake his jet-black hair out of his face. He would've been a handsome man if hatred hadn't made his eyes so cold. "Caden was my mentor from birth, Avery. I was born to lead our people someday, and you made me look weak. I was in the hospital for three days because of you. I *hated* you. Every taunt from the males in our class, every Get Well Soon card from the females who saw me as pathetic—that was your fault.

But as we grew up, I began to see you differently. I wanted to punish you for what you'd done, sure, but there was something more. You're the prettiest trinket here, Avery. The most dominant female raven, and you'll be the most fun to break." Benjamin's lips curved up wickedly. "Do you know who you remind Caden of, Avery?"

She shook her head, then murmured, "No," so the camera could catch the audio.

"Aviana King."

"You mean Aviana Novak?"

"I mean Aviana King!" he screamed, his face turning red. "Caden told me everything. She was too independent for her own good, too. She fancied herself above the flock, like she didn't need us. Like she didn't need Caden. She left him for a filthy bear shifter. A filthy Gray Back. She left Caden with no heirs, no nest, no mate. And then you came along. A late Changer, and when your animal finally got her shit together and showed herself, she came out dominant. The first and only fucked-up female since *her*. Since Aviana. Every time Caden put you in here—he was punishing *her*. Every time he heard you scream to let you out—it was *her* screaming. Every tear, every pathetic sob, every heartbroken sound—that was his revenge until he could get to her offspring. Her pride and joy. Her only son. Her only raven child. You were his revenge until he could reach the Novak Raven."

Avery swallowed the bile that crept up the back of her throat. "But he didn't," she whispered.

Benjamin cupped his hand around his ear. "What's that?"

Avery cleared her throat and made her voice stronger. "He didn't get the Novak Raven."

Benjamin's lips curved up into a predatory smile. "Wrong again. You never stopped being the bait, Avery. I've read all his letters to you. We all have. Weston Novak fell for you when you were kids. He was so fucking predictable. All we had to do was give you a few weeks with him to revive the bond and then bring you back. Your mom messed up by telling Aviana about the council's involvement ten years ago, but Caden is the best hunter in the whole flock. All he had to do was wait patiently until you convinced the Novak Raven to forgive you. He just had to wait until he could draw Weston out of the protection of his people." Benjamin lifted his chin and looked down his nose at her. "You brought him straight to us, just like you were born to do."

No. They didn't have Weston. They didn't! He was strong and smart, and he wouldn't let them. But Benjamin looked so triumphant. So sure.

Fuck! Now Raven!

Pain blasted through her as she pushed her Change. It was death in an instant, and then there she was, her black-feathered phoenix. Avery struggled out of the neck of her tank top, costing her a precious second. The camera was right in front of her on the tile, and Benjamin was looking at it with a deep frown. Now that dumbass was starting to get it. He was the fucking bait. Not her!

Avery snatched it up in her beak as Benjamin rushed to pull off his shirt. Stretching her wings, she flapped furiously for the door. That crack was her salvation. Stupid Benjamin, so scared of locking himself in here with her. Caden would've never made that rookie mistake.

"Caw!" Benjamin cried out from behind her when she tucked her wings and shoved the door open with a vicious jerk of her beak. The camera loosened, but she held on tighter. She would not let go, she would not fail, she would not let her mate down. She would not let her Bloodrunners down. She would not let herself down. As Avery flew past, she checked the other two rooms in the basement. If Caden had Weston, he hadn't brought him here. Fuck, where would he be keeping him?

Benjamin was right on her tail feathers. She could feel him getting closer, so she blasted up the stairwell and into the first floor. Frantically, she searched for an open window, open door, something. She made two desperate passes through the dining room and living room.

The house was locked up tight, though. The bedroom doors were closed, and the windows were covered with blinds that would tangle her up. She ducked sharply out of the way of Benjamin's outstretched talons, flittering this way and that to avoid him. *There!* The small window above the kitchen sink only had two thin curtains over it, no blinds. Her raven was big, and the window was small. It would be close. She could get trapped and bleed out on the glass, but there was no other way. Benjamin would get her if she stayed in here, and she was running out of time. She had to find Weston. She had to help him.

He was her heart, her blood. She couldn't live without him.

Avery gained speed, flapping furiously as she angled toward the window. She clamped her beak onto the camera and hoped to hell she kept it secure. And then like a torpedo, she dove for the window, Benjamin right on her tail. She tucked her wings as tightly as she could and smashed through the window. The pain was blinding, not only on her face, but when she opened her eyes and the glass was raining all around her, something sharp and excruciating radiated through her right wing.

The camera slipped out of her grasp, and she watched in horror as it catapulted toward the ground. Determined, she dive-bombed, but something hit her on the back like a cannon ball, and she blasted into the dirt.

Before she even could right herself, Benjamin was on her, pecking, slashing, raking his nails across her breast feathers. Fury rocked her. All these years, they'd trained her raven to be small and submissive. Fuck that. This was where Avery took her raven back and let her be as aggressive and dominant as she wanted. This was where Avery gave her raven permission to be a War Bird like Weston was.

With a battle screech, she rolled him over and slammed her beak into his neck, into his eye, against his skull. He fought, but not like her. And the second she gained ground, dominated, hurt him, she stretched her wings, ignoring the horrible pain that arced like electric currents through her body, and she hopped to the camera sitting in the middle of the sea of glass.

Benjamin was flapping in the dirt, righting himself, but he was shaking his head hard, as though she'd knocked him straight into confusion. Good. Fucker deserved that and worse. One of his eyes was bleeding bad, and the other flashed with hatred and pain in the glow of the kitchen light, but Avery couldn't conjure a single solitary fuck right now. She needed to get to Weston.

Camera in her beak, she flapped her wings hard and was nearly immobilized by the pain. Something reflective flashed right by her face, scaring her, and when she banked to the left and arched her gaze, she could see it. A huge shard of glass was lodged in her wing, right at the base, glistening with blood and moonlight. But something else flashed in the reflection of the jagged glass as she flapped upward into the sky. Something orange and glowing.

Avery searched desperately across the tree line. A bonfire had been built in the woods of The Hollow. Bonfires were only for special occasions. They signified Change, or were built when a severe punishment was being decided on.

She wanted to scream in agony with every beat of her wings, but she could hear it now. She could hear the collective *caw, caw* of the flock. Something awful was happening. And as she struggled over the last line of trees, Avery saw him. Weston leapt into the air, human and naked, covered in crimson gashes, muscles flexing as he reached for a dive-bombing raven. He grasped the bird and slammed it to the ground, and mid-jump, his raven exploded from him and continued to battle. A hundred ravens swarmed around him, pecking and slashing. They surged onto him in a ball of violence as he thrashed and fought. He couldn't even spread his wings, so he was falling with the rest of them.

Caden was standing to the side, glowing like a demon in the firelight, chin lifted high, eyes full of raw triumph as he watched his people bleed the Novak Raven.

She would kill them all to see Weston live. Kill them all to save one.

Avery swooped lower, dropped the camera into a fern, and flapped furiously toward the battle, pain be damned. Weston Changed into his human form right before he hit the ground, and he fought savagely. His face was full of intensity, not fear, as though he knew exactly how to fight a war like this. The hoard of ravens lifted as Weston ducked, hit, and grabbed. He never missed, and he was so fast he blurred.

And when he ran and leapt into the air with ravens trailing, Avery tucked her wings and smashed into the closest two. Their talons had been out, ready to hurt him mid-Change, but as Avery barreled into them, the power of Weston's shift blasted through her. Everything slowed as she stretched her wings to catch the currents and Weston, just under her, flipped upside down and stretched for her, war in his eyes. She cawed at him. *It's me, my love. I'm here.* The death-bringer in his eyes softened. He answered with a strong, bellowing battle cry, and then he arched his back and fought the hoard following them. Taking his cue, Avery bowed her back and flew over the flock of blood-lusting ravens. She caught one by the outstretched claws and spun the raven around, slammed it into a tree trunk and searched for the next. Weston was engaged with three, flapping his wings desperately, trying to keep them all from slamming back down to earth. He couldn't bear more weight, so she dive-bombed the fourth, knocked it off course. Above, ravens circled, cawing constantly, drawing more and more of the flock into the battle, and it was her and Weston against the entirety of Raven's Hollow.

She was hit from behind, and another raven clashed with her front, holding onto her with nails dug deep into her flesh. Avery ducked the sharp beak as she flapped desperately under the new weight. Her wing was injured, though, and she wasn't as strong as Weston. She was going down hard. In a desperate move, she Changed to her human form right before she struck the earth. She slammed into the ground, and the air was shoved forcefully from her lungs. She was too close to the bonfire, and heat flared up her legs as she thrashed and grasped for the ravens.

There were too many now, but she could see him coming—Benjamin. He was naked and streaked with dirt and blood. His eye was swollen closed, and it looked as if he was crying rivers of crimson, but hate flashed across his entire face. When the ravens lifted from their attack on her body, she could see Benjamin was holding an ax in his hand. Avery tried to force her body to move, to scramble away, but the wind was still knocked out of her, and her body was frozen in fear.

Three more long deliberate strides, and Benjamin lifted the ax gracefully over his head, an evil smile on his face, the fire illuminating his ruined eye. This was it, the end, and it would hurt so bad to die this way. Avery drew her hands over her face and flinched as the ax began its arch toward her.

And then Weston was there, human, his great weight covering her body protectively. He cupped her head tightly against his shoulder, shielding her.

A sick *thunk* sounded, and Weston's body jerked.

"No!" Avery screamed, tears burning her eyes.

After a horrifying second of silence, Weston eased up, his eyes wide with shock. He jerked his gaze over his shoulder, and Avery could see it, too.

The ax wasn't buried in the man she loved. It was hanging limply from Benjamin's hand, and he was looking down at his chest in shock. The handle of a knife was lodged against his sternum.

Benjamin sank to his knees, and above, the battle song of the ravens wrenched up in volume.

Weston looked behind Avery toward the woods, flickering in an orange bonfire glow. Avery followed his glance, grasping his tensed arms desperately.

A man stood there with blazing green eyes and dark hair. In his hand was another blade, ready to be thrown. He stood to his full, imposing height and bared his teeth. His face looked like a predator's, twisted and wild. In a booming voice, he said, "You won't be layin' another hand on my boy."

A woman stood behind him, long, dark hair streaked with silver and waving down her shoulders, her eyes the pitch black of a raven. Avery recognized her from the picture she had. Aviana Novak. And that meant the man—the wild one who'd just saved Weston from an ax blade—was none other than...

The man opened his mouth and yelled as an enormous silver grizzly bear ripped out of his skin. His bellow tapered to a roar that shook the woods.

Beaston.

Above, the ravens' battle song turned panicked and disjointed.

Beaston and Aviana weren't alone. Harper melted out of the woods flanked by Lexi. Then another bear answered Beaston's call, and another. Alana's dark-furred bear followed Wyatt's and Aaron's out of the tree line, and a massive snowy owl stretched its wings against the wind and landed on a branch above Beaston.

"Move," Weston said low.

The instant he grabbed her arm, she gasped at the pain. His eyes flashed wide when he laid eyes on the glass sticking out of her shoulder. Look away."

After she squeezed her eyes tightly closed, he pulled the glass from her in a quick jerk. The pain drew a sharp yelp from her lips, and then he was pulling her up, pulling her away from where Benjamin had fallen to the side, his one eye staring vacantly at her. It was still filled with hate, even in death. Caden was walking closer, flanked by the rest of the council, but Weston picked her up like she weighed nothing and strode toward the Bloodrunners.

Avery stared in horror over his shoulder at the council coming for them.

Rage-filled eyes on Aviana, Caden screamed, "Kill them all!" to the ravens above.

But something moved just beyond the trees, and Weston skidded to a stop, his heart pounding hard against her shoulder. "Holy shit," he murmured.

Avery twisted in his arms. In the shadows of the trees, barely lit by the bonfire, behind Beaston, Aviana, and the Bloodrunners, something massive and serpentine moved through the woods. A low rumble filled the forest, and a huge eye opened, the elongated pupil constricting as it focused on Caden. The eye was the color of gold fire, and the scales of the monster dragon were as dark as night.

Terrified, Avery whispered, "Is it Kane?"

"No," Weston murmured. "That's Rowan of the Gray Backs."

The gray-scaled dragon pushed up on massive legs until her back blocked out the moon. Her long neck unfurled, and she lifted her enormous head into the air. Long, arched horns extended from face, and her back was covered in razor sharp spikes. A few terrifying clicks sounded, and she bellowed a roar, blowing a stream of fire and lava into the air.

The circling ravens scattered like ashes in the wind.

"That's as much warning as you'll get," Harper shouted at Caden, fury tainting every word. "Come another step closer, and you'll get a war you aren't prepared for." She planted her feet near Aviana and Beaston and leveled her glowing gaze on the leader of Raven's Hollow. "You've done enough." She gestured to the limp ravens scattered across the clearing around the bonfire. "You've caused great loss to your people in the name of vengeance. Save what remains of The Hollow and let us go in peace."

"She's mine!" Caden screamed, jamming a finger at Aviana. "And she's mine." He pointed to Avery.

Beaston's bear snarled and circled his mate tightly, his glowing green eyes promising death to Caden. Weston set Avery down and held her protectively behind him as he backed her toward the safety of the crew. Weston's voice came out a feral snarl. "My mother was never yours. My mate was never yours. You'll let them go for good, or your last breath will belong to me."

Caden was alone in the clearing now, his

countenance enraged, his thick crop of silver hair disheveled, his chest heaving, fists clenched at his sides. His council was on the run, his protégé was dead, and his War Birds had abandoned him, yet still he faced the Bloodrunners, insanity in his dark eyes. And in a flash, his glare on Weston, he leapt into the air and burst into a raven.

Weston took two steps, jumped and morphed into his raven in an instant. He hit Caden full in the chest, locked his talons onto his and flew them up higher and higher.

Heart in her throat, Avery moved to Change, but Harper was there, hand resting on her forearm. "Let him end this," she murmured, power in her words.

And her animal wanted to listen. She wanted to obey Harper, not because she was bullying her into submission like the ravens had done. She wanted to listen to Harper because her words were wise. Weston needed to defend Avery, to end her hurt because that's what real mates did. She'd had the same instinct, to protect him from everything. But also Harper's words had fused with some deep instinct to expose her neck and obey for the good of Weston. For the good of the crew. She'd always wanted to fight submission to the ravens, but this felt so right. So important.

Harper was Avery's alpha now.

Lifting her eyes to the sky, she squeezed Harper's hand as hard as she could and watched her mate avenge her. And when the birds tumbled from the clouds, locked in war, beating their wings and slamming their beaks into each other, she didn't run to fix this herself. Weston was good at battle. He was capable. Avery winced when they reached the ground, but with a booming thud, one raven lay limp near the fire, and the other, the biggest raven of all, spread his wings, arched upward, and ghosted the ground before lifting up on the air currents victorious.

Caden and Benjamin were gone, and never again would Avery have to fear The Box.

Never again would she have to fear anything.

TWENTY-FIVE

Weston glanced over at Avery again, just to make sure she was okay for the hundredth time. She was huddled into herself, staring out the window as the Smoky Mountains blurred by.

"We're almost home," he murmured, wishing he could take her pain away.

She rolled her head across the seat and gave him a tired smile. There were ghosts in her eyes, though.

Today had been hell. She'd gone to battle with the flock, been hurt escaping The Box and defending him, and then she'd spent the entire day in the Damascus Police Department, making her statement and answering questions.

She'd done so fucking good getting the video. On

it, Benjamin had admitted so much, not only for himself, but he'd unknowingly testified against Caden, too.

She was a phoenix now, just like he'd always known she would be.

"What will happen to the ravens?" she asked in a hoarse voice.

"Caden and Benjamin are gone, and the council has been arrested for their involvement in what happened, not only when you were growing up, but in the calculated manipulation of law enforcement and the attack on both of us. The leadership of The Hollow has been dissolved, and the raven shifters have a real shot at changing their ways. They can grow, join modern times, and respect their women, or they can fail and fall back into darkness. The choice is theirs, Avery, but at least they have a choice now. You gave them that."

"My mom said she's proud of me," she murmured. "She said she hopes that someday she can be strong like me." Avery sniffed and wiped her cheek on her bandaged shoulder. "I never thought she would say something like that to me."

Weston slid his hand over her thigh and

squeezed. Avery didn't see her worth, but he did. She had so many layers to her. She was sweet and sensitive, caring to a fault, but when it had come time to let her inner raven loose, she had no fear. She'd viciously fought her own people to protect him. She'd willingly gone into The Box to protect the crew. She didn't realize how tough she was yet, but she would someday, and he was so damn proud that he got the chance to watch her rise up from the ashes of her past. He was so damn proud she had chosen him to hold onto all these years. So proud she'd chosen him as her mate.

He pulled to a stop in front of 1010 and gave a two-fingered wave at the truck that passed carrying the other Bloodrunners.

It was full dark in Harper's Mountains, but the glow of 1010's lights beckoned, welcoming them home.

Avery slid from his truck like she was boneless. She looked exhausted. All Weston wanted to do was bury himself inside of her and make her forget the horrors of the past couple days. He wanted to empty himself inside her and banish how close they'd come to losing each other. But Avery looked wrecked, and he wouldn't relieve his needs on her when she was so raw.

She stumbled, but he was there, picking her up and cradling her against his chest as he made his way into 1010. With a soft sound, she slipped her arms around his neck and buried her face against his chest. "I don't want you to leave tonight."

"I won't leave, Ave. I won't hide from you anymore. I know you can handle me after the visions now." Little phoenix. He wished she could have seen herself in action tonight. She'd been a beautiful, relentless weapon. She'd bought him time, but also time for his parents, Rowan, and the Bloodrunner's to reach them. Da had dreamed of circling ravens and Benjamin swinging the ax at Weston's back, but nothing more. Nothing to tell him the fate of his son was sealed. He'd brought Ma and Rowan with him for back-up. Weston had told the Bloodrunners to stay back while Avery was in The Box. He thought they would draw too much attention while his raven would blend in. Weston had been ambushed, though, as if the ravens had known exactly where he would be waiting for her.

If the ravens had succeeded in killing him,

Rowan and the others would've laid waste to the entire shifter species to avenge his death. The inhabitants of The Hollow didn't realize it, but by Avery saving him, she'd saved them as well.

He carried his mate inside and readied for bed with her, watching her out of the corner of his eye. He was so fucking worried about her. What if she had bad dreams tonight? What if she'd been scarred even more on her insides? What if she started crying and he couldn't help her to stop?

But she didn't. His brave little phoenix crawled under the covers and lifted the comforter up for him to slide into bed with her. She didn't cry or moon over what had happened. Instead, she told him, "Tomorrow I'll give you my letters, and you can see all of me. And tonight, if you have a vision, you can wake me up and tell me about it, and I will love you even more."

And after she laid her cheek on his chest against his drumming heartbeat, her breathing evened out and she fell asleep. Weston sighed and looked up at the dark exposed rafters of the bedroom and sent up a silent prayer that he would have no visions tonight. Because he wouldn't hide from her anymore. He would tell her about every vision, the good and the bad, because she deserved to see all of him, even the dark parts.

If the Fates could let him rest easy tonight, Avery would be able to sleep peacefully beside him. And after everything she'd gone through, his Avery deserved peace.

****

Weston flinched under her, and Avery's eyes flew open in the dark. Every muscle in Weston's body was tensed. He felt like a stone under her searching hands.

"What's wrong?" she asked, sitting up in bed.

His heart was pounding hard under the palm of her hand, and his chest heaved with each breath. In the dim light of the bedroom, Weston's eyes were wide and shocked.

"Is it a vision?" she asked, panicked. God, what if he'd sustained more injuries than she'd thought. His body was covered in cuts and gashes now from the raven war. What if he'd been damaged internally? "Weston, say something. Are you okay?"

"I'm fine," he huffed out on a breath. He grabbed her hand and brought it to his lips. "It was a good one."

Avery sighed with relief and sagged against his side. Slowly, she straddled him and locked her arms against his chest. "What was it about?"

"You," he uttered in his deep, sexy sleep voice. "It was short, just a small glimpse of a bigger scene. You and I were dancing, and you were smiling so big. You were so fucking beautiful and happy, I couldn't keep my eyes off your face." Weston swallowed hard and brushed her long hair off her shoulder to expose her claiming mark. "You were wearing white."

Avery didn't want him to see her tear up at that beautiful vision, so she curled her arms under her and cuddled against his strong, warm chest. "Maybe ten-ten really is magic, like you said."

Weston rubbed gentle circles against her spine. "What do you mean?"

"Ten-ten gave you a good vision for our first whole night together. It might not always be like this, but it gave us a gift."

Weston chuckled, the deep sound vibrating against her cheek. God, she adored that sound. Feeling emboldened by his vision, Avery sat up and arched her back, rocked her hips against his.

Weston groaned and gripped her hips so desperately, his fingers dug into her skin. His dick was hardening by the second under her so she offered him a wicked grin. She loved that he was sensitive to her touch, always ready for intimacy in seconds. Leaning forward, Avery sucked on his nipple, flicking her tongue against his piercing. His body turned to water, rolling against her like a wave. She lifted up just enough to pull his briefs down his powerful hips. His bright white smile flashed in the dim lighting as she pulled her sleep shirt off and tossed it to the ground.

Cupping the back of her head, Weston pulled her down to him, pushed his tongue past her lips immediately, then sucked hard on her bottom lip. He stroked into her mouth, setting a fast, hard rhythm that had her rubbing against him. He dragged his rough kisses down her neck and grabbed her breast. He sucked on one nipple hard as he bucked his hips against hers.

She let off a long, helpless moan and arched her back, giving him better access. Weston laved his tongue over and over her sensitive skin to the pace he set with his hips, and she was getting closer, the pressure building until she was right on the edge.

As if he could tell how close she was, Weston grabbed her hips and pulled her forward until she was hovering just above his face. Before she could balk, he pushed his tongue deep inside of her.

Avery was already gone. All she could do was grip the headboard and roll her hips to meet his deep thrusts. She cried out as he plunged into her time and time again. Orgasm pulsed through her, but he didn't stop. He ate her until every aftershock was done. Until she was twitching and bucking erratically against his mouth. Until her grip on the headboard was weak and shaky and she was panting his name mindlessly.

Oh, they weren't done yet, but she needed to buy her body some recovery time. She locked her gaze on his and then worked her way down until her breasts brushed his dick. It throbbed between her cleavage, and he let off another sexy sound, lifted his hips to her. Weston rolled her over on her back so fast her stomach dipped. He gripped her hair and straddled her chest, shoved his huge dick between her breasts. How was this so fucking sexy? Dominant brawler man burying himself over and over between her boobs. This should do nothing for her, but she was getting wetter and wetter. Avery moaned and arched against the mattress, shoving her tits together to make it tighter for him.

"Fffuuuuuck," Weston moaned, smoothing out his thrusts, making them shallower. "How do you want me to come," he gritted out. "Tell me quick."

She was desperate for him to touch her. To bury himself balls deep inside of her and make her come again. His dick was so hard against her, so tempting. "In me," she gasped out.

Weston pulled away from her breasts and positioned himself between her legs. He wasn't gentle or slow. He slammed into her wet heat, his eyes riveted on their connection. She could see it, too, his wet dick sliding in and out of her, pounding her. His abs flexed every time he pumped his powerful hips. So fucking sexy.

"Ooooh, right there," she groaned as her release built up hard.

Weston dropped down to her, wrapped his arm around her ass and hit her deep, kept it there with shallow thrusts, hitting her clit over and over, so fast. He gritted out her name, slammed into her, and froze.

As her orgasm exploded through her, his dick pulsed inside of her, shooting heat straight to her middle. Avery sank her nails into his back as he pushed into her erratically, his shaft throbbing, filling her as he rammed her up the bed.

His lips went to her neck, sucking hard as he grunted and pushed into her again. He drew out slowly, then rammed into her. Over and over, he did that until both of their aftershocks were through.

Weston rubbed his cheek against hers, his short stubble scratching her. Rough mate. He held her hands over her head as he worked his lips up her throat along her jaw to her mouth. Affectionate mate. He ran his fingers down her ribs and massaged her breast as he kissed her gently. Perfect mate.

He adored her until her body buzzed. Until her eyelids grew heavy and her chest hummed with the heat of their unbreakable bond. Happy and satisfied down to her marrow, Avery nipped his neck possessively. "Mine," she growled.

He chuckled deep in his throat and rolled them over, squeezed her against his impossibly strong chest. "Possessive little beasty," he accused.

"Damn straight," Avery murmured. She nuzzled

his throat, inhaling his scent.

Weston brushed her hair off her cheek. In the dim, dawn light, his expression turned to one of surprise. "You make me happy."

He said it so tenderly her heart thumped faster in her chest, and the butterflies in her stomach beat their wings double-time.

With her fingertips, she traced the sharp lines of his jaw and whispered, "Good."

"Just good?" he asked, eyebrows arched high. He tickled her ribs until she squirmed and laughed.

"I mean you make me happy, too. You make me happy, too!"

He released her, but her giggling trilled on. This complicated, incredible man had her whole heart. As she settled on her side, facing him, Weston drew his arm under his cheek.

His smile reached all the way to his eyes when he said, "I can tell you're happy here."

"How?"

Weston brushed his fingertips over her cheek, as though he was memorizing her face. "Because when you first came here, your eyes were hollow and scared. You smelled sad, and when you walked, you looked like you had the weight of the world on your shoulders."

"And now?" she asked.

"And now you look like you're free."

And she was. Avery kissed Weston's palm and pressed it against her cheek. He was right. She was different now. She'd felt it for a while, but she'd undergone massive growth since she'd come to Harper's Mountains and dared to give her heart to the Novak Raven.

She'd always thought freedom meant being away from her people and on her own.

But freedom wasn't being alone as she'd assumed.

Freedom existed in moments like these that she shared with the man who protected her heart.

TWENTY-SIX

Avery wiped the fog off the mirror and studied the angry, red gash right beside her claiming mark. Raven shifters didn't heal as fast as predator shifters, but already it was halfway sealed and hurt a lot less. Her culture encouraged perfect skin with no scars. A couple months ago, this new adornment on her body would've devastated her because it would've made her even more different from the ravens she had so desperately tried to fit in with.

But today, she stood a little straighter, lifted her chin a little higher, and was proud of the scars she now bore. She was mate of a former Gray Back, mate of a Bloodrunner. *She* was Bloodrunner, and scars were a part of this life. They were brush strokes on the canvas of her body, showing that she'd lived. Showing that she'd endured. The claiming mark would always be her coveted scar, but the other she'd gotten saving herself, and then fighting for Weston.

She'd earned these.

When she'd awoken late, Weston had already left, and his side of the bed had been cold. She missed him, even though she would see him at work in a couple hours. It was early to get ready, but as she fixed her hair and put on her make-up, she already planned on showing up to Big Flight early, just to see Weston sooner.

Avery wrapped her towel tighter around her and padded into the bedroom to get dressed.

On the bed, resting on the shorts and tank top she'd laid out, there was a pocket knife, neatly folded, the handle a rich walnut woodgrain and polished. Avery lifted it gently in her fingers and read the inscription Weston had carved onto it. *W + A*. She smiled, deeply touched at his gift. He'd told her he would make her a knife and teach her to use it. She opened it carefully, and the blade gleamed in the soft light streaming through the window. It was beautifully crafted. She would carry it in her pocket always.

Full of emotion, she closed the blade and picked up the folded letter that had been resting under the knife.

Ave,

I hope you like it. I made this out of a wood that reminds me of you. It's pliable where it needs to compromise, but it's strong, just like you. I have put together something for you today. Don't freak out, it'll be fun. I hope. I told you I would write you a lot of letters, and this is the beginning of that promise. Today you will get a couple. This is the first clue of a little scavenger hunt. Come find me, little phoenix. I'm waiting for you where you first saw me, back when we didn't trust each other yet. Things are different now, and I trust you with my life, but come find me at the beginning.

Later gator,
Weston

A scavenger hunt? This was awesome! Avery hurried to dress, shoved the knife deep into her pocket, shoved her feet into her hiking boots, and barely bothered to tie them up before she bolted outside and climbed into her Civic. She took the shortcut through Harper's mountains to reach Big Flight and skidded to a stop in front of the shop.

Weston was sitting on a bench, elbows resting on his knees and a slow, stunning smile for her. He'd shaved his jaw, and his dimple showed easily. That was just for her. He wore his favorite camouflage baseball cap and a black T-shirt under a red and black plaid shirt with the sleeves rolled up his muscular forearms. He wore dark wash jeans over his work boots. Why was he so dressed up? They had a tour starting in an hour.

With a confused frown, she jogged up the porch stairs and said breathlessly, "I got the knife. I got it, and I love it so much."

"God, you look beautiful," he murmured in that deep, rich timbre she adored.

"Thank you," she said softly.

He pulled her hips until she was standing close to him on the bench, and then he looked up at her and said, "Do you remember the vision I had last night?"

She nodded, confused. "It was a good one, right?"

"It was the best one. But I didn't tell you part of

it."

"What happened?"

He smiled and traced the scar from the glass on her shoulder. "This mark wasn't yet healed. It was red and angry, just as it looks right now."

"I don't understand," she whispered, shaking her head.

Weston sank down to one knee on the porch, right in front of her. In his hand was the turquoise ring she'd been admiring in the shop.

"Weston," she whispered, shocked.

"You deserve more, and I'll get it as soon as I can afford it. I'll get you whatever ring you want, but this one felt right for some reason. I kept looking at it, thinking about it. About how pretty it would be on your finger. About how pretty it would go with your eyes."

"I love it, I love it," she said, her eyes filling with tears.

Weston licked his bottom lip and slid his palm against her left one. "I bonded to you when we were kids. I clung to your letters and fell in love with your voice through them. I didn't want other girlfriends after you because all I wanted was what we'd had.

Your people convinced you that you were flawed, but to me you are *perfect*."

Avery's face crumpled, and her shoulders shook. How those words filled her heart. How she'd longed to hear that she was good. That she was okay. "You're perfect to me, too," she forced out past her tight throat.

He smiled up at her, the morning sunlight highlighting his chiseled jaw and that dimple that said he was happy. "I choose you. For now, for always, I want you to be the one I wake up to. I want you to be the one I share my visions with, and hold, and laugh with. and struggle with, and grow old with."

"I'll protect you always," she whispered.

"I know." Weston's voice broke on the last word, and his eyes rimmed with moisture. He laughed and looked away. Over and over, he swallowed, shaking his head like he was trying to gain control of himself again. In a steadier voice he said, "I know you will. And I'll protect you for always, too. My body is yours. My heart is yours. It has been for a long time. Avery, you are my match. I've claimed you, and you already feel like mine, but you said once that claiming marks aren't recognized by ravens. And I want you in every way. Ave, will you marry me?"

She was already nodding because she wanted nothing more than to bind herself to him completely. His eyes full, he slid the ring onto her finger. Clenching her fist around the new weight, Avery fell to her knees in front of him and hugged him up. A long sob wracked her body as he rocked her back and forth, back and forth. Weston eased away and kissed her. Clinging to him hard, she kissed him back, tears streaming down her cheeks. She didn't know how long they sat like that on the porch of Big Flight. Maybe it was only minutes, but it could've been hours. Time had never made sense when she got lost in his arms like this. Mate, mate, mate. He'd chosen her. How had she gotten so lucky? Their story was long and winding, and so much had conspired to keep them apart, but look what had happened?

Love had won.

Weston leaned back and cupped her cheeks, wiped away her tears. "You're not through."

"What?" she squeaked out.

He laid another peck on her lips and pulled something out of his back pocket. It was another letter. She unfolded it and read it aloud as best as her shaking voice would allow.

"Ave, I love you. I wanted to say that first before anything else because you should hear it all the time. You deserve to know how I feel about you, and never have to question it." Her voice hitched, and she had to clear her throat before she continued. "This is the second clue to your scavenger hunt. This is going to be one of the biggest days of our lives, so enjoy this. Take stock of every moment. I want you to go to the lair of the dragon. And no questions. I know you'll have a million. I won't answer them. Just play the game. Later gator." She looked up at him. "I have to go now?" she asked, wanting to spend more time with her newly betrothed.

Weston chuckled and said, "Trust me. You'll want to do it now."

"Okay," she said, wiping her damp cheeks. It was then that she saw Ryder. He was holding a big camera and taking pictures of them. Ryder was giving them a gift—pictures of their engagement that she could treasure for always.

Avery kissed Weston once more, and when she disengaged, he held her hand, admired the ring on her finger. It fit perfectly. With a boyish grin, he helped her up and swatted her firmly on the ass. "Go on now, or you'll be late."

"Late for what?"

Weston shook his head, denying her answers just like his letter promised. With a giddy laugh, she bolted down the steps, the clue clutched in her hand. She wrapped Ryder up in a big hug.

"Selfie proof that I was here for my first best friend's big moment," he said and turned the camera on them.

Avery cheesed so big. She'd taken a dozen selfies with Ryder for his social media over the weeks, but this was the best one.

"Oh!" he said as she ran off. "I got you something!"

She ran back as he dug in his pocket. Ryder pulled out a purple bear paw beer bottle opener, just like his and Weston's. And now as Avery held out her hand for it, the tears were back.

"It felt right that all three of us have matching ones. You make my best friend happier than I've ever seen him. You're all right, Avery Foley." The jokester ruffled her hair as she blew out a steadying breath and tried to hold herself together.

Ryder sent her on her way, and she jogged to her car, her hands full of some of the most important trinkets of her life. The keychain that said Weston's best friend accepted her, the letter with the next scavenger hunt clue, and the most important thing she possessed—a ring that said Weston wanted her to be his everything.

Avery sped through the backroads of Harper's Mountains, her heart soaring as she raced for the cabins. She drove past 1010, then past Aaron's cabin and the double cabin Weston and Ryder shared. At the top of the hill near the cliffs, she parked her car and made her way onto the sprawling porch of Harper and Wyatt's cabin. She'd never been inside the lair of the dragon before, but Lexi, Harper, and Alana were waiting for her at the open front door.

Lexi was crying, and for a moment, Avery hesitated, uncertain. "Are you okay?" she asked.

Lexi nodded and pulled her inside where a beautiful white dress adorned with sparkling beadwork hung against the log wall.

"It's for you," Alana said softly.

"What?" Avery asked, fingering the gorgeous

material.

"Weston bought it from me this morning. It's the extra dress I had for my wedding. He said you didn't want much fuss for your big day. He told us you said you wanted a wedding that didn't take away from my big day." Alana's dark cheeks turned rosy, and she ducked her gaze. A tear splatted against the wooden floor. "I can't tell you how sweet that is, but you deserve a big day, too."

"I-I don't understand," Avery stammered, looking from face to face. The women all had their make-up done and their hair in beautiful cascading curls. They wore sundresses in different pastel colors.

"If you want it to be," Harper said, "today is your wedding day. Weston has planned everything."

Avery put her hands over her mouth to control her sobbing. Her shoulders heaved as she took a few steps back and shook her head. This couldn't be happening. Something this incredible didn't happen to people like her. But it was, and now all the girls were tearing up. Harper hugged her up tight, and then others wrapped their arms around her, too.

Sniffling, Avery asked, "Will you be my

bridesmaids? I want all of you to be up there with me."

"Of course," Harper answered. "We're your crew. There is nowhere else we'd rather be. Now," she murmured, easing away. "No more tears because your make-up will be shot to hell. Are we doing this?"

Avery laughed thickly and nodded her head. "Yeah, we're doing this. Today is my wedding day."

TWENTY-SEVEN

Avery's hands were shaking so bad the bouquet of wild flowers in her hands made a rustling sound. She caught a glimpse of her reflection in the window of the Bryson City Town Hall. The final scavenger hunt clue had led her here.

The dress fit snugly, emphasizing her figure, and Harper had done a quick, temporary hem of the bottom so it wasn't too long. It was fitted and flared out just below her thighs. Alana had done her hair in curls, pinned shining tresses with pearl clips, and Lexi had re-done her make-up.

Avery felt like a princess. She sighed and wondered what was taking so long. Harper had asked her to wait here for some cue to make her way through the doors. Maybe Weston hadn't been able to secure the last-minute wedding license as he'd hoped.

The door behind her opened with a pretty *ding* of the bell. She turned and froze.

Weston's fearsome father, Beaston, strode toward her, his bright, inhuman gaze locked on hers. For a moment, she seized in fear, but he smiled and took her empty hand in his rough, calloused palm.

"You don't have no worthy daddy to walk you down the aisle," he murmured. "Weston said you wanted a quiet wedding, just you and him, but I wanted more. My Ana wants to see her boy married." Beaston shifted his weight and dropped his eyes to Avery's flowers. "You smell scared, but you don't have to be. I won't hurt you. My boy loves you." He lifted that terrifying gaze back to her, but he angled his face, giving her his neck. "I only have one raven boy, and he had my heart from the first second I laid eyes on him. My Ana gave me girls after Weston, all bears. So you see," he said softly, "you will be my only raven girl. You can't be the daughter of my blood, but you can be the daughter of my heart. You take good care of my boy. You will make him feel steady when the visions get bad, and you'll keep Harper from putting him down. You'll save him, and he'll fix your inside scars. I don't want you going down the aisle alone when you meet him. I want to be the one to walk you."

Avery bit her lip hard so she wouldn't lose it. She'd been terrified of Beaston and shifters like him all her life, and now he was telling her she was his girl. Her own flesh-and-blood father had never declared as much. Jerkily, she nodded, and slipped her hand into the crook of his strong arm. "I would be honored," she whispered.

Beaston gave her a crooked smile, one that looked so much like Weston's, and pushed the door open.

Her eyes locked on Weston, waiting in front of the Justice of the Peace in a dark suit, his smile stunned and taking up his whole face. Her lip trembled as Beaston led her past the tiny crowd. Mom was standing next to Aviana, tears in her eyes. She must've defied Dad to be here, and for that, Avery was so proud of her. On the other side, Officer Ryan and Officer Hammond stood out of uniform with their hands clasped in front of them, easy smiles on their faces. Kane stood leaned against the far wall, hands in his pockets, his sunglasses on, and a slight smile curving up his lips. He nodded a greeting, and she waved her flowers gently at him. Up front, the Bloodrunners stood for her and Weston, looking so proud, as though she was a welcome member.

Everything was perfect.

She kissed Beaston gently on the cheek before he left to stand by his mate, and then Avery handed Harper her bouquet of wildflowers. With a happy sigh, Avery slipped her hands into Weston's. And as she looked up into his eyes, lost in how deeply she loved him, they repeated the simple vows, and each said their I do.

Weston kissed her for so long Ryder told them to "get a room." Avery giggled against her mate's lips when he lifted her off her feet and hugged her tightly. The others were clapping and whistling, and Avery had never been happier than in this moment.

They signed the certificate, Avery's heart banging against her chest the entire time. She was married to the man of her dreams. No, neither one of them was perfect, but they were perfect for each other.

"I'm starving," Weston said after a few pictures.

"I'm hungry, too, and it would be fun to go out to eat all dressed up," Avery said.

"I could eat like...seven cows of steak," Ryder announced, reviewing pictures on the camera.

"Gross," Lexi teased from where she was hugging his waist.

"I have one last surprise," Weston murmured against Avery's ear.

"More surprises? Weston, you've already given me the best day of my life."

"Best day of *our* lives, Ave." He grabbed her hand and led her across the street, the others following and chattering happily. Up a few shops, he pulled her into a fancy looking restaurant on the corner called The Cork and Bean Bistro. It looked unassuming enough on the outside, but inside, it was beautiful. Rustic iron chandeliers hung from the ceiling, and the walls were paneled in polished wood. There was a bar along the back wall with three tall chairs in front of it, and chalkboards with drink specials and sprawling mirrors adorned the wooden walls. The tables looked hand-carved, and the chairs were all made of polished thick wooden branches. Avery would've never guessed this gem lay hidden in the heart of this quaint town.

A server was waiting for them and smiled brightly when she saw Weston. "Perfect timing. We just opened up the kitchen to serve dinner for your party. Right this way," she murmured.

Weston led them into a back room where the tables had been pushed away from the center of the room and soft music played over the speakers. Two of the walls were covered in the same polished wood as the bar room, but one was made of exposed red brick. A huge iron chandelier hung above, and matching mirrors and sconces decorated the wall. The last wall was made of windows, and natural light streamed in, casting a beautiful glow on the wooden floors and tables.

"You have this room for three hours," the server said to Avery with a beaming smile. "We don't usually do private parties, but your man was very persuasive. You got yourself a good one."

"He paid her to say that," Ryder joked.

"Shut up," Weston said, shoving his friend in the shoulder. He twirled Avery onto the dancefloor and chuckled, his eyes on her smiling lips. "It's just like my dream."

She laughed and slid her hands up around his neck, swaying side to side with him. "Well, I didn't even have enough imagination to dream of something this amazing. You listened to me. You gave me the wedding I told you I wanted. And I didn't have to plan or stress. I just had to get dressed and show up. You're so fucking awesome. Best husband ever." She squealed and repeated it. "Husband! You're my husband. I can't believe this. After everything we've been through…"

"Woman, you fought for me. You hung on when I wasn't worth hanging onto. I'll spend the rest of my life hanging on to you back."

Avery lowered her voice and teased, "You keep talking like that, and I'll let you fuck my boobs again."

Weston arched his dark eyebrows high. "By the way, they look amazing in this dress." His eyes glazed over as he stared. "All big and pushed up to your chin. Hide my boner."

She cracked up as he pulled her closer and nipped her neck.

"Weston, Avery, what are you drinking?" Wyatt asked from beside the server.

"Champagne," Avery said.

"Ew, no." Wyatt scrunched up his face. "She'll have a long island iced tea."

"I'll have the same," Lexi and Alana said at the same time. Oh, it was going to be one of those parties.

Weston snorted, and Avery giggled. "This is so freaking perfect. It's exactly how I would want it to be. Just me and you and the most important people in our lives."

"Getting drunk," Weston said, his eyes dancing. "We'll be lucky if they don't kick us out of this place."

"Harper is drinking orange juice. She'll keep us in line." Avery hoped.

Their alpha pulled Wyatt onto the dance floor, and now they were slow dancing side-to-side next to Avery and Weston. Wyatt had his hand resting on the tiny swell of Harper's stomach, and he was murmuring low against her ear. Harper had the sweetest smile on her lips as she hugged her mate closer.

Lexi and Ryder were dancing inappropriately, and Alana was grinning up at Aaron as they two-stepped, the scar on her lip stretching with how happy she looked. Beaston, Mom, and Aviana were sitting at a table, talking easily. She had a feeling Aviana would be a good support for mom in the coming months.

"I don't know how I got so lucky," Avery murmured.

Weston frowned at where Lexi was doing a shimmy dance with her butt against Ryder's pelvis. "Yeah, super lucky."

Avery swatted his shoulder. "You know what I mean."

He ran his fingertip lightly over her claiming mark and then the scar from the glass below it. "So you don't have any regrets?"

Avery shook her head and looked around, still in disbelief that this day was hers. Didn't Weston see? She'd been hollow before. She'd been a shell, and he'd given her so much, filled her up with emotions she didn't know existed. He'd given her himself, his heart, and then he'd gone and done even more. He'd given her friends who had come to her aid, no questions asked. He'd given her a place in the best damn crew in the entire world. He'd given her confidence and made her want to be stronger. He'd gone to battle for her, banished her ghosts, banished the ones who had hurt her.

He'd pulled her from the mud, cleaned her feathers, and told her to *rise up, little phoenix*.

And because of him, she had.

"Of course I have no regrets. I'm right where I belong." She traced the silver claw mark scars on his neck. "We fought for each other, Weston. I love every mark on me and every mark on you. You laid your body over mine, under the swinging blade of an ax, just to make sure I lived. Just to save me from pain. Just to make sure I was okay. Every mark on our bodies is proof that we're in this. No matter what comes now, we'll face it together, for always."

Her mother had used those words once when she'd admitted Avery was born to betray the Novak Raven. She'd hated them then, but now she was taking them back.

The ravens had failed.

Avery hadn't been born to betray Weston.

She'd been born to love him. *For always*.

Weston leaned down and kissed her claiming mark, then kissed the mark from the shard of glass. And then he straightened, cupped her neck gently, and pressed his lips to hers.

Resting his forehead against Avery's, he softly repeated her oath. "For always."

Want more of these characters?

Novak Raven is the fourth book in a five book series based in Harper's Mountains.

Check out these other books from T. S. Joyce.

Bloodrunner Dragon
(Harper's Mountains, Book 1)

Bloodrunner Bear
(Harper's Mountains, Book 2)

Air Ryder
(Harper's Mountains, Book 3)

Blackwing Dragon
(Harper's Mountains, Book 5)

About the Author

T.S. Joyce is devoted to bringing hot shifter romances to readers. Hungry alpha males are her calling card, and the wilder the men, the more she'll make them pour their hearts out. She werebear swears there'll be no swooning heroines in her books. It takes tough-as-nails women to handle her shifters.

Experienced at handling an alpha male of her own, she lives in a tiny town, outside of a tiny city, and devotes her life to writing big stories. Foodie, wolf whisperer, ninja, thief of tiny bottles of awesome smelling hotel shampoo, nap connoisseur, movie fanatic, and zombie slayer, and most of this bio is true.

Bear Shifters? Check

Smoldering Alpha Hotness? Double Check

Sexy Scenes? Fasten up your girdles, ladies and gents, it's gonna to be a wild ride.

> For more information on T. S. Joyce's work,
> visit her website at
> www.tsjoyce.com

Printed in Great Britain
by Amazon